LEAVE ME BREATHLESS

LEAVE ME BREATHLESS

WOLFF BROTHERS

DARA GIRARD

ISBN: 978-1-949764888

LEAVE ME BREATHLESS

ILORI PRESS BOOKS, LLC

www.iloripressbooks.com

BOOKS BY DARA GIRARD

Wolff Brothers

Seeing Red

Leave Me Breathless

Kayode Sisters

The Language of Flowers

Sooner or Later

This Time Forever

Ladies of the Pen

Words of Seduction

Pages of Passion

Beneath the Covers

Duvall Sisters

The Glass Slipper Project

Taming Mariella

A Reluctant Hero

The Black Stockings Society

Power Play

A Gentleman's Offer

Body Chemistry

Round the Clock

Return of the Black Stockings Society

Playing for Keeps

After Hours

A Private Affair

Just One Look

Private Lessons

Henson Series

Table for Two

Gaining Interest

Careless Rapture

Dangerous Curves

Familiar Stranger

It Happened One Wedding

Unexpected Pleasure

Midnight Promise

Sweet Temptation

Always and Forever

Clifton Sisters

The Sapphire Pendant

The Amber Stone

The Emerald Ring

Fortune Brothers

A Tempting Proposal

A Seductive Arrangement

An Unforgettable Moment

Novels

Best Laid Plans

Dream of Me

Honest Betrayal

The Daughters of Winston Barnett

Remember My Name

Illusive Flame

Winterwood Lane

Mum's looking for you.

A wolfish grin touched his lips as Lucas read the text. He should be afraid, but he wasn't. Let her come looking. He hadn't made himself that hard to find. He wasn't going to give her the satisfaction of chasing after him. He'd learned early that running only prolonged a game he planned to win.

"Yes, Mum. I'm here. And I'm ready." Lucas mumbled the words to himself, although the stillness of his father's living room made the words seem louder.

The animal had been let out of her cage. She had served her time and now she was after him. He doubted she wanted a family reunion. She wanted something from him. To own him. But he was his own man now. With a new life and a new name. The problem wasn't what she could do to him, but what she could do to those he cared about. He'd have to be cunning to keep them safe.

"Is what you grinning at?" his father said, dropping the

Standard English accent he'd honed for business to the one from his island background.

Lucas turned and replaced one grin with another: He flashed his father a smooth, polished grin as he put his phone inside the inner pocket of his new calico colored jacket, which cost more than his father's living room set. Although, to be fair, his father didn't take much interest in interior decoration (to Lucas's continued dismay) so it wasn't much of a stretch.

While the mustard colored walls made the room bright (his father saying they reminded him of his favorite mango smoothie) the walls could use a second coat of paint. The coffee table, Lucas knew by memory—old oak with a chipped edge—rather than sight because, presently, it was buried under stacks of newspapers and magazines. One magazine page was folded to a slick, glossy picture of a designer watch. Since his father wasn't into watches—or fashion of any sort— Lucas could safely assume it was the gorgeous female model wearing the watch that had caught his father's attention, which gave him an idea of how to answer his father's question. "A new love interest. What else?"

His father frowned. "You're usually better when you lie to me."

Lucas softly swore. Perhaps news of his mother's release had rattled him more than he was willing to admit. "Sorry."

"I know about her."

He would. His father knew about a lot of things. Eldin Wolff had saved Lucas and his two adopted brothers, Damian and Ian, from grim futures. The Caribbean born businessman had connections that stretched as long and far as shadows cast by a mountain. His father had a dark past Lucas still couldn't figure out and didn't want to. When

Eldin Wolff decided to become a father in his forties, he'd separated his former life from his sons and they'd let him, out of respect, because they all had pasts they wanted to forget. New lives they wanted to live.

Lucas pulled out his phone and showed his father the message. When he saw his father's frown increase he quickly assured him, "I can handle it."

"I know."

"If she contacts you first, you tell me."

His father sent him a long, probing look. "I also know how to handle her."

Maybe, but time had passed and his father was older now and Lucas worried that—

He didn't even feel the attack—only the after effects.

Lucas woke up with his cheek pressed against the coarse grey rug, his body twisted like a wooden toy and his neck throbbing like he'd been struck with a hot iron. Lucas cautiously lifted himself to a sitting position, trying to focus on the couch to stop the room from spinning. He fumbled for his glasses, which he found between one of the legs of the coffee table and the new luxurious travel bag he'd bought for his father's upcoming holiday abroad. Lucas shoved the glasses back on his face before he gingerly touched his neck. He blinked up at the bulky silver haired man whose diamond stud earring glinted in the afternoon sunlight.

"Dad, what the hell—?"

His father folded his arms, unapologetic. "Look at me like I'm a fragile old man again and I'll make sure you're knocked out for longer than a few seconds."

Lucas stumbled to his feet and groaned. "A stern warning would have also been sufficient."

His father narrowed his eyes. Lucas held up his hands in

surrender. His father might be shorter and older than him, but Lucas would rather wrestle two hungry crocodiles than this man. "Point taken. I'm sorry." It was moments like these when his father's unspoken past roared into the present. Lucas had no desire to face it. He liked keeping things in their place and that past should stay the past.

Lucas looked around the living room and saw where he'd dropped his phone when his father had struck him. He picked it up and kept his voice light and teasing when he said, "I guess I should stay here for protection."

"You're always welcome."

He shot his father a glance. "It was a joke."

"I wasn't joking."

"I know." Lucas sat down heavily on the worn couch, sinking into the soft cushions, rubbing his neck. He softly swore. He was going to be sore for awhile. "Don't tell the others, okay?"

"They're your brothers. They'd want to know."

"When the time's right—"

"The timing will never be right. They'll have to be warned." Eldin studied his son before he quietly said, "You know she won't come to you first. She'll try to reach a weakness."

Lucas gritted his teeth. He hated the idea of thinking of his brothers as a weakness, they had gotten him through so much, but she could hurt him through them.

"Alright. I'll tell them. Give me a week."

"You have until tomorrow."

"But—"

"When you're young you think you always have time. But when you get older you realize time is the enemy. The longer you wait, the stronger she gets. Time feeds fear."

Before Lucas could tell his father he wasn't afraid his father said, "This isn't someone you can wait on. You don't know when she'll strike. Or why. You can't protect your brothers by keeping them in the dark. There are still things they don't know."

Lucas pretended to look offended. "I'm an open book."

"With invisible ink."

Lucas feigned a look of pain, placing a hand over his heart in an exaggerated show of grief. "Father...you wound me."

Eldin held back a grin trying not to be enchanted by his son's charm and ability to make light of serious subjects. "We both know I'm right." He paused, cleared his throat then said quietly, "They wouldn't judge you if—"

Lucas leaned forward, cutting off his father's words. "I know that. I'm not hiding anything—much," Lucas quickly corrected when his father narrowed his eyes, "I just don't like talking about it."

His father shrugged. "Now you're lying to yourself too." He rested a hand on Lucas' shoulder. "Speaking of ladies."

"Were we?"

"Your mother isn't the only one looking for you."

Lucas squeezed his eyes closed and groaned.

"You have to stop avoiding her."

He looked up at his father. "I'm not avoiding her. I'm just really, really busy."

Eldin shook his head. "Lie number three and you're out."

"It's not really a lie. I've been busy trying my best to not have to see her."

His father tightened his grip. "I didn't raise cowards."

Lucas felt the grip on his shoulder and sighed, resigned. His father was right. He wasn't acting like a Wolff. He wouldn't shame his father's name. It was a possession he prized. "No, you didn't raise a coward. I'll see her sometime next month."

"You'll see her today."

Lucas shook his head. "And have to talk to my brothers tomorrow? That's too much."

"I'll give you a week to tell your brothers. You'll see your aunt today."

Lucas opened his mouth to argue but the hard glint in Eldin's gaze made him reconsider saying anything more. He closed his mouth and hung his head in defeat.

His father patted him on the shoulder. "Good boy."

Lucas barked.

His father frowned and shook his head with a sigh. "I don't know how I ended up with you."

Lucas grinned. "You couldn't resist my charm."

"That's true."

What was also true was that Eldin Wolff had rescued him from living a lie.

"You have nothing to be ashamed of," his father was saying, although Lucas was trying to think of a way not to visit his aunt. Eldin paused for a moment then said, "Don't start acting like Damian—"

Lucas stared at his father and shivered with mock horror. "Never."

"About this," Eldin finished. "You have a family that wants to be there for you."

Lucas smiled. "I know."

Eldin folded his arms. "Put that dangerous grin of yours away. You know it doesn't work on me."

Lucas continued to smile. "Doesn't stop me from hoping."

His father affectionately patted him on the cheek. "When are you going to start smiling for real?"

Lucas felt his smile waver. That hurt. "I'm not a fraud, Dad."

"I didn't say you were."

"I have a naturally sunny personality. It's shocking, but true."

Lucas knew how he appeared to others. It was a carefully crafted image, but with his family he was always himself. At least he thought he was. He prided himself on being the light and heart of his family. Damian was too serious, too morose. Ian too insular and enigmatic. Lucas liked to think of himself as the bright one, the happy one, the one who had survived and helped his brothers. He wasn't as wounded as them. He hadn't suffered like them.

Although he had suffered.

And the one who had caused the most suffering was now out and looking for him.

"I didn't mean it like that," Eldin said with a note of regret.

"I know. It's okay." Lucas kept grinning because that was his nature to keep smiling no matter how much something hurt him. He wasn't pretending. It really was okay. He was fine. He'd forgive his father anything.

"Damian isn't the only one who can find someone."

And now it was time to exit. Lucas stood. "I'm not lonely."

"Didn't say you were. What happened with Lania—"

"Who?"

"The flight attendant."

"Dad, that was nearly five years ago." *1,725 days, 10 hours and 36 seconds.*

"Exactly and there hasn't been anyone since then."

Lucas flashed a sly grin. "No, there've been *plenty* since then."

"But no one serious."

Lucas's mind briefly flashed to the satin, gold colored thong that had ended up on his chandelier. That had been a fun night. "Oh, it was *very* serious for about—"

"Lania was wrong for you. What she did was...unforgiveable. You don't have to forget that, but running from it won't help either. There's a woman out there you can trust."

Lucas smiled. "Sure," he said keeping his voice light. He snapped his fingers as a thought came to him. "And before I forget we need to do something about the kitchen. When I was putting away the chocolate digestives I bought for you, the cabinet handle came off and the sink—"

"My kitchen's fine. It's my son that needs work."

"Don't worry, Damian's got Rosaline now and Ian is...Ian." Lucas shoved his hands in his pockets and said, "I'd better get going."

Eldin looked a little sad, as if he didn't want to see him go. "Don't do anything reckless."

Lucas playfully clicked his tongue, pretending that the sad expression on his father's face didn't wound him. "That sounds like a challenge," he said, hoping to encourage a smile.

"Lu," Eldin said the word softly, but the nickname hit Lucas hard. It was too close to what he'd been called in the past. The name he'd shed when he'd been given a new life. His father wouldn't use that nickname without reason. It was a warning. Eldin was worried. He'd been the first to call Lucas that instead of the other name. The name that tied him, locked him, in a lie.

Lucas grinned as he quickly texted his PA to let him know his plans had changed. "I'll do my best to behave." He put his phone away and turned, letting his smile fall. His father knew him too well, but what he didn't know was that Lucas also had patience.

He'd been waiting for this day.

A chance to get his revenge.

If his mother crossed him, if she hurt anyone he cared about again, if she gave him the barest of excuses, he'd already considered ten different ways of killing her and getting away with it.

2

From a distance the house on the edge of what had been Maryland farm country looked small.

It sat like a matchbox turned on its side. It was bright red with white shutters, bracketed by large shrubbery that nearly reached the roof. But as one drove closer to the house, the quaint matchbox feel fell away replaced with a tinge of awe. The house loomed, the greenery turned out not to be shrubs at all but large trees carefully trimmed to give that impression. The large arched windows gave the house a look of surprise, the door painted black like an open mouth caught in a scream.

Lucas really hated visiting that house.

The woman inside it was no different. From a distance, his aunt also appeared smaller than she was. She sat in a large high back armchair, back ridged, her round figure appearing soft and inviting (like a brown teddy bear) everything the real woman was not.

At her feet sat, Benton, a black mutt as sweet as guava

jelly and as old as Methuselah (also his nickname), his muzzle a shocking white compared to the rest of him.

Although officially Wynette was Lucas's great aunt, she bristled at the term and preferred to only be called 'aunt.'

She was eighty years old and only six years older than her nephew, Lucas's father, Eldin.

This late-in-life surprise, to a couple that never imagined having a daughter after a succession of three boys all in their twenties, decided at six years of age that she would take the role of aunt seriously and made it her mission to check up on Eldin. She was the one who'd encouraged him to go into business with her. She knew early on that men had a hard time taking a woman seriously, and in the era she grew up in, it was more prevalent than now, so she'd primed and schooled her nephew to do what she wished and he willingly followed. The family found it sweet and adorable that a little girl would take it upon herself to look after her younger relative. They thought it was a sign of a girl's natural 'mothering instinct' not understanding that this little girl had ambitions and that she had a grander plan for both of them.

Wynette had no desire to become a domestic or work in a factory or be a teacher. She wanted power. And she knew that Eldin was a ticket out of the small island where they'd both been raised. She had little tolerance for school and was too restless to be a man's wife and too ambitious to be his mistress. However, she only discovered that fact after she'd married and divorced (twice) and been the mistress of a government official who referred to her as his 'tasty grater cake' one too many times. By her mid-thirties she came to the conclusion she wanted to be her own person and not tied to anyone.

She learned to buy what others didn't want. She saw

potential in everything. Like taking old dresses she'd bought in thrift stores and have others turn them into gowns, which she'd turn around and sell at a tidy profit. She knew how to organize others. From dresses to cars to houses, soon she had made enough money to buy whatever she wanted.

With her cunning and smarts, she and Eldin both invested in profitable extra legal activities and became very successful and rich.

"You've been avoiding me," Aunt Wynette said when Lucas entered the room, the slight lilt of her island accent softening the accusation.

She had a pleasant voice—soft, melodic, alluring. Her voice always shocked Lucas the most. It quickly helped him to forget his unease and he found that she wasn't as frightening as he remembered.

But it didn't shake the feeling that he wished he were somewhere else. He blinked and took a seat, careful to look respectful rather than bored. No point denying the obvious. He glanced at the tea set on the coffee table and the selection of biscuits—most powdered with confectioner sugar others covered with lemon crème, he could tell by the scent.

"Have you lost weight?"

Lucas sighed, tugging on the cuffs of his jacket. That statement also didn't warrant a reply. She didn't do small talk either.

"I need a favor," she said.

Yep. That was why he wished he wasn't here. His aunt didn't ask for favors. She rarely asked for anything, she gave commands and expected them to be obeyed.

Lucas folded his arms and waited. He looked around. "It's awfully quiet. No servants?"

"You know why."

Lucas lifted an eyebrow. "I do?"

"I know it's best to keep them away from your...seductive charms."

Lucas rolled his eyes. "It happened once."

Wynette frowned.

"All right. Three times, okay, maybe four, but that's all. I can't help that I have a certain...appeal."

"You stole Alex from me."

Lucas pointed to his face. "This is the look of no regrets. You were wasting his talents. He's doing well by the way." Alex was his excellent new PA.

"Of course he is."

Lucas shrugged and fell silent. He glanced at an old painting from a modern artist, priced the cost of a sculpture he hadn't seen before, yawned.

Wynette frowned. "This isn't like you."

"What do you mean?"

"You're not usually so quiet."

Lucas shrugged again. "I learned when facing a storm it's better to wait it out than to fight it."

"So you see me as a storm?"

"A typhoon."

Wynette grinned, pleased. "Thank you."

He bowed his head. "You're welcome. What's the favor?"

"I have three properties I want you to look into."

He let his hands fall. "I don't cross that line, Aunty. I don't do property management. No threats, no evictions, no way."

Her tone hardened. "I don't threaten people."

"You don't have to."

"All my tenants are very happy."

"I wouldn't doubt it."

"The network needs another location and they reached out to me. I want you to assess the properties to see which one would be best."

"Oh."

He didn't know too much about the network and really didn't want to. His father and aunt had always gotten into dealings with people with nicknames like Mango Juice, Ska Joe and Duppy Man, who he'd rather not know about.

"Still not sure I can help you," Lucas said, eying a biscuit. It was easier than facing the woman in front of him, "but I know of people—"

"I need this kept in the family."

Lucas lifted the sugar biscuit and took a bite. "I have a really busy schedule."

"And it won't take you too long."

He finished the biscuit and grabbed another. They were better than he'd expected—sweet and crispy, a hint of nutmeg and vanilla. "I'm afraid I don't think I'm the right one."

"Your brother asked me for help."

The cookie crumbled in his fist, leaving crumbs all over his lap. Lucas softly swore as he brushed the crumbs off his lap into his palm then placed them on the napkin. He should have been on guard. The sneaky snake didn't even need to touch him and yet she knew how to bring him to his knees. With one word: brother.

She didn't even need to mention his brother's name. Ian didn't have a dangerous side hustle so that left Damian. All Wynette had to do was mention that and then she'd harness Luca's weakness. He'd do anything for his brother.

"Of course I can say no," Wynette said softly, the velvet

threat as powerful as his father's iron grip had been. Her tone said: If you don't do this, your brother will be disappointed. He won't even know why.

"Why does it have to be me?"

"Because I said so."

Lucas shook his head. "Doesn't wash. You never make a decision without a valid reason."

"True."

He waited.

"Your brother needs you."

Lucas gritted his teeth. "Stop bringing Damian into this."

She looked surprised. "Did I?"

Lucas counted to three. He couldn't believe that she thought by not mentioning Damian's name she could pretend they weren't talking about him. "What do you need from me?"

"Your gift."

Lucas shook his head. "It's not a gift."

"You're one of the best. You look at buildings in ways that I've never seen before. It's a special talent. It's a way you can help your brother."

It was dangerous when family knew your weakness, she could keep twisting the knife and he'd let her.

Lucas leaned back in his seat trying to appear more relaxed than he actually felt. "You could have told me this over the phone."

She winked. "I wanted to see your face."

"Did you enjoy the look of horror or shock?"

"I'm being sincere."

He doubted that. He bet she got a special delight shocking him, but he decided to play it off by stroking his jaw line with mock vanity. "Then again, a man this good looking can't blame you for that."

"I do like seeing you."

No, he wouldn't fall for that. He was a means to an ends that was all. It wasn't the first time he'd been used as a tool. "You just want a report?"

"You know the drill. What to look for, what needs work, the like." She pointed to the table where a large manila envelope sat. "I don't want to take up anymore of your time."

His hint to leave. He wouldn't delay. Lucas jumped to his feet.

Wynette tilted her cheek up at him.

He frowned at her. "You must be joking."

She tapped her cheek with a manicured finger, it glittered silver.

Lucas released a long sigh then placed a kiss there. "We both know you hate being kissed on the cheek."

She grinned. "I know, but you hate doing it even more."

He turned her face and kissed her other cheek. "Hate is too strong a word," he whispered. "It would mean I cared."

Wynette laughed. "That's why I wanted to see you," she said with delight, "you only show your fangs with me."

He quickly patted Methuselah then straightened.

"You have two weeks."

"Two weeks! I told you my schedule was busy."

"And I told you your brother came to me so that means it's urgent."

Lucas paused. "When did he ask you?"

She lowered her gaze as well as her voice, looking unnaturally, scarily, subdued. "I don't remember."

"Yes, you do. I bet you can remember the last time Methuselah farted. Nothing escapes you."

She met his eyes. "I was also busy and the request escaped my mind."

Lucas slapped the manila envelope against his thigh. "When?"

"Perhaps six months ago."

Perhaps six months! She'd kept his brother waiting for six months? Why had Damian even gone to her in the first place? Lucas could have helped him. If he'd told his brother once, he'd told him a thousand times...

"I'm sorry. Truly." The sneaky snake was apologizing, if only he could truly hate her but he didn't. She got focused on something else and the request had probably skipped her mind.

Lucas flexed his fingers, reining in his temper. "Fine. I'll do it in the time given. Then I'll tell Damian—"

"You'll tell me. There's no need to involve Damian or Ian. They don't need to know anything yet."

Lucas paused, cautious. Strange that she'd mention Ian too. "Why?"

"That's my business."

He set the papers down. "It's mine too. I won't do anything that might harm my brother."

Her eyes flashed fire. "Watch your tongue, child. Don't think you're the only loyal one in this family. You may not be my blood but you are my nephew's child and that means everything to me. I keep things from him—from you—to keep you safe. So if I say it's my business I mean it. You are not the only one in this family your brothers can trust." She paused, drummed her manicured nails on the arm of her chair then said, "And I know how you feel about women."

"I love women."

"I know how they've hurt you," Wynette continued as if

Lucas hadn't spoken. "How you were treated. Your past. What your mother did..." She let her voice trail away. "I make no apologies for who I am, but I will never betray you."

Lucas lifted up the papers, shame making it difficult to meet her gaze. There were many things he didn't know about her, but to accuse her of disloyalty was a low blow. He cleared his throat then looked at her and said, "I'm sorry." He opened the folder and flipped through to get an idea of the three properties. "These are all businesses?"

Wynette nodded. "Makes a good cover, no?"

The first property was a hair salon. Been in business ten years.

The second property was a dental office.

The third was a contractor's office. He didn't think he'd get far there, since the property seemed to house two other businesses while the others were single focused, but he'd still look around.

"Will they be expecting me?"

"I'll let them know."

Wynette tilted her cheek.

Lucas closed the folder and shook his head. "I'm not kissing you again."

She laughed. "Worth a try. How about a hug?"

This time Lucas laughed, relieved that she'd forgiven him. She was his family and that mattered to him. His father loved her and he didn't want to disappoint his father. He knew that his aunt would give his father a report about their visit and he wanted to make sure it was an admirable one. "How about I leave?"

"That's a good idea. Tell Ian it's time he visited me."

"What do you want with him?"

She lifted a brow. Lucas sighed. "I know, I know, none of my business."

"Take the biscuits with you."

He quickly wrapped them in a napkin and shoved them in his pockets since he couldn't get a maid to properly wrap them for him. He then shocked her by kissing her on the cheek and dodging out of reach before she could smack him.

He waved as he backed towards the exit. "Bye, Aunty. Hope not to see you anytime soon," he said then laughed and added, "Love the manicure," when she slowly and sweetly lifted her middle finger.

Wynette didn't watch Lucas leave. She stroked Benton's head and waited.

She waited until she heard her nephew's Mercedes-Benz roar to life then disappear down the drive before she pulled out her cell phone and called her nephew, Eldin.

"You winning?" he said.

She rested back, satisfied. "Yes, he behaved better than expected."

"Are you sure this is the right thing to do?"

"I'm rarely sure of anything," Wynette said her gaze falling on the three crumbs Lucas had left on the rug, she'd have someone clean them up immediately, "but I like to take risks."

"If he ever finds out..."

"He'll find out when the time is right. For now he only knows what we want him to. Keeping things hidden is what we do best."

"You're still sly."

She heard the smile in Eldin's voice and a devious one touched her own lips. "Is there any other way to be?"

3

Maya's Hair Salon had started its life as a funeral parlor, situated on the toe end of a lower middle class suburb—a suburb that was only a few apartment buildings away from being a city (although eager developers were hoping to change that). While the solemn air that had once surrounded the building's delicately manicured surroundings and brick face had faded, somehow the heavy square windows and massive door continued to intimidate with a gravitas that its bright purple accents and poster sized pictures of various black hairstyles couldn't erase.

It didn't help that the shuffling grey clouds spit down a drizzling rain, making the row of tulips droop their yellow heads as if depressed, the neon sign had several letters unlit causing it to read 'ya air lon' as if one were trying to do a poor imitation of a Caribbean accent or a English person who tended to drop their h's.

Lucas stepped underneath the awning just as the last customer was exiting into the early evening drizzle. He'd scheduled his visit to be late and near closing. While he enjoyed people, he didn't want them around when he was inspecting a building because their energy could get in the way of a reading.

He held the door open for the heavyset woman sporting new reddish-brown highlights in her pressed black hair and smiled, she smiled back and Lucas was about to say something flirtatious before he noticed the bulldog of a man in the parking lot waiting for her. *Not worth the effort.* Lucas kept his smile in place and his mouth shut, as her gaze shifted past him. He noticed her dismay.

It took only a second to realize why. The rain would ruin her style. He shot another look at the bulldog to see what he would do. But the man seemed clueless to his lady's predicament, Lucas inwardly sighed and decided to take a risk.

He opened his umbrella and held it out to her.

She looked up at him as if he'd offered her an engagement ring. The expression on her face got the bulldog swiftly moving in their direction.

Time to disappear.

Lucas winked at the woman and quickly made his escape inside. And crashed into a pair of pink colored overalls. The owner of the overall swore as Lucas—in horror—watched the scene that was about to unfold. He saw someone falling backwards, brown arms flailing helplessly in the air, he reached for the first thing he could, a tool belt, and yanked it forward. Too hard. Suddenly, the pink overalls were coming at him and before he could do anything, he was struck by them again, knocked flat; his face buried in-between two large breasts.

He inhaled the scent of paint thinner, sawdust and blueberry muffins.

Then it was gone as the person swiftly rolled off of him

and lifted him into a sitting position as if he weighed no more than a ragdoll. They checked the back of his head and he felt broad, calloused hands brush the back of his neck, which briefly, strangely made him wonder how it would feel to have those hands skitter down his back—and front—before he dismissed the thought.

He heard a soft sigh of relief before a low, surprisingly soothing voice said, "There's no blood, but you may have a bump." He felt a hand on his sleeve. "Don't worry. That will come out in the wash." Lucas looked down vaguely aware of the oily paint stain there, surprised he wasn't annoyed by the sight of it. "They'd told me everyone was gone and they were closed for the day. I'm sorry I scared you."

This person was sorry? Wasn't he the one at fault? Lucas wasn't usually without words, but the person left him speechless as he watched them stand. They turned their back and picked up a pink cap, they placed it over a head full of black twists, gathered back into a ponytail, shielding the owner's face.

With calm efficiency, Pink Overalls stowed away tools in a box to the side Lucas hadn't noticed. A step ladder was tucked under an arm then the pink overalls left.

The scent of rain and a slight spring breeze that drifted through the open door helped Lucas come out of his stupor.

He scrambled to his feet. He felt the back of his head expecting to feel a tender section, but he felt nothing and then he remembered that he didn't recall hitting his head at all, as if the person had cradled his head and cushioned the blow with their hand or arm, he wasn't sure which. But how had they been that quick?

Lucas took a deep breath and shook his head. It didn't

matter, he was glad it hadn't been worse. He dusted off his trousers and looked around him.

The foyer of the salon had been turned into an elegant sitting room with a sleek reception desk to the left side. The air held the scent of lanolin, shampoo, relaxers and hot curlers. Further down the hall Lucas saw the salon and the startled face of a woman the same color and width of a straw broomstick.

She had long black hair parted in the middle and looked as if the breeze of a hand fan could topple her over. She stood perhaps an inch taller than him, with cheeks that threatened to disappear completely. Each ear had three piercings; she wore a shapeless blue dress and clunky brown shoes.

Smiling at her took only a bit more effort than the woman with the highlights because she unnerved him. But he quickly recovered and flashed one of his most engaging grins.

The moment he did so the woman burst into tears.

It was a new reaction for him. He'd had women faint. Even scream but he wasn't a man to make a woman cry.

"He found me," the woman wailed in a pitch so high Lucas held up his hands as if she'd sounded an alarm and he expected the police to rush in. It took a few moments to realize what he was doing and let his hands fall to his sides.

"I'm sorry?" he said, confused.

"I never thought it would come to this. What do you want? How much? How soon?"

Lucas held up his hands again, this time to assure her. "I don't know what you're talking about."

Before she could reply another woman, older, perhaps mid-forties, dressed in black with the careful movements of a ninja, came up behind her and held up a pair of scissors letting the blades catch the fluorescent lights with an ominous gleam.

"There doesn't have to be any trouble," Lucas said.

"What do you want?" the older woman said.

"Nothing," Lucas said, trying his best not to laugh at the absurdity of the situation. They were clearly scared and he didn't want to make it worse. "I mean...Didn't Aunty... excuse me Um..." His aunt used many different names. Lucas searched his mind trying to remember the name she used with her tenants. What ex-husband's name had she decided to keep? He finally seized on it, "Mrs. Clemmens tell you I was coming?"

The two women looked at him with blank expressions.

"I'm her nephew Lucas."

The older woman blinked at him, doubtful. "You're the nephew of sweet little Mrs. Clemmens?"

Sweet? His aunt was about as sweet as a bowl full of vinegar mixed with cayenne pepper. "Yes, ma'am," he said, although saying 'ma'am' didn't come naturally to him. He sensed it was a term the older woman was used to. "I am."

"Not much of a family resemblance."

He shrugged. It wasn't their business to know he was adopted. "You can call her now and let her know I'm here."

The two women shared a look. The older woman put her scissors away into the pocket of her black apron that sported the salon's name. "I'll do that." She pointed to a black, three legged stool in the salon. It looked as if it were built for a toddler. "You can sit over there."

Lucas glanced at one of the more comfortable waiting room chairs, with their plush green seat cushions and metal armrests. "I think I'll—"

"You'll sit where I tell you to. I'm keeping my eye on you."

He nodded, said "Yes, ma'am," again in order to stay on her good side and obediently made his way over to the stool, hoping it wouldn't break. His aunt was going to pay for this.

The older woman narrowed her eyes. "Where are you from?"

"Why?"

"You don't say 'ma'am' right."

"Didn't realize there was a right way," Lucas said with a smile, keeping his tone light in order not to cause offense. It was also a way to deflect his inner tension. He hated his 'outsider' status being noticed. Although he was more than twenty years away from his island upbringing, he'd picked up some of the cadence in speech and mannerisms from his father and the various people in his father's world.

The timid broomstick woman tugged on the older woman's sleeve. "We should call Mrs. Clemmens."

"Yes." They both disappeared into a room further in the back, the office he imagined.

Seconds later, Lucas heard laughter. He shifted on the child size stool, annoyed that his aunt was likely having a great time at his expense. Clearly 'sweet' Mrs. Clemmens was giving them the go ahead. His aunt was a crafty woman.

The two women returned. "Sorry for the misunderstanding," the broomstick woman said, looking far more confident than she had only a few minutes before, "But I'm sure you understand. You look like a thug."

Lucas surged to his feet, hurt. "A what?" He worked hard on his image, especially today. He'd selected a subtle custom made wool/cashmere navy suit and Fendi shoes that were as carefully chosen as his black framed glasses (which gave him a more studious look). No one had ever confused him for a thug before.

"That's not what she meant," the woman with the scissors clarified. "It's more you look like an underworld crime boss."

He winced. The woman didn't need scissors to wound. Lucas tugged on his collar and adjusted his glasses, trying his best to appear nonchalant. He knew criminals but he certainly wasn't one—anymore—and didn't look like one. Damian sure, perhaps even Ian, but Lucas prided himself on looking like a successful, *legitimate* businessman.

He smiled. Although the expression came easy, the following words did not. "It's okay."

His expression lightened the room. The broomstick woman said, "A free haircut on us, if you're interested."

"Thank you..." He let his sentence trail off to allow her to fill in her name.

"Samantha," Brookstick said, "and this is Deena."

"Where's Maya?"

"Retired. We bought the place from her and kept the name."

He nodded. "A pleasure to meet you both. Now, I don't want to waste anymore of your precious time. Let me get to work."

Samantha blocked his path. "No, I mean." She lowered her gaze, licked her lower lip as if gaining courage before she met his eyes again. "I'm really, really sorry for the misunderstanding. Is there any way I can make it up to you?"

Lucas was not naïve enough to misunderstand her, but he was still surprised. There was no reason she should be this...grateful. When he glanced to see what Deena thought of the situation he was only partially surprised to see she'd disappeared.

Lucas cleared his throat. "Did my aunt explain why I'm here?"

Samantha lightly touched his collar, her fingers brushing underneath his chin, soft as a butterfly's wings. "Yes," she said in a whisper. "She explained." She paused. "But did you know I live upstairs?"

"No."

"Would you like to start there first?"

Lucas swallowed, trying to resist the faint scent of lavender that clung to her skin. He was a sucker for lavender. He should say no. He hadn't come here for this kind of distraction and his brother was counting on him. He should nod and walk away sensing that she was embarrassed about mistaking him for a thug and, more than that, eager for the male gaze of appreciation.

Lucas wondered what her body would feel like when he pulled away that shapeless dress, plus he felt a little sorry for her. Along with lavender he could smell the biting acrid scent of desperation. An overeager hunger for connection and validation. If she wanted to indulge and he could make her feel a little better about herself, what was the harm in that? Fortunately, he always came prepared.

The inspection could wait.

"Absolutely," he said.

4

———————

Samantha's ear piercings didn't prepare Lucas for the pillows. Her bedroom upstairs was choking on them. She had large life size pillows with cartoon characters brandishing swords in the two corners and a shocking amount—it felt like a hundred but was probably ten—on her king sized bed. Eerily bright fixed smiles and black, brown and green eyes stared back at him, the black blanket had a gold circle and sword that pierced the center.

Samantha pulled off her dress and got into bed, where Lucas quickly lost sight of her as the bedspread and pillows swallowed her up.

One skinny brown arm appeared and she crooked her finger forward.

Lucas shrugged, ready for the challenge, stripped down and joined her.

He was a bit surprised by how quickly she came. He'd barely touched her before she was writhing in ecstasy, enjoying an orgasm he was certain he hadn't brought about.

He felt a flash of annoyance, wondering if she was toying with him, until he soon realized all her sounds and movements were real. This was a woman hungry for the slightest crumbs of affection. Ravenous for it and the barest amount— a brief touch on her arm, the lightest taste of her lips—sent her senses swirling. Lucas felt even sorrier for her. So he whispered words he didn't really mean, but knew he had to say because she needed to hear them. He told her she was beautiful, that she deserved to be loved, he felt like a con man but the way she responded to him, the joy in her gaze, pushed him to continue the charade.

Thin, eager fingers swept across his back like the legs of a tentative caterpillar and he briefly thought of blueberry muffins and imagined the sensation of calloused fingers sliding down his back with a cool confidence before he pushed the thought away.

Samantha's stamina seemed to be as long as the lengths of a goldfish bowl. She didn't last as long as he thought she would, but Lucas managed to leave her sighing with satisfaction before he left the room. "You're beautiful," he said once more, the final time.

She smiled. "When can I see you again?"

Lucas felt his blood go cold as tiny icicles of panic scattered over his skin. Had he pushed too hard? Said too much? Given her the wrong impression? He saw her hopeful expression and swore. Clearly he had.

"The first instinct you had about me was right," he said with regret, "I'll break your heart. You deserve better."

Her smile was a little sad, but she nodded in agreement. "I don't know how to choose them, do I?"

It wasn't a question that required a response so he

grabbed the jacket he'd draped over one of the large pillows in the corner and left.

When Lucas reached the top of the stairs he had to steady himself. His senses were more alert than usual—everything about the building spoke to him at once, the age of the hard wooden railing, the fragrance of the replaced carpet (cheap but durable) that went down the hall, the rough texture of the walls, where someone had painted over hastily removed wallpaper, the soft groan as the building settled against the drizzling rain. He briefly shut his eyes. He should have known better than to succumb to Samantha's desire, but he hadn't been able to resist a woman who needed a little cheering up.

When Lucas opened his eyes, he'd managed to ground himself and buttress all the sensations that threatened to overwhelm him. As a child it had been terrifying—to have an aged door almost demand it tell you its history, to smell a wooden pipe that hadn't been lit in centuries but had many stories to tell—as an adult he'd learned to manage his gift. He lived by sensing energy, not only the structure of a building, but it's potential.

The inspection took less than twenty minutes.

The building (like the women who occupied it) held certain surprises, but was easy to read and told him a lot. Lucas lingered longer than he needed to in the redone upstairs bathroom next to Samantha's bedroom. Unlike the rest of the building, he saw that a true artisan had taken pains to update the space. He let his hand run across the smooth, cool surface of the marble patterned wall tiles sensing the care taken with the placement of each square. This had been the work of a professional who had used a quality sealant and sturdy high end material that would last for years. The shower fixture and faucets also got his attention—both installed with functionality and style in mind. The room had been constructed by someone who cared, who took pride in their work. It wasn't something he saw regularly. He made a mental note to ask who they'd used.

Overall the place was solid. If the owners agreed, and he was pretty certain they would, the hair salon could be a great location for whatever Damian wanted.

Lucas softly swore when he realized the building had a basement, seldom used. The owners kept the door sealed and Lucas would have preferred it that way, but then he thought of his aunt nagging him and made the unwanted descent into a place he knew offered no windows and only one exit.

He hated walk-in closets, small cupboards, large pantries, crawlspaces, attics, enclosed showers, storage spaces underneath stairs and especially basements.

He worked quickly and efficiently, tamping down his nausea and fear, reminding himself he was doing this for his brother, until he could rush back upstairs. His hands were still shaking as he closed the door, but, thankfully, there was no one there to notice.

The building had extra space if the network found it necessary, plus some of the closets and upper rooms could have double uses.

Lucas made his notes and headed to the front door.

Deena met him there, seeming to materialize out of the shadows, the apron and scissors gone. "You're done?" she said.

"Yes."

"Are you sure?"

"Absolutely."

She leaned against the door, blocking his exit. "Sure you don't want to rethink that?"

Lucas thought it was an odd question but it took him the span of two heartbeats to realize that wasn't what she was really asking.

Lucas adjusted his glasses, trying to mask his disbelief and interest. He couldn't believe his good fortune. "Maybe I could be a little more thorough."

Deena pushed herself from the door. "That's what I thought."

She didn't take him towards the stairs, instead leading him through the salon to the back and a short hallway with two doors. One led to a tiny office the other to the storage closet, which was the one she opened. She pulled him inside then closed the door behind her, when she wasn't looking Lucas opened it up again just a crack.

The space was well organized with neat wire shelves that stored all the items that kept the salon running.

Lucas barely had time to slide his rubber in place before Deena was on him like hot wax, taking him between shelves that held boxes of endpapers, rollers, straight pins, jars of relaxer crèmes, hot oil treatments and hair dyes. While Samantha had been ravenous for affection, Deena expressed a primal lust. She didn't need any words of encouragement. Didn't want them. Didn't give him a chance to say anything, even do anything. She took control and Lucas happily let her.

She was rough, wild, a little terrifying in a way that heightened his enjoyment. He wouldn't have to worry about her feelings. This was pure sex. Pure pleasure. Just the way he liked it—uncomplicated and fun.

Several minutes later, Lucas staggered out of the salon into the rain scented evening pleased by his recovery and stamina; he only felt the weight of his exhaustion when he found it a herculean task to press the button on the fob for his car. When he finally managed to get the car door open, he sank into the driver's seat and released a long sigh. Deena was at least a decade older than he was. He needed to get in better shape.

He jumped when his phone rang. He glanced at the salon door with a mixture of fear and delight, wondering if Deena was following up. He cautiously pulled out his phone from his inner jacket and looked at the number. He recognized it and felt his unease disappear. The phone rang with dominant insistence just like the caller. He thought of ignoring it because he wasn't in the mood, then succumbed to guilt and answered. "Yes?" he said with all the enthusiasm of a held captive denied work release.

Wynette laughed. "Is that any way to greet me?"

"What do you want?"

"How did it go?"

He paused. That wasn't like her. "I'll give you my report when I'm finished."

"What did you think of them?"

"Who?"

"The owners, who else?"

"I don't know. They seemed nice."

"They're both single."

Good to know, but he'd already suspected that. He was proud of the 'no stealing' vow he'd honored since he was a child. He was different now. He didn't take what belonged to someone else, no matter how willing... "I have to go."

"And not bad looking."

"Not having this conversation." He disconnected and tucked his phone away. It couldn't be that his aunt was trying to set him up, could it? He shivered at the thought.

He started the car, the headlights coming to life, piercing through the darkness. One property down and two to go. Tomorrow he was going to the dentist.

5

—————

*L*ucas could smell the fried roti and curry from a block away. He made a mental note to stop by the Caribbean takeaway after he did his inspection. After a busy day running errands, he hadn't realized he was hungry.

The building that housed the dentist office sat on the tail end of a strip mall squashed between an auto parts store and game depot. As he headed there he passed someone carrying a stepladder, whistling an old tune he couldn't place, but remembered with fondness. He turned and saw the back of grey overalls and a pink colored cap. He caught his breath.

Could it be the same person? The height and build seemed right, but what were the odds? He had to be imaging things. Why did it matter anyway?

The whistling grew faint and soon the person turned the corner and disappeared from sight.

Lucas shrugged and headed to his destination.

When he stepped inside the dentist office, the reception

desk appeared longer than it should have been but not alarmingly so and the chairs in the waiting area were neatly organized along the peripheral of the room. Then he and saw the large sign with a wide smile showing pearly white teeth and the phrase "Smiles begin here" in black letters on the soft blue walls, he had a desire to race back out again. Something didn't feel right.

"Can I help you?"

Lucas turned and stared. He wasn't into men, but he actually did a double take. The tall, brown skinned man was so good looking he didn't seem real, and he could make any man feel inadequate with his powerful physique. He was at least a head taller and forty pounds heavier than Lucas, made of pure muscle. His dentist smock looked made to order and yet...something didn't feel right.

"Can I help you?" the man repeated this time in Spanish.

"I'm not sure," Lucas said in English, finally finding his tongue. He hadn't felt this awkward since he'd been a child and had to pretend...no he wouldn't think about that. It was long ago.

"It's okay," the man said. "Not everyone feels comfortable coming to the dentist."

"Right," Lucas said with a light laugh. Something was wrong. He could feel it but it didn't make sense. Was it the building? What was it telling him? And why would he think he was there for an appointment when it was already after hours? "No...I'm here because—"

The man laughed then pointed at him. "Right of course. The nephew, right?"

Lucas nodded, wondering what the man found so amusing. "Right, Lucas Wolff."

"She told me you were coming," the man said, his gaze roving over Lucas like a land surveyor.

Lucas was used to getting the once over, but wanted to make things clear. He cleared his throat, determined to be polite. "I'm not—"

"Neither am I, most times." When the man smiled, Lucas found himself smiling back not even knowing why. There was something strangely relatable about him, and yet...something still bothered him. "Tell me what you need to me do," the man said.

"Nothing," Lucas said wondering why the man hadn't given him his name yet. Lucas already knew what it was, Jamie Noeworth, because it was on the paper, but wasn't it usual for someone to introduce themselves? "I don't want to be in your way and I'll be thorough and quick."

"Good to hear. Do you need help with your equipment?"

Lucas frowned. "I don't need any equipment."

The man gave a low whistle. "That's a new one. How will you prove anything?" Before Lucas could reply, the man said, "Of course now anything can be faked with computers so you likely won't be believed and you only came here to make an assessment. Am I right?"

No, he wasn't right. But Lucas didn't know how to translate the statement the man had just made, so he smiled and nodded then went to work.

The feeling of unease only intensified. Outwardly, the office would also make a fine location for Damian's plan (whatever it was). But there was something that bothered Lucas and he wasn't sure what it was.

"You sense it too, don't you?" the man said behind him.

The man who still hadn't given Lucas his name, the man who seemed too adept at sneaking up behind people, and startling them, but although Lucas hadn't heard the man's footsteps, he'd smelled cedar and spice and felt the heat of his body. Lucas wasn't startled by the man's sudden presence, but he was on alert. He slowly turned and faced the man who was closer than he needed to be.

Lucas took a step back, not out of fear, but rather strategy. Distance was his ally, plus tilting his head back put him at a disadvantage.

"Sense what?" Lucas asked, meeting the man's steady gaze.

"This dark energy. She said you were the real deal. Sorry, I didn't believe you at first. You weren't what I was expecting."

Lucas frowned. "I don't know what you mean."

"But with your insight," the man continued, ignoring him, "I might be able to convince the owner to let me break the lease. I'm losing clients."

"My insights?"

"About the ghosts."

Lucas blinked.

"They're scaring the clients. I didn't believe in them until this place and now I can't wait to leave."

So that's why he'd given him the once over. He'd thought Lucas was a ghost hunter. He didn't know how to tell him that he didn't believe in ghosts, but there was definitely a dark energy here. But what exactly was he sensing? It didn't feel ancient; it felt present, fully in the now. He wouldn't be recommending this place to Damian.

"Unless you think there's a way to get rid of them," the man said.

"There's been a misunderstanding," Lucas said, lowering his gaze to jot down some more notes. "I'm not here for the ghosts." He paused when he realized that the energy had shifted. If, moments before, he hadn't been so taken by the whistled song from his childhood and the sight of the pink baseball cap he may have seen it sooner. The energy wasn't coming from the building. It was coming from the man. There hadn't been a misunderstanding. The man had been trying to distract him with his talk of ghosts.

Lucas' gaze shifted to the mirror where he saw two stockinged feet from behind the counter. Then he realized why the counter had seemed longer than it should have. Two 24 by 36 large rectangular white boxes sat side by side giving an illusion that they were part of the reception counter.

He hadn't seen her before. The man had probably tried to move her when Lucas had been in another room, but Lucas hadn't given him time to finish what he'd started and he'd made a mistake.

The man clicked his tongue. "I really wished you hadn't seen that."

6

---

*B*efore Lucas could reply, the man lunged at him, his large powerful frame giving him the advantage, but Lucas was quick. He couldn't let the man catch him unless he wanted to be snapped like a twig.

Fire flooded his veins as he inhaled the scent of survival and rage. One of them was not going to see the dawn of tomorrow.

He escaped the handsome giant by mere inches and knew that was more due to luck than tactic. He couldn't depend on getting lucky the next time.

The man didn't move, watching Lucas, weighing his next move. Lucas took those precious seconds to think.

He could escape. He saw a way he could dash out and outrun the giant, but he wasn't the type of man to flee and wouldn't give this beast a chance to hide the crime he'd committed. The man must pay.

Lucas thought of killing him. It could be swift and neat, but then there would be questions.

Wounding him was another option. It wouldn't be as

swift, but then the bastard could be punished for what he'd done.

Lucas took off his glasses and tucked them in his jacket pocket. "Let's not act hast—"

He didn't get a chance to finish. Lucas leaned back as he felt the breeze of a ham-sized fist brushing millimeters away from his nose in an attempt to smash his face.

The man's movements were wild and uncoordinated. He'd grown use to the element of surprise as an advantage, but didn't know how to fight when that advantage was gone. Instead, he depended on his size and brute force. Lucas noticed that the handsome giant didn't look around and study his environment. He didn't look for ways to potentially trap Lucas (there were plenty of corners to do so), he didn't grab things to use as either projectiles (a chair or small side table) or weapons (the pens and pencils on the counter). Lucas liked that pattern, it made the giant predictable. That meant Lucas could control the giant's movements.

He contemplated breaking his nose, a couple fingers, maybe take out an eye.

He dodged another swing of a fist that sliced through the air and hit nothing. He heard the giant growl. Swear.

Lucas tried not to laugh. Tried not to enjoy himself. He shifted side to side in a calculated bouncing motion, keeping the giant's gaze on him as he lured him to where he wanted his enemy to be.

He loved a fight; although that was a part of himself he tried to hide. He was desperate to forget it—but not now.

Another swing, this time the fist made contact with Lucas's shoulder, he winced, stumbled a bit, but didn't stop moving.

Saw the man's eyes, beautiful brown eyes that were too

bright, the pupils too dilated. He was high on some sort of drug. Lucas silently swore, annoyed that he hadn't noticed, but it would also work in his favor. The giant felt invincible. He'd be careless.

One of us will lose.

And that prospect thrilled Lucas even more: Power, dominance, hierarchy were all at play.

Men are beasts. Brutes. Should be strangled at birth, a tormenting voice from his past whispered.

A woman's torment. A handsome man is most dangerous of all.

On the man's face, Lucas saw what he'd been taught to hate. What needed to be destroyed. But to his shame, Lucas also saw a reflection of himself, he saw the weaknesses and primal desires he'd been taught to despise. He saw what had lured Lania and had also driven her away. *You're an animal. I thought you were different.*

Lucas tried to clear his mind from the truth of the words, the truth it said about him because Lania was gone and he wasn't going to lose.

The handsome giant lunged at Lucas again, which put the giant off balance and gave Lucas the advantage he'd been planning. Lucas darted to the side and let his fist plunge into the man's granite jaw before he kicked the man's knee from under him. The giant fell forward and the side of the wooden counter did the rest. His head hit the corner of the counter with a sickening, gruesome thud before he collapsed to the ground with the force of a marble statue.

It hadn't been the outcome Lucas had wanted, but he appreciated it.

He checked the man's pulse. Clearly dead. Too bad, he

would have been popular in prison, but at least he couldn't hurt anyone anymore.

Don't get too proud, a voice of censure whispered. *You're one of them. A filthy beast. A man not to be trusted.*

Lucas shoved his glasses back on then raced over to the motionless woman. Her eyes were closed, her wrists and ankles bound and a red scarf wrapped around her mouth. Purple bruises, a garish souvenir left on her arms and face by her attacker, marred her light brown skin.

Lucas reached to check her pulse not expecting much. Her eyes flew open.

He jerked his hands back, shocked she was still alive.

"It's going to be okay," he told her, quickly removing the gag before unbinding her. "My name is Lucas."

7

———

When her arms were finally free she hugged him fiercely. "I thought I was going to die."

Lucas patted her back then tried to pull away, unsure who was shaking more—her or him. "You're safe now, Jamie."

She gasped. "How did you know my name?"

He quickly explained about his aunt and the inspection.

Jamie held him tighter. "How can I ever repay you?"

"You can start by not squeezing the life out of me," he said only half joking.

She didn't listen. "You saved my life."

He patted her arm, then pinched her, she let go and he moved away.

Lucas stood and held his hand out to her ready to help her to her feet. But she ignored his outstretched hand, her grey gaze fixated on the body of the man who'd attacked her. She wasn't pretty or cute, but had average features that could show a cascade of emotions. Her straightened brown hair was cropped too short, emphasizing a slight overbite and strong jaw line.

"He hit his head," Lucas said unsure of how she'd feel about the man's demise. Domestic disputes were complicated as were the feelings involved. She looked dispassionate.

"Do you think you can walk?"

Before the woman could speak, the man groaned.

She looked up at Lucas alarmed and accusatory. "I thought you said it's going to be okay."

"It will be, but—"

"It can't be." She scrambled to her feet, grabbing onto the counter for support. "Not if he's still alive."

"Listen, he—"

She tentatively pushed herself from the counter. "Either he dies or I do."

"You don't have—"

"And if he's not dead yet," she grabbed a swivel chair and began to raise it over her head. "Then he soon will be."

Lucas snatched the chair from her. "You don't want to do that."

"Yes, I do." Fierce eyes met his. "More than you can imagine."

He knew that look, remembered that feeling.

The man groaned again. Lucas walked over to the man, punched him and left him still once more.

Lucas turned to the woman and saw tears shining in her eyes. "He told me that he loved me. I know, fool me. A man like that, why would he look at someone like me, but...he made me believe him. He's taken everything from me. He didn't want a divorce he was going to make me disappear, then he could have everything."

"That's not going to happen."

"What am I going to do when he wakes up?"

"He's not going to wake up."

"But he—"

"Groaned, I know. That was air escaping, but the hit on the head killed him and the drugs will take care of the rest. I punched him so you don't have to, but he's already gone."

The woman breathed a sigh of relief. "So it's finally over."

Lucas nodded.

She kicked the body for good measure then smiled.

Lucas turned to leave.

"Do you have to go?" she asked him.

"I'd rather not be here when the police arrive."

"But how will I explain what happened?"

"The marks on your wrists. The security cameras will all tell a good narrative."

"He said there are blind spots."

"He's right, but I lured him into the ones where he'll be seen. You don't need me to..." He let his words trail off as her face fell. He sighed. "But if you need someone, I'll wait with you." *It's the least you can do, you bastard,* the voice of his past whispered. *You dog. Go on and pretend that you didn't enjoy that fight just like you pretend everything else. Animal.*

Her face brightened. "Thanks."

The police initially didn't believe her story, and it didn't help that the giant had disconnected the cameras, but the man's past came to her rescue when the police ran the dead man's prints and discovered his other identities. He'd been conning women up and down the east coast for more than a decade.

The next morning, when the ordeal was finally over, Jamie invited Lucas over to her apartment to thank him.

They never got to the black tea and nibbles she's spread out on the kitchen table. Not that it mattered, Jamie had been drinking something a lot stronger than tea by the time Lucas had arrived at her modern style apartment—sophisticated muted colors, lots of chrome, minimal furniture—he could smell the whiskey on her skin, her breath, see it swimming in her eyes. Her slightly unsteady movements made the satin material of her floral dress seem to sway from an invisible breeze.

She was more vulnerable than Lucas usually liked his ladies and told her so, but she grabbed his hand and told him she was alright, begged him not to leave her.

He should go. But she looked so sad. A couple of minutes wouldn't hurt, would it?

He expected to hold her and comfort her on the couch, but she had other ideas.

She unzipped her dress and revealed nothing underneath.

He needed no more encouragement.

8

———————

She took him on the ground. Lucas would have preferred the couch but the floor offered more space, although he quickly regretted the choice when he felt the rough texture of the area rug scratch against his bare back like tiny nails. While aesthetically pleasing, the rug was built for durability rather than comfort. It was better suited for a high traffic area like a hallway than a living room. It offered no softness. The rug burns would be brutal.

He considered flipping positions but decided against it when he saw the hope in her hazy gaze, she thought she was in control, she felt powerful, and he wouldn't take that illusion away from her.

He learned she was a multi-lover: the kind that could do two things at once with the same intensity.

Jamie rode him like a bronco while she also drenched his chest in tears, twice calling him by someone else's name (not the dead guy's, thank goodness) but Lucas didn't mind. That made leaving her that much easier, she wouldn't miss him. Plus, he enjoyed new experiences and she'd be memorable.

When they finished, Jamie sat curled up on the couch—still naked. She wiped her eyes and watched Lucas pull up his trousers.

He lifted her dress off the ground, surprised by how stiff and inflexible the fabric felt, and held it out to her. She shook her head.

"Put something on," he said. "You're shivering."

"I don't care."

He did.

Lucas left the living room and found her bedroom—it held the same modern minimalistic feel as the rest of the place except for a rustic rocking chair in the corner that housed an empty birdcage. He took the blanket off of the bed, returned to the living room and draped it over her.

"You're a good man," she said.

He pulled on his shirt. "Hmm."

"But not one for commitment."

He sent her a look, she laughed. "I know, I know, after what just happened I shouldn't even be thinking of starting a new relationship. Even one on the rebound."

Lucas sat on the couch and put on his socks.

"Who are you running from?"

He paused, turned to her. "Who says I'm running?"

She leaned on her side, resting her head in her hand. "I can tell. Who is it?"

Dog, the voice of his past whispered. *Animal. I'll find you. You belong to me. You'll always be mine.*

No one had asked him that before. He didn't have an answer he wanted to give. He wasn't running. He thought of his mother, his past, his family. He wasn't running. He wasn't hard to find.

He stood. "Nobody."

"I don't believe you."

He didn't care. He grabbed his jacket.

"Did you see it?"

"What?"

"The cage in my room."

He nodded.

"I was going to surprise him with a pair of lovebirds. Isn't that pathetic?"

Not pathetic, just sad, but he didn't want to say so. Instead he smiled and said, "You'll find another use for it one day."

She bit her lower lip. "I hope one day you'll find someone worth running to."

He doubted that but didn't want to dampen her spirits. "You take care of yourself."

"Do you feel sorry for me?"

He paused, curious. "Why would you ask that?"

"You're a good looking man. Why would you waste your time on a woman like me?"

He grinned. "I don't waste anything, especially my time."

"You don't trust women, do you?"

Not a question he needed to answer.

"I wouldn't trust them either if I were you."

She flashed a watery smile that drifted along the edge of hope and sorrow before she turned away.

Lucas didn't move. Part of him wanted to comfort her more, another part wanted to run, a final part wanted her to explain what she meant. He was eager for a connection deeper than sex.

But logic took over feelings. Sex was enough. There was nothing more a woman could offer him. Nothing more he'd ask for. Jamie didn't understand him, he didn't need her to. His scars were meant to be hidden.

Only his family knew of them and even his brothers didn't know everything.

Lucas turned and quietly left.

He wasn't running.

He was ready. Ready for his mother's return.

Ready for the battle that would begin.

He decided the final property would be the easiest. It was a three level building that housed three businesses. His aunt wanted him to look at Gardner's Contractors on the third floor. Why? He no longer cared. He was going to make this job easy. He'd be in and out—no distractions, no fuss.

If this property didn't work out, the salon space was fine or he'd find Damian something else.

Lucas was so busy typing some notes into his phone and thinking of what he was going to say, that he aimlessly walked across the lobby into the elevator. Forgetting how much he hated them until too late.

9

_W_heezing.

At first Patricia hadn't been able to identify the sound and once she did, she hadn't known where it was coming from. There were only two of them in the elevator and she didn't think the tall, well dressed man could sound like wind pressed through a slit in a door. But the sound was definitely coming from his direction.

She stole a glance at him. He didn't look good either. Under different circumstances she could see that he was probably very good looking. But right now his hazelnut brown skin looked ashen, his lips without color, a sheen of sweat glistened on his forehead. He was excellently dressed —a designer checkered suit with a black shirt and slender tie only a man with a lot of money could pull off (he made it look sexy rather than gaudy), and expensive black shoes polished to a shine. He felt vaguely familiar but she couldn't place him.

Patricia didn't know if she should notice his discomfort or pretend that she didn't. It had only been ten minutes since the elevator had jerked to an ominous halt, leaving them stuck between floors. Fortunately, she'd managed to call and alert the emergency service of the problem.

"At least we're only stuck on the second floor," Patricia said, trying to keep her voice light and casual, "Even if we'd made it to the third floor we wouldn't have to worry about plunging to our deaths, perhaps we'd fracture a few bones but..." She let her words trail off and swore. The man hadn't moved but he looked even paler than before. So much for making him feel better. What was wrong with her? Why did she always say the wrong things? She wasn't good at comforting people. She was more use to taking action, but trying to pry open the doors wasn't necessary—yet.

She stole another glance at the man. If she didn't do something soon he'd likely collapse, fall face first like a felled tree if she guessed correctly, and she wasn't sure she could catch him without staggering under the weight of him. Best to take control.

She grabbed his hand, it felt cold to the touch, and pulled him towards the ground. "Sit."

He looked startled, but did as she said. He was so weak it hadn't taken much to move him. As she'd suspected, he was close to collapse, at least with him closer to the ground she could better manage him.

Up close, she saw he had brown eyes and, although he looked to be in his late twenties/early thirties, they fixed on her with the trust of a child. His humanity bare, he was beautifully vulnerable as his gaze held her as if he had been a drowning man and she was now his lifeline. His path to safety. Why was he terrified?

"It's going to be okay," Patricia said, lightly patting his hand, unnerved that it felt so cold.

His eyes fluttered closed and he whispered something.

She leaned closer. "What?"

"Hit me. I don't want to pass out."

"But—"

"Please."

He sounded so pathetic and looked worse. She didn't like violence but he had asked so...

She hit him hard across the cheek. It was only after his glasses flew across the space and hit the left wall that Patricia realized she should have taken them off first. He toppled onto his side.

She stared at him stunned. Had he fainted anyway? Before she could check his face, his shoulders started to shake. She waited for the rest of his body to start convulsing but it didn't. Only his shoulders. The man slowly sat up rubbing his jaw. It took her a moment to realize he was laughing.

Patricia crawled across the ground, grabbed his glasses then held them out to him. "Are you okay?"

He grinned. A blindingly beautiful grin that shocked her. She usually wasn't affected by men, but this one made her take notice. His grin wasn't cynical or calculated, he was truly amused. What was so funny?

"I didn't expect that," he said as if reading her mind. "I thought you'd just slap me." He glanced at her hand. "You've got quit a punch."

Patricia looked down at her clenched fist horrified. Of course, that's what he'd meant! Why hadn't she slapped him? Why had she slugged him? She was so used to protecting herself she usually didn't think of other ways to interact with people. She'd always had to use her fists. So when he'd asked her to hit him that had been the first thing that had come to mind.

She covered her fist with her other hand, ashamed. "I'm so sorry."

"It's okay. I'll be bruised but..." His gaze darted to the ceiling. "I'll be bruised but..." His gaze darted to one wall then the other. His breathing became erratic again and she realized he'd asked her to hit him as a distraction. She didn't want to hit him again, but she didn't want him panicking either.

She grabbed his hand, held it between hers, trying to get it warm. "What's your name?"

He shook his head.

"You don't know your name?"

With his free hand he tugged at his collar as if it was choking him. He swore. "I-I can't."

She helped loosen his tie and undid the top button of his shirt. "You're going to be fine. Now breathe. Take deep breaths, slowly. There's plenty of oxygen. We can be stuck in here for hours and...no never mind. We'll be okay. We'll get out soon."

But he didn't seem to believe her. He continued unbuttoning his shirt.

"Wait, what are you doing?" Patricia asked as he tore off his tie and stripped off his shirt.

"I need a favor."

10

Patricia held up her hands. "I'm not hitting you again."

He mumbled something.

"What?"

"E-even if I ask nicely?" he managed to say barely above a whisper.

"No."

He shook his head. "No worries... not going... to ask that." His labored breathing made his words difficult to hear. She reluctantly leaned closer.

"I need you to tie me up."

She jerked away. "Is this some sort of joke? You have some strange sexual fantasy you want to play out? That's fine with someone else, but I'm not—"

"Please." His voice grew weaker. "I-I can't pass out. Please."

It didn't make sense, but he didn't look as if he was playing with her.

"Okay."

"Wrap the shirt around my mouth and bound my hands with the tie."

"Are you serious? Couldn't you—?"

He took a deep breath, as if speaking took effort. "I...I would if I could...trust me." He held out the shirt with a shaking hand. She bit her lip. If he was faking this attack, he was a good actor even if the remedy was strange.

"Hurry," he whispered. "I can't pass out. If I pass out... she can hurt me."

Now he was beginning to hallucinate. Poor man.

Patricia quickly rolled up the shirt then used it to gag him. Once that was done, he dutifully held his hands behind his back.

She paused unsure. "This is the strangest—"

The man moved his hands with impatience. Reluctantly, Patricia picked up the tie and fastened his hands. There that was done.

She sat back and looked at her handiwork. It shook her to see this well built man tied up. He must be uncomfortable...but when she reached to loosen the tie he shook his head and turned to face her, keeping his hands out of reach.

"Okay, I won't touch them," she said, "but it's unnerving to have you looking at me like a victim of a kidnapping."

He didn't look away, instead, he held her gaze as if trying to calm her. To let her know he was alright. Strangely, his eyes were clear and focused. Nothing like they had been only seconds before. He certainly knew what he needed to do to keep from passing out, but facing him was too much for her.

She found herself glancing down at his bare chest to see how he was breathing. He was more lean muscle than she'd expected him to be. She noticed under his right nipple a mark she couldn't quite make out. Was it a scar? A birthmark? A tattoo? She glanced up and saw his amusement. He raised a brow in question as if to say: Want to know what it is?

She folded her arms and turned away.

He made a sound. When she turned to him he lifted his brows again.

"Okay," Patricia said, "I admit I'm curious. But how can you tell me anything with your mouth gagged?"

He glanced at his right shoulder, lifted it then looked at her.

Patricia sighed. "You want me to scratch your shoulder?"

He shook his head before he lifted his right shoulder again.

He glanced down at his chest, then at his right shoulder then met her gaze.

"You want me to look at your shoulder?"

He nodded.

She hesitated. "This feels wrong."

He blinked as if to say: You have something better to do?

"You're right. What else is there to do." She leaned close and looked at his shoulder and saw a tiny star. She glanced at his chest again. "Oh, so it's a tattoo."

He shook his head.

"It's a birthmark?"

He shook his head again.

"It can't be a scar. They're both too precise." She peered closer, ran her fingers over the scar on his shoulder. "Like they were burned into your skin." She moved to explore underneath his nipple, ignoring his quick intake of breath as she did so. She let her fingers slowly sweep over the scar. "I've never seen anything like it."

She heard a low growl of warning. She pulled her hand back, more out of instinct then fear. Then she realized what she'd been doing.

She kept her gaze on the ground. "I'm sorry. I got carried away."

He didn't move. He didn't make a sound.

Cautiously, she lifted her gaze and met his. The amusement was back mingled with something else—something secret, dark, alluring. Something mischievous in the depth of his gaze that made her face grow warm.

This was one of the most outlandish situations she'd ever been in, and yet this man made it seem...okay. As if he was encouraging her to talk to him. She didn't do chitchat. "Please turn around." She held up her hands. "I won't touch the ties. I promise."

The stranger thought for a moment then turned away. After a few seconds he moved his shoulders then looked at her.

"What?"

He moved his shoulders again.

"You want me to look at your shoulder again?"

He shook his head, lifted his shoulders up and down.

"Does your back itch?"

He nodded.

"I can untie your hands—"

He fiercely shook his head.

"Okay, okay." She scratched his upper shoulder, he tilted his head to the left, she let her hand follow until she was in the center of his back. He nodded and sighed with pleasure.

She leaned closer and whispered, "I swear if this is some sexual fantasy you've been having I'll make you—"

The elevator jerked to life, cutting off her words and causing her to fall forward, resting her chin on his shoulder.

And that's how her sister, Monica, and emergency personnel found them when the elevator doors finally opened.

11

——————

*L*ucas didn't make it to Gardner's Contractors. He barely made it home.

After getting his hands untied, he'd dashed out of the elevator before she could remove his gag. He raced out without looking at anyone, not because he was embarrassed —few things embarrassed him—and he didn't half stagger and half run to his car because he was shirtless with a gag around his mouth.

He ran because the threat wasn't over. He couldn't depend on adrenaline or pain to keep his mind clear. He felt the edges of panic crawling up his skin as the threat of losing consciousness still loomed. Then he'd be vulnerable and that scared him. He hated being scared.

Three minutes. Three minutes in an elevator, that had been a hard-won victory. In three minutes he could keep his breathing steady, keep his thoughts controlled and ride the steel cage like everyone else.

Usually, if a building had too many floors, and too many

stops, he'd get off after small, predictable intervals until he reached his destination. He'd managed to deal with his aversion to elevators for years this way.

No breakdowns, no anxiety—until today. Today, he'd shot way past his maximum level of five minutes. Three was fine. Four was unnerving but five was unbearable. Beyond five his mind couldn't take it and in spite of his tactics to keep him from a complete meltdown-—pain helped—his mind was still fighting him.

Lucas continued to make his way towards his car, but he felt as if he were running in mud, his steps taking forever to reach the black Mercedes arrogantly stationed near a lamppost.

Breathing hurt. Every breath took valiant effort as if he were trying to breathe through a slightly bent straw. The car felt far away, the traffic sounds blending with the scent of newly laid asphalt, the descending evening breeze too cool and yet not cool enough.

He slammed into his car, holding onto the hood to keep himself upright a few seconds more. He opened the handle with shaking fingers and crawled inside as the world continued to spin.

Then...thankfully...it stopped, dropping him into darkness.

SHE HAD to make sure he was okay.

Patricia had ignored the startled look of the elevator operator and her sister's giggles to run after the stranger.

He wasn't hard to find.

He was the man who'd collapsed half way inside his car, his top half hidden while his legs dangled out like a dropped toy left hanging on the rim of a toy box. She would have laughed if she wasn't worried. He could suffocate if he'd fallen face down on the seat.

Patricia dashed across the parking lot until she reached the man. Had he fainted? He'd seemed fine only seconds ago. Now he was completely still. With two trembling fingers she touched his neck and checked his pulse.

It was strong, thank goodness.

She undid the gag then hesitated, wondering how she would get him inside the car. It wouldn't be the first time she'd had to deal with a man who'd passed out. She would be methodical and quick.

She turned him over onto his back, pointedly ignoring how warm his skin felt in spite of the cool day. She took off his glasses and rested them on the dashboard then she lifted him up and he fell forward against her, like a crash test dummy. She automatically cupped the back of his head, her hand sinking into the soft give of his short black hair, wondering why the gesture felt familiar. She quickly moved her hand and let his head rest on her shoulder, the warmth of his bare chest seeming to seep through her shirt. He smelled nice too, like rosemary and peppermint, which surprised her. She would have expected him to smell like expensive cologne not some handmade soap blend.

She told herself she didn't care. She didn't want to see him as a person. People were complicated.

He was someone who needed help.

Even though he proved heavier than he looked, she reminded herself that she was used to carrying heavy objects

—4x4s, bags of cement—and refused to think about the many times she'd had to help her father when he'd passed out.

She struggled to push the seat backwards before she managed to lift the man so that he was flush against the back of the seat then she swung his legs inside.

His head was turned away from her, which made it easy for her to look him over in amazement. That such a strong, healthy man could be so weak and vulnerable.

She knew vulnerability too well and despised it.

She was the daughter of a happy-go-lucky alcoholic who'd died in a puddle of water because he'd been too drunk to save himself. Her father had been a kind, funny, tenderhearted man who found life too hard to bear without the help of liquid courage. The dependency went through several stages. First it appeared as a casual friend, then a possessive mistress, then a jailer before it killed him: A biochemist, a philosopher, a dreamer who was both too big and too small to handle the beauty and terror of being alive. He wrote numerous papers, taught, inspired and despaired that it wasn't enough. That he wasn't enough, as if through each drink he was swallowing his imagined inadequacies, while hiding from the real ones. Swallowing fears, hurts, helplessness, soon he swallowed happiness as well. That's when Patricia knew she'd lost him. When his laughter turned into a false almost hysterical giggle, instead of the deep, rich laugh he used to have.

Her mother's best way to cope had been to berate her husband and turn her heart against him—more out of survival than cruelty, which was how Patricia had seen her mother's behavior as a child. Her two younger sisters had stayed out of the house as much as they could.

It was only when Patricia was a teenager, when the almost mummified version of her father—the one with the hollow eyes and sunken cheeks, the one whose bones jutted out from under his skin like large tree roots after a rain, because he'd stopped eating—that she realized her mother's pain. How devastating it was to see someone you love on the long slow path to death. A path littered with desperate denials and angry promises, tears and apologies.

Patricia remembered one night having to help her father up the stairs and him telling her a ridiculous story while giggling and her trying not to resent him, to remember who he used to be, who he could be.

She remembered reaching his bedroom, her parents no longer shared a room, and him collapsing on his back and whispering 'I'm sorry' over and over again, each apology causing Patricia to die a little inside because he still sounded like he was giggling, like it was all a joke.

She took off his shirt and trousers then covered him with a cotton blanket, wondering why he couldn't love them enough to change. Others had overcome, why couldn't he? Why couldn't he face it?

"Don't fall for a weak man," her mother liked to warn her.

Patricia decided not to fall for anyone—weak or strong. Both tended to hurt you in the end. She'd never open her heart to anyone.

But she was surprised by how angry she was right now. Her feelings were too real, freshly familiar. She didn't know this man, but it annoyed her that he was so vulnerable. He should take better care of himself. She resented this stranger for making her care, for making her heart shift even with the barest amount of concern, when she didn't want to feel anything. When she was used to feeling nothing. She wanted to feel nothing.

Then she remembered his eyes. How he'd looked at her with a calm that was almost otherworldly. He made her feel as if everything would work out. How he managed to do that with his hands tied and his mouth gagged she couldn't understand.

But she felt a connection, as if he really saw her and cared about reassuring her. People didn't care about her like that. She was the strong one in the family. The one that had held it together so that her mother could fall apart. She liked that role. She liked being the one people depended on. She'd never depend on anyone, but, for a moment, she wondered what it would be like to rely on someone else's strength, to lean on someone and know they wouldn't let her fall.

But that was for fairy tales, not real life. She didn't need anyone else.

She lightly tapped the man on the cheek. "Hey, wake up."

He didn't move. She thought of hitting him a little harder then decided against it, she could already see bruising where she'd struck him the first time. She was probably the last person he'd want to see when he finally came around.

Patricia bent down and lifted his shirt from where it had fallen on the ground and folded it then laid it on the passenger seat, then she used his jacket as a blanket to cover him. From a quick glance he looked like an ordinary man taking a nap.

She heard him release a soft sigh, pleased. She chose to ignore how her heart responded, how it shifted a little with the barest amount of joy. She hadn't made him sigh like that. He wouldn't remember this moment or her.

She'd never seen a phobia and panic attack that bad, it would take a lot for him to recover, but at least he looked peaceful and his breathing was normal.

Satisfied, she'd done all she could for him, Patricia gently closed the car door and left.

12

———————

*L*ucas woke to the sound of steel drums. It took him a moment to realize it was his phone ringing. He absently fumbled towards were the sound was coming from, pulled out his phone and answered it.

"Where are you?"

Lucas shot up out of his seat at the sound of Damian's voice. He felt his jacket slide off his chest and settle onto his lap. He glanced around frantic, wondering where he was. And why was everything hazy and out of focus?

It took him a moment to realize he didn't have his glasses on. He saw them sitting on the dashboard and put them on. The world came into focus.

One question answered. Now the second one: Where was he?

The sky was a muted dark hue that still held a cascade of pinks and blues, which meant it was evening but not night yet. His gaze fell on a black Ford Explorer, a yellow Nissan and three sparrows fighting over a dropped French fry. Okay...he was in a parking lot.

And he was in his car because…

His mind flashed back to the memory of a low, soft voice, followed by the image of a lovely face, the cold interior of an elevator, and collapsing in his car, but he couldn't remember much after that.

How long had he been out? He glanced at the time and swore. That's right he was supposed to meet his brothers for dinner. He'd invited them over so that he could talk about his mother's release. He'd managed to convince his father to give him a few more days to tell them. He'd wanted to treat them to a nice meal and assure them that everything was alright.

This wasn't a good way to start.

Lucas lifted up the back of his chair and said, "I'll be right there so—"

"What's going on?"

It wasn't a simple question. Damian didn't ask simple questions. His questions were usually heavy with meaning, which meant his brother was worried. Lucas hated worrying anyone. "Nothing," he said, forcing a laugh. He reached to smooth down his tie then remembered he wasn't wearing one. He wasn't even wearing a shirt. He inwardly swore. "I got caught up with business. I'll finish up and—"

"Say the word."

Lucas felt his mouth go dry. As children they'd come up with a code word that they could tell each other in case they were in trouble. Needed support emotionally, physically, mentally. Didn't matter, it was a symbol of their bond. It reminded them that they had each other. Lucas had never used the word and never planned to. He would be his brothers' support, not their burden.

"I don't need—" When he heard his brother sigh, Lucas quickly added, "Really. It's okay."

"If you can't make it—"

"I can make it." He wasn't going to cancel. His brothers had taken time out of their busy schedules (and their wife in Damian's case) for him, he couldn't let them down. "It's all planned." He'd worked on the menu with his personal chef.

"Lucas."

"I'll be right there." He disconnected before his brother could argue then called his chef to apologize for the inconvenience and requested she make sure the appetizers were served.

"Your brothers look worried," Julia said. "Should they be?"

Lucas briefly shut his eyes. "No, no everything's fine."

AND THAT'S EXACTLY how Lucas felt when he walked into the kitchen a half hour later and greeted his chef, Julia Salinas, who was checking something in the oven. When she turned to him she stared at him openmouthed. Julia was always cool in the kitchen, but now looked at him as if he'd come into her presence carrying a bag from a fast food restaurant. She'd been in the restaurant industry for six years before deciding to venture out on her own.

Lucas wondered if her expression was because he hadn't straightened his tie or something. He was usually pristine when it came to his attire, but had been too preoccupied to care. "I'm really sorry about this," he said.

Julia blinked.

Lucas turned at the sound of hurried footsteps coming up behind him. He waved at his housekeeper, Carter Bukoski, who gasped in response and covered his mouth as if he'd found a grime stain where it shouldn't be. Carter took pleasure in his job. He'd been a househusband for nearly twenty years then found himself unmoored when his two sons went off to university and his wife filed for divorce. He signed up with a maid service and Lucas used him for one day and decided to keep him on the payroll indefinitely. Few things rattled him.

What was wrong with them?

Carter lowered his hand from his mouth then sent Julia a furtive look.

Lucas cleared his throat, "I know I've caused you both a lot of trouble. Don't worry, you'll both get a bonus."

"But your—" Carter began to say before a low warning hiss from Julia stopped his words.

"Your brothers are waiting in the dining room," Julia said, coolly professional again. "I'll follow with the first course."

"It's okay," Lucas said, "just leave instructions and I'll take care of the rest." It was only on rare occasions he'd have his chef both cook and serve. His brothers weren't big on formality.

"No," Julia said giving Lucas a stern look. "I think you should see your brothers first."

That wasn't like her, but Lucas wouldn't argue, he had kept his brothers waiting long enough. He patted her on the back and smiled. "Thanks," he said, but Julia didn't smile back nor did Carter who looked near tears.

Lucas left the kitchen and glanced down, doing a quick survey of his clothes. Everything was in place. He hadn't misbuttoned his shirt, his jacket was in good order. He couldn't fathom why they'd look at him so strangely.

He waltzed into the dining room with his arms

outstretched and a wide smile on his face. "Sorry for the wait," he said to his brothers who were seated at the stone-top table, "but I promise the food will be worth it and of course the company."

Damian surged to his feet as if propelled by a rocket, his large size appearing to be even more intimidating than it usually was, Ian remained seated but his body stiffened as if he'd been turned into a marble statue. But while his brothers' physical reactions were polar opposites, their expression was the same—their eyes read rage.

13

Lucas swallowed and stumbled back stunned by their fury, fear scattering over his skin. He didn't like to make people angry—he knew too well the price of that—especially his brothers. They meant the world to him.

Guilt twisted his gut. He knew he'd let them down by being almost an hour late, but he'd never imagined he'd make them this angry. He noticed the plate of tomato bruschetta had been left untouched. They hadn't even eaten the appetizers. He let his hands fall as quickly as his smile.

He took a cautious step forward, smoothing down his tie because he didn't know what to do with his hands. He took a deep breath then said in a low voice, "I know I messed up—"

Damian pointed at him. "Shut up and give me a name."

"What?"

"You heard me."

"But—"

"Why did you lie to me?"

Lucas frowned. "I didn't lie."

"You said nothing was wrong."

"It wasn't. Isn't. I swear."

"Then what happened to your face?"

His face? What was wrong with his face? Lucas touched his cheek and winced at the shock of pain that followed, gingerly he let the tips of his fingers register his swollen, tender skin. Oh, right. The punch. He'd forgotten about that. Fear fell away as dawning took place. Now he understood his brothers' anger. "I asked for it."

Damian shook his head. "I mean what did you do?"

"I know what you mean," Lucas said, taking a seat, feeling more at ease, "I literally asked for it. I told someone to hit me."

"Why?"

He paused. He really didn't want to share what had happened, even if they did deserve the truth.

"We waited," Damian said, "You owe us."

"You're right," Lucas said.

At just the same moment, almost as if they'd been waiting, Julia and Carter appeared with the first course.

Lucas inwardly groaned. He really wasn't in the mood for an audience but they'd been just as shocked as his brothers so they deserved an explanation too. "I got stuck in an elevator."

Carter and Julia froze as if unplugged; Damian swore and collapsed into his seat. Ian looked the most unaffected when he sighed and clasped his hands together as though he were conducting a business meeting.

Lucas took the plate of basil scented creamy pasta and chickpeas from the frozen chef and said, "This looks wonderful."

That took Julia out of her paralysis and she placed the

other plate she held in front of Ian while Carter served Damian.

Damian absently thanked him, barely glancing at the food before he leaned forward and said, "Where? How long? Who were you with?"

Lucas noticed that Julia and Carter had also taken a seat and were looking at him, waiting for the answer. While he enjoyed treating his staff like family, he wondered if he'd become too lax in his dealings with them.

Lucas stretched his arms then let them fall to his side. "I'm not going to answer any of those questions."

"Why not?" Julia demanded.

"Because it doesn't matter now," Lucas said. "And thank you for your—"

"Of course it matters," Carter added.

"I invited my brothers here for another reason," Lucas said, hoping the two would take a hint and leave.

They didn't.

"What happened?" Damian said, clearly not caring who was around to hear it.

Lucas sighed. "I just told you what happened."

Damian shook his head. "Half your face is purple."

Lucas shrugged. "Doesn't bother me. You know I'm used to bruises."

He smiled. No one else did. He sighed. "Not even a chuckle? You're a tough crowd."

Damian frowned, scratched his beard. "It'd help if you were actually funny."

Lucas rested a hand over his heart and looked pained. "You wound me."

"How big was the guy?"

Lucas shifted in his seat. He twirled the pasta onto his

fork and took a large bite. It was rude to speak with one's mouth full. Unfortunately, they waited for him to finish. He swallowed and said, "Delicious. This food is my reason for living. Eat up before it gets cold."

"How big was the guy?" Damian repeated.

Lucas kept his gaze down on his plate. Twirling enough pasta onto his fork until it was nearly the size of a tennis ball. "It wasn't a guy."

"You mean you're unsure?" Carter asked.

"No," Lucas said, resting his fork down. "I'm sure."

Damian's brows shot up. "A woman did this? Did you upset a boxer?"

Lucas flexed his fingers, lifted his fork then set it down again. "No, like I said, I didn't do anything. I asked her to hit me, but she definitely hit me like she was used to punching things." Lucas smiled remembering the shock and surprise in the woman's voice when she apologized. "She kept me from...she helped me."

"You know pain isn't the only way—"

He wasn't in the mood for a lecture or advice. "The monster's looking for me."

His words got the response he wanted. Damian's face changed and Ian stilled like a predator on alert. His brothers knew about his mother, although he'd never thought of her as one after his father had rescued him. Calling her Monster made it bearable. One could escape a monster, but a mother held more of a tie. More of a weight and burden. They shared the same blood, but that was all.

"I'm okay," Lucas said. "Dad knows but I thought you should be prepared. She doesn't know everything about me, but it won't take her long to put the pieces together."

"How big was she?" Julia asked.

Lucas shrugged. "I don't know, I was a kid."

"To hit you like that," Carter added.

Lucas looked at them amazed. "You're still thinking about the punch?"

"It's impossible not to," Damian said. "It's impressive. Are you sure you didn't do something to piss her off?"

"No. At least I don't think so and if I remember correctly, though most of it was a blur, she seemed very sorry afterwards. But that's not why—"

"Did you get a name?"

"No...and I know what you're doing. I don't need a distraction. I've been prepared for this day." He paused. "You don't seem as surprised as I thought you'd be."

Ian picked up his fork and began to eat, Damian looked away.

Lucas swore, "Dad told you."

"It doesn't matter," Damian said. "We're still here. Tell us what we need to do."

"Ask Rosaline to come over," a deep voice said.

The room fell silent. Everyone turned to Ian, surprised. Because Ian spoke to infrequently, when he did he always managed to make a room stop and stare.

"Why?" Damian asked, wondering why his brother would mention his wife.

"She needs to look at the bruise."

A private looked passed between them and Lucas knew they were no longer talking about his bruise but the elevator experience.

"I'm fine," he said. "I can take care of it myself."

Ian ignored him. "She'll have a cream for him."

"And see if she can bring that bread she made last time," Julia piped up.

"Oh and bring some of that essential oil I was able to use in the study," Carter added.

Damian nodded. "Right. Okay."

Lucas shook his head amazed he had so little control over his household. He didn't want or need Rosaline. She'd see more than he'd want revealed. "Why won't anyone believe me? I told you I'm fine."

Damian took one of the tomato bruschetta's and finished it in two bites, before he leaned back satisfied. "We'll let Rosaline decide that."

14

The sun had long disappeared by the time Patricia had finished installing the shower for her chatty client, Mrs. Chen. Her body ached on the edge of collapse, every muscle feeling as if she'd gone a couple rounds in a boxing match. She'd been fighting corroded pipes all day, but finally the job was finished and she could go home.

She packed up her things just as Mrs. Chen popped her bright cheery face, framed by a stylish perm, in the door and showered Patricia with praises on a job well done. She again told Patricia (for the fifth time) about how important it was to have new appliances in the old house because her grandson was coming out of rehab and trying to get his life back on track. She told Patricia (for the sixth time) about how bright he was and the high marks he used to get in elementary school. But from looking at a photo lovingly resting on the woman's side table in the living room, of an unsmiling man in a black shirt that held all the charm of a framed mug shot, it looked like the bright young grandson was pushing way past thirty.

Patricia smiled at Mrs. Chen's enthusiasm. She picked up her tools and headed down the picture lined hallway, hoping to escape before she bumped into Mr. Chen who was ten times chattier than his wife.

But neither could compete with the old house that had been telling Patricia more about the couple than they'd probably want known. To Patricia, people and houses were like notes on a keyboard that offered either discord or harmony and this couple blended with their home like a string quartet.

Patricia could sense the harmony and love that filled it and hoped their grandson would be able to sense it too. (Her own home had been filled with chaotic cacophony, although it hadn't always been that way).

Mrs. Chen again thanked her and then asked her to recommend someone to help fix a broken porch step. Patricia heard the slight anxiety in the woman's voice, the concern that it couldn't cost too much, that she didn't want her grandson coming to a house that wasn't up to par for fear he'd slide back into addiction again.

It was a fear she could relate to. She understood the need to try to fix something when you can't fix the ones you love.

Patricia's exhaustion momentarily faded away when she assured Mrs. Chen she knew which step was a problem and that it wouldn't take too much time to fix.

Mrs. Chen thanked her again, then, thankfully, left Patricia alone to work in peace.

Patricia stepped out onto the porch, adjusted her pink baseball cap then pulled out a stick of sugar-free gum from the front pocket of her overalls. She folded the stick of gum in her mouth, reminding herself that chewing gum was better than smoking.

The gum was supposed to taste like lime but oddly

tasted like lemon. Smoking had never given her surprises like that, but, then again, a long-term smoking habit could end up giving her some surprises in the future she didn't want to face. After three years as a non-smoker, she had already been able to last longer on jobs than she had in the past.

She unpacked her tools and got to work on the porch step.

Work was good.

It was distracting.

When she was working she didn't think about *him*.

She *would not* think about him.

She would think about why she'd been outbid on three jobs in spite of her stellar reputation.

Patricia was pleased she'd finished the Chen job on time and on budget and had another project lined up. But it wasn't enough. She preferred to have three projects at a time. That was the most she could handle, since presently, she had to handle everything herself including managing timelines, workloads, conflicts, resource availabilities, finances and the regular issues of running a business like hers. She wanted more work, but her current pace of one project at a time sequentially was better than nothing at all and kept the lights on and the plants fed.

Because she already had enough on her mind, she would not think about the man she'd met in the elevator.

Or the one who'd fainted in his car.

It didn't matter that they happened to be the same man.

She wouldn't think about him.

She'd learned early that caring was dangerous.

She'd had to build bricks around her heart starting in elementary school. That was where the torment began.

In fourth grade she'd transferred to a new school, when

the family moved for her father's new job. She'd been a shy kid hoping to make friends, which she hadn't managed to do at her old school.

Her name was Patricia Irene Gardner, and for some reason—to this day she still can't understand why—the teacher decided to introduce her to the class using Patricia's full name. One kid, who fancied himself the clever class clown, realized that the first initials of Patricia's full name spelled PIG.

He decided it should be her nickname and soon others joined in. It didn't help that she was chubby and on that day, when the clown proclaimed what Patricia's nickname should be to the other kids on the playground (cleverly out of earshot of any adults), her father had casually tossed one of his new red socks in the wash with Patricia's white blouse and when she saw the socks' destruction (it was the first time she heard her mother swear), instead of being upset, Patricia had actually liked the new pink blend and decided to wear it to school.

Little pink pig. Little pink pig. They'd sing on the playground.

She thought of never wearing pink again until she overheard her father talking with a colleague about the colors in some foreign flag. He said that red stood for passion and white stood for hope.

In that moment, pink became the color of strength.

It was a color she'd need when she entered middle school where the verbal taunts turned into physical assaults. One bully made it her mission to hurt Patricia every way she could. She'd put her trash on Patricia's lunch tray (when she wasn't spitting in her food), have one of her followers trip Patricia in the hallway. The group would take turns beating

Patricia up after school, and at times they'd leave used feminine products in her locker.

Until one day, a week after her thirteenth's birthday, Patricia decided she'd had enough. This little piggy wasn't going to cry anymore, she was going to fight.

She watched videos, started lifting weights and running in her neighborhood while also doing odd jobs around the house like mowing the lawn, and painting the hallway. She also got to know her Uncle Orlando who was a contractor. He gave her advice and helped her with some home projects and also taught her some fighting moves.

This secret training took nearly a year then one day, when one of the tormentor's minions was making pig noises, and the leader tripped Patricia in the hallway before third period, Patricia pretended to stumble.

The group started to laugh.

Their laughter turned to screams when Patricia spun around and punched their leader with all the rage she could muster (which had been years in the making). One punch probably would have made the point, but Patricia gave her tormentor two—one broke her nose, another knocked out three teeth.

She ended up being expelled.

Patricia tried to keep her head down at the next school. But was—again—seen as an easy target.

When the taunting and bullying began, she ended it by shattering someone's jaw. The parents tried to sue but when Patricia sent pictures of their precious daughter's exposed breasts, which she'd sent to a boy she'd liked (who of course shared with others) the parents left her alone.

The school didn't. She was expelled again.

She managed to make it to high school where her reputation preceded her, with some hyperbole of course. Not only could she beat people up but, apparently, she could also toss them across the room.

She didn't care about the truth of the rumors.

All that mattered was that she could walk the halls, enter a cafeteria, or sit in a classroom without anyone bothering her. Nobody messed with her. She never heard someone mimicking pig noises again.

But high school wasn't for her. She did poorly on every test given (and honestly couldn't care less) and with her father's health declining she wanted to start working to help her family. Plus, she'd become a target for something else: bets.

Before she caught on, she'd gone out with three guys without knowing they had only chosen her because of a dare. She'd wondered why none of them ever wanted a second date. Finally, through the help of her only friend, Jeremy, she learned the truth.

He'd been stripped of his gym clothes and shoved into the equipment closet (having been too big to fit into a locker) when he'd overheard two guys taking a bet on who could date her, mentioning the other three guys who'd managed to succeed.

Patricia wrote down all the names Jeremy had mentioned and came up with a plan. She decided to let one of the boys win the bet then the following day when the 'winner' tried to pretend she didn't exist, that they hadn't even gone out the Saturday before, she dropped a pregnancy test in his backpack that he couldn't explain to his girlfriend.

She knew it was a risky move because he could have removed it before his girlfriend found out. But what he didn't know was that she was the jealous type and checked his backpack after every period.

Their hallway fight became epic.

The other guys also had unfortunate ends.

At seventeen she sensed the family needed the extra money she could bring in and fortunately, got a chance to become an apprentice with her Uncle and had worked for him until he retired last year.

She'd hoped he'd hand over the business to her, having worked with him for sixteen years, but to her dismay, he left the business to his eldest son: The one with the shiny college degree and hands as soft as butter. The only time she'd seen her cousin pick up a hammer was to move it out of his way to pour himself a drink.

She'd never felt more betrayed. She couldn't believe her uncle hadn't even considered her as a successor. And he'd disappeared to some island hideaway without giving her a chance to confront him.

The one bright spot was that her cousin (out of guilt most likely) had given her some money and rented an office for her so that she could set up her own business: Gardner's Contractors.

She wasn't too proud to take him up on his offer and it had helped her, but she felt as if she were starting from zero. Not even her reputation as a dependable, hard worker came to the rescue because all of uncle's contacts preferred to work with her cousin instead.

Her uncle was the last proof she needed that she was better off on her own. With every brick thrown at her she'd built up a hard inner core. Her survival depended on it. On being strong.

Her family depended on her.

Patricia finished the porch step then packed up her tools.

No, the man in the elevator, the one who smelled like rosemary soap, the one who held her gaze, she'd never think of him again.

She wearily climbed into her truck and was about to close the door when Mrs. Chen called out to her. She raced over to the truck and held out a container of homemade dumplings.

Patricia graciously thanked her—glad she wouldn't have to cook dinner tonight—then drove away.

No. She would not think about him.

15

———

There were times when Lucas had to remind himself that his beloved sister-in-law, Rosaline, wasn't a witch.

She didn't talk much (only slightly more than Ian, but the bar wasn't high) could read auras and heal using different lotions and concoctions she made.

Plus, she managed to bewitch his staff. They always materialized the moment the attractive dark skinned woman with shoulder length cornrows pulled into a low bun entered the house and eagerly took whatever she gave them. Julia held the fresh baked bread close to her chest, as if given an ancient secret recipe before she returned to the kitchen while Carter floated up the stairs tightly holding onto his jar of essential oils.

Now, Lucas sat with Rosaline in the living room, absently listening to her as she gave instructions on when and how to use the cream. If he paid too much attention she would read his aura and reveal things about him that he didn't want her to.

"...and I plan on leaving Damian..."

Lucas sat up in the chair and turned sharply to her. "What was that?"

Rosaline laughed, her eyes bright with humor. "Glad that got your attention."

Lucas frowned and sunk back into his seat. "That's not funny."

Rosaline covered her mouth to hide a giggle. "I'm sorry."

He folded his arms unable to hold his frown. "Then why are you still laughing?"

"Because of your expression."

"I enjoy being entertaining, that's my reason for living," he said, any trace of annoyance now gone. He could never stay upset for long. Especially when it came to his family. He pulled off his glasses and pinched the bridge of his nose. "Speaking of entertaining, I'm going to host a bon voyage party for Dad." His father was going on a three week holiday around Europe and Lucas wanted to send him off in style. "Tell Damian I'll take care of everything, all he has to do is show up."

"Are you sure you'll be up to it considering...?"

Lucas replaced his glasses on his face. "Considering a monster's after me?" he finished. He pulled out his cell phone and waved it at her. "I hire people. There's nothing for me to do."

"Except organize everything."

He grinned at her concern. "I hire that out too." He tucked his phone away. "So. Do I pass?"

"I'm sorry?"

"You're going to give Damian a report about me, right?"

She folded her arms.

He'd put her on the defensive. He hadn't meant to do

that. "It's just he and Ian worry too much and I wouldn't want you to worry them more," Lucas said, trying to soften his tone and the expression on her face. "I've known them longer than you."

She kept her arms folded.

He silently swore. This wasn't going well. "Okay, go on," he said with a sigh of defeat. "Tell me what you see. Am I on the verge of despair? Is a dark abyss looming to swallow me whole?"

"Why did you ask her to hit you?"

He blinked. "What?"

"In the elevator," Rosaline clarified, her tone soft. "Why did she need to hit you?"

Lucas hesitated. He didn't want to talk about it but knew she wouldn't leave until he did. "As a distraction."

"She hit you harder than she needed to. Did that make you angry?"

Lucas grinned in memory. "No, actually the opposite. You should have seen her face. I felt sorry for her. I really regret putting her in that position, but she was...easy to..."

"To what?" Rosaline asked when he didn't finish.

He was about to say, To talk to, then realized they hadn't really talked at all. "To be with," he said.

"How so?"

"I don't know," he said growing impatient.

"Did you get a name?"

"You're not usually this chatty."

"Did you get a name?" Rosaline repeated.

Lucas sighed dramatically. "No."

"If you could give her a name what would it be?"

"Does it matter?"

Rosaline pulled out her cell phone. "Should I call Damian right now?"

Lucas waved his hands. "Okay, okay. I'll play along."

She put her phone away and waited.

He sent her a helpless look. "I really don't know."

"Try. Do you remember what she was wearing? What she looked like?"

"She was dressed in jeans and a grey shirt with pink nail polish. I'd say she was cute rather than pretty, medium height with nice curves."

"Your type."

He flashed a slow smile. "If she's female and she likes men, she's my type."

Rosaline narrowed her eyes.

"What?"

"You're lying."

His brows shot up. "I'm not lying." Growing up with Ian, the human lie detector, had been bad enough. He didn't need this too. "I like women."

"You desperately want to."

"What's that supposed to mean?"

"Nothing."

His tone sharpened. "What have you heard?"

"Nothing."

He believed her, but she was reading something about him he didn't want her to know. He stood ready to be honest. "Okay, we both know..." He took a deep breath. "You cannot tell anyone this."

She nodded.

"I like women, but...I'm not good for them."

"Who told you that?"

"It's something I know."

She opened her mouth as if ready to argue then closed it and he felt relieved. She saw it too. Part of that knowledge hurt, but he was glad she wouldn't lie to him. "Okay." She stood. "I'll tell Damian you're fine."

"Thanks." He walked her to the front door and held it open. "That means a lot."

She met his gaze, held it for a moment longer than she usually did, before she nodded and left.

Lucas closed the door behind her almost wishing she had told him he was wrong. That there was someone out there for him. Instead she'd left him with the grim reality, the one he'd always feared, the reality that he would always be alone.

16

It took all of Rosaline's strength to keep walking to her car. She wanted to run back inside and tell Lucas he was wrong. So very, very wrong. He was wonderful. Amazing. Any woman would be lucky to have him. Why would he think otherwise? But there were reasons and she didn't want to pry, not yet.

Damian didn't like talking about his past, let alone those of his brothers. But what she'd managed to learn about Lucas's sounded pretty nasty and dark. All at the hands of someone they referred to as the monster. And now the monster was back and Lucas had trusted her with his hidden pain.

She wouldn't betray him and tell Damian what his brother had told her, but she also wanted to find a way to shift the colors of anguish that swirled around Lucas. There had been slight traces, but they hadn't been so prevalent before.

I like women, but...I'm not good for them.

Who hurt you, Lucas? Who made you believe that? His

statement was not the product of a childhood wound he was talking about, but something newer, fresher, and more recent. Rosaline had almost said something after he'd spoken those words, but she sensed silence was the best. Lucas had grown accustomed to manipulating people with charm and words (and she wouldn't be able to outmaneuver him there, he was too good with his sly smile and witty words), but he didn't know what to do with silence.

He wouldn't have believed her anyway, although she could sense he wanted her to argue with him. She saw it in the depth of his steady brown gaze. She wasn't the one to convince him otherwise. Someone else had to.

And if she was right, she knew who that 'someone' could be.

When she returned home, Rosaline barely made it through the front door before her husband pounced. "Well?" Damian said, taking her jacket from her.

Rosaline slipped out of her shoes. "She definitely made an impression on him."

"Who?"

"The woman in the elevator."

"Of course, she did. You can see the big bruise on his face."

Rosaline shook her head and headed for the living room. "No, that's not what I meant. I mean she's good for him. She's affected him in a good way. When he talks about her his colors are bright."

Damian groaned.

"What?"

"That means she's bad news."

Rosaline looked at him confused. "Why would you say that?"

"Because my brother has great taste in most things, except women. He likes pain."

"Damian—"

"So he chooses the ones who will hurt him."

"I don't think it's that simple. At least not this time."

"It is. You'll see." He paused. "Do you think he knows her and isn't telling us?"

"No, she really is a stranger to him, but his description of her...he really paid attention and he's not even aware of how much of an impact she's had. Other than that, he's not lying when he says he's fine. His colors are stable. He's emotionally balanced." Although he's carrying a raw pain he has to work out on his own.

"That's good," Damian said with a relieved sigh. "I hope he never sees her again."

17

Patricia was not having one of her best days when her twin sisters, Melody and Monica, rushed into her office. They were fraternal twins but acted like one mind.

They were both working on their graduate degrees. For some reason, beyond Patricia's understanding, her sisters actually enjoyed school, and volunteered their free time helping Patricia around the office, usually addressing technical issues, acted as a receptionist on the rare occasions a possible client dropped by and used any down time to study.

But they weren't in study mode as they stood in front of Patricia's desk.

"There's a man," Monica said, her long dangling earring, which nearly reached her shoulders, swaying against her skinny neck. She wore a blouse of neon orange and red trousers.

"Out front," Melody said, tugging on the skirt of her light pastel dress, which flowed against her curvier form, while tiny pearls graced her neck.

"Who's related to the landlord."

"Mrs. Clemmens."

"He wants to look over the place."

"He said we could call her to verify."

"And that he'd be quick."

"But we thought we should talk to you first."

Patricia sighed. She wasn't in the mood to talk to anyone and she'd sort of remembered Mrs. Clemmens talking about her nephew, but hadn't paid much attention about the reason. All that mattered was that her lease wasn't being cancelled. She had enough on her plate and the business was barely scraping by. The one thing her cousin had been good for was getting her this office and paying the rent.

Patricia made a dismissive wave with her hand. "Let him do what he needs to." When her sisters didn't move she said, "What?"

"We think you should talk to him," Monica said.

"Why?"

Monica looked at Melody before she said, "He's a little terrifying."

"But charming too," Melody added.

"He mentioned having a house he's considering renovating."

That got Patricia's attention. A possible client?

"Yes," Melody said reading her thoughts.

Patricia gestured to the door. "Then why aren't you selling our business to him?"

The sisters shared another look.

Patricia felt her patience thinning. "What? Tell me quick."

Monica bit her lower lip. "It's seems like a big job."

"I've done big jobs before."

"True," Melody said. "And it could be the start of some-thing bigger if you do this right, but..."

Patricia sighed when her sister trailed off. "But what?"

"We have a bad feeling about this," she said.

Monica nodded. "There's something he's not telling us."

Melody nodded too. "Or something wrong with the house."

"We're not sure."

"We were thinking of giving him a reference to—"

Patricia stood. No way was she going to lose an opportu-nity like this. "I'll deal with it."

Monica delicately cleared her throat. "We don't think you should."

Patricia patted her on the arm. "I'll assess the situation. If he's better off with one of our competitors that's fine."

"You're so much braver."

"Than we are."

Patricia had to resist the urge to dash out of the office. She hoped her sisters hadn't dissuaded the man to leave, even unintentionally. They were good at reading people, but so was she and she needed the work.

Patricia struggled to keep her steps measured and confi-dent as she left her office and walked into the main lobby, where she found a man staring up at one of the corners and then a light fixture as if they both were the most fascinating things he'd seen.

He seemed neither terrifying nor charming. He had his back to her, his hands clasped behind him, so all she could make out was a tall, trim brown skinned man wearing an expensive dark blue suit with light brown shoes (that shouldn't have worked but strangely did) short cropped black hair, and manicured fingernails.

The scent of money swirled around him and she had to keep herself from salivating. She was not used to having clients like him, but something about him felt familiar.

She cleared her throat.

He turned.

She stared.

And stared.

And stared.

It couldn't be *him*. She was not supposed to meet him again. She'd pretended to not think of him for days, never imagining he'd be here looking so...normal. She was surprised her sister, Monica, hadn't recognized him, but he'd dashed out of the elevator so fast (not to mention shirtless with a gag around his mouth) he could have been mistaken for anyone.

But not to her. Whether half-naked or fully clothed she'd recognize him.

However, he didn't seem to recognize her. The man smiled—no, he did more than that. He blinded her with a row of straight, marble white teeth and moved with the casual confidence of a con man as he held out his business card as if they'd just met. "Lucas Wolff."

18

—————

$\mathcal{P}$atricia didn't move. Lucas. He now had a name and it suited him.

"She's Patty," Monica said behind her in a cool business tone, reminding Patricia that she and the man—Lucas— weren't alone although he made it feel that way.

"But she prefers to be called Patricia," Melody added.

Monica nodded. "Yes, Patricia Gardner."

Lucas continued to hold out his business card, his tone almost teasing when he said, "Nice to meet you, Patricia Gardner."

Patricia took the card from him. "Uh, right, yes, same."

"Nice cameras."

"Cameras?"

Lucas paused so briefly that for a moment she wondered if she'd imagined it before he gestured to the display of different finished projects hanging on the wall and said, "Camera angles of your work. I see you specialize in kitchens and baths—"

"But I've been involved with large renovation projects,"

she quickly added, "and have a great list of suppliers I work with so don't hesitate to ask me about anything."

An unreadable look entered his gaze that worried her, he had appeared to be pretty easy to read. Had she said something wrong?

He glanced away and she noticed a slight down turn of his lips, something bothered him, but before she could worry about what she'd seen, he returned his gaze to her face, warm and inviting. "I believe my aunt told you about me?" he said then started to explain why he was there.

Patricia barely listened. It all sounded like such banal pleasantries. How could he be so smooth? So unaffected by seeing her again? And what had she said that had bothered him? Perhaps he hadn't liked her interrupting him? Perhaps he wasn't the same man. He must remind her of the man in the elevator.

But then he did something unnerving. He briefly lowered his gaze then met hers and slightly raised a brow. She didn't know how he did it, whether it was a trick of the light or the way he slightly tilted his brow upward but suddenly, it was as if a mask fell from his face, revealing the man underneath, one with probing brown eyes that made her feel calm.

She noticed the tiniest bit of bruising beneath one eye, cleverly covered by makeup, and felt guilty all over again.

Wordlessly he let his eyes say, *It's okay, relax, trust me,* and in spite of herself she did. Although she didn't know why. At least she knew she hadn't been wrong about him. His eyes were something she'd never forget. The way he focused his full attention on her made all her senses come alive. Made her notice him in a way she didn't want to. Her gaze fell on his pillow soft lips, the angle of his jaw, the shape of his ears.

She searched to see if he'd lost weight, curious to see how the incident had affected him, then she became annoyed that she'd cared. That she'd worried at all. He looked fine. More than fine. It was as if nothing had happened.

Then he blinked and the mask was back in place. With the skill of a magician he became a stranger again. A man pretending he didn't know her, while also letting her know that he did. A man of contradictions. "You must have some jealous exes."

Was he making fun of her? "Why would you say that?"

"Because you're good at what you do. This kind of talent can intimidate people."

"Not my problem."

Lucas sent her a long searching look before he said, "I'll get to work. This won't take long." He lightly brushed past her, the scent of rosemary trailing him, but when his arm touched hers it burned her like an electric shock. When she jumped he gaped at her a mixture of horror and dismay on his face. "I'm sorry," they said in unison, and Patricia forced a laugh that didn't ring true and he smiled in a way that didn't reach his eyes. But it wasn't unkind, it was sad, as if he felt his mere touch disgusted her.

But how could he think that? He didn't seem like the kind of man women rejected or if they did the kind of man who would care. But he did. The hurt was brief, but she'd seen it. She didn't know why she'd reacted to him so strongly, but she didn't want him to think that he was at fault. She'd touched him before, why had it felt so different this time? "I guess I'm too big to miss," Patricia said to lighten the mood then instantly regretted her words because they were corny and she usually didn't talk about her size, because it was easy to notice and not something to be pointed out, plus it sounded flirty and she didn't flirt.

But instead of lightening the mood, her words seemed to make the energy between them grow more intense. Lucas didn't say anything, he barely looked at her (his gaze shifting to the floor then the wall), but somehow he loomed larger, every aspect of him capturing her attention, drawing her closer. She wanted to touch him again, to feel that burning heat of his skin, he made all her senses spin. Her mouth felt dry, her heart continued to pound.

This was no ordinary man. Inside him lurked something hot and powerful that seemed to radiate around him and when his gaze finally met hers the intensity of fire and light-ning that mingled there took her breath away.

This wasn't the man from the elevator, or the one who had fainted in his car, nor was he the businessman who'd smiled at her only a few moments ago. This was someone wholly new, someone she found fiercely, dangerously attractive.

She made a move to step back, but he gave a low growl of warning and narrowed his eyes as if to say, *Don't run or I'll chase you.*

The warning surprised her, as if he sensed her fear. She'd never been this afraid before, but not because of him. But herself. Of her strong attraction to him. What she wanted to do to him—with him. She gripped her hands into fists, although her first instincts had been to run, she didn't feel like running now. *You think you can catch me?*

He blinked, slowly. *Yes.*

She bit her bottom lip. *I'd like to see you try.*

His gaze dipped to her mouth then back to her face. *Is that a challenge?*

It's whatever you want it to be.

And she wanted to strip him down and—amazingly—he looked like he wanted to do the same. She felt the heat of his gaze as if he were slowly undressing her and enjoying every moment of it.

Careful.

Why should I be careful when I know your weakness?

Suddenly, he lowered his gaze and quickly said, "Excuse me," in an octave so deep it was as if the sound had been pulled up from the bottom of the ocean, before he disappeared down the hall.

19

She'd lost him. She'd scared him off. Been too much. She shouldn't have even tried.

She must have imagined his attraction: The touch, the look, everything. It had all been in her head. All one sided. She'd thought there had been a moment between them, but she'd been wrong. Instead, Lucas couldn't get away from her fast enough. She was too strong for him.

Another weak man. She should have known better, but it hurt all the same.

Patricia barely had a moment to recover from her overactive imagination before her sisters rushed up and stood on either side of her.

"We told you he was scary," Monica said, standing on her right side.

"And terrifying," Melody said, standing on her left.

"I don't think we said that," Monica gently chided her sister.

Patricia shook her head, wishing she had a moment to

gather her racing thoughts and pounding heart. "I don't think that."

Melody patted her on the back. "You could barely speak."

"And you're having a hard time breathing," Monica added.

"You don't have to pretend not to be scared."

"We're here for you."

"But I'm really not," Patricia said.

"That isn't like you," Monica said.

Melody rested her hands on her hips as if coming to a decision. "This proves it."

Patricia frowned. "About what?"

"We can't help him with his project," Monica reminded her.

"We don't even know what it is yet," Patricia said. "Let's wait and see." Patricia didn't want to disappoint them but suspected that Lucas Wolff would change his mind about hiring her. Especially because of the strange way she'd responded to him. She inwardly groaned at her foolish actions. That wasn't like her to let emotions take hold. She wished she knew a way to win back his trust.

Fortunately, she didn't have to. Nearly five minutes later, he knocked on her open office door. Patricia glanced up from her computer surprised. She stood. "Did you need to look around here?" She was ready to leave the room, eager to keep distance between them until she could figure out how to make him feel comfortable with her again.

He motioned her to sit back down. "No, I've finished my inspection."

She didn't sit. His voice was still an octave deeper than it had been when they'd first met and it stirred something wild within her—like the desire to jump over her desk and rip off his shirt and...

That would be inappropriate.

As would grabbing his hand and leading it down her front until her cupped her...

No, she had to keep standing because if she moved even an inch she might do something that would embarrass them both. She rested a fist on the top of her desk. She would not scare him away.

Everything that had passed between them when he'd accidentally touched her in the main office area had all been in her mind. Of course, there was no way she'd be interested in a man like him or he in her, even casually. Business was all that mattered. Fate had given her a second chance and she'd seize it. This was her chance.

"That was quick," she said.

She'd thought the inspection would have taken much longer. Although she hadn't really asked or cared about what the inspection was for as long as it meant she could keep the office.

"I work fast," Lucas said in that same disturbing voice then fell silent as he looked around her office. She waited for him to say more, but he didn't. Instead he walked over to her arched built-in wall unit and touched one of the light wood accents that complemented the dark blue hues.

He ran a hand along one of the shelves, with the sweep of a slow, soft sigh. And Patricia watched his hand and her mind went where it shouldn't have as she imagined his hand sliding down her—

"You?"

Patricia blinked, coming out of her wayward thoughts. "What?"

"Did you build this?"

"Yes," she said surprised. "How could you tell?"

He shrugged, a quick rueful grin came and went. "You wouldn't believe me." Before she could ask him more he said, "I'd like to talk to you about a project."

"Sure. I have a few minutes," Patricia said trying to sound casual. Her schedule was completely free. She had the rest of the day—the week—if he needed it.

"Unfortunately, I don't," Lucas said sounding genuinely regretful his voice returning to normal. He held out a folded piece of paper. "Can you come to this address tomorrow? Say around two?"

Patricia took the paper from him and read the address amused that he'd felt the need to write it down in the first place. "That sounds fine." She sighed relieved that things were better between them again. She folded the paper then slid it in her trouser pocket.

He waited.

"Is there something else?"

"You don't have any questions?"

"Not until I see what you want me to do."

He nodded. "And you don't have to write the time down? I don't want you to forget."

"Tomorrow at ten, right?"

Lucas opened his mouth to correct her then slowly began to grin, recognizing her teasing. "I wasn't questioning your professionalism. I'm sure you get that a lot."

More than she'd care to admit. "I will take very good care of you and your property. You don't have to worry."

Lucas adjusted his glasses and she noticed the slight downturn of the corners of his mouth. "I'm not worried," he said.

He was a smooth liar, but she wouldn't fall for it. Patricia sat down, feeling more at ease and leaned back in her chair. "Yes, you are." He looked startled and she smiled in response. "It's okay not to trust me yet. I have a lot to prove."

A glint of humor entered his gaze. "I'm not worried."

This time she believed him. Again, she didn't know how he managed to be two different people at once. He'd managed to say the same statement twice but in two different ways—one sounding like a lie and the other ringing true.

The second time sounded true because he didn't seem the type to worry, but whatever had passed only a few seconds ago hadn't sat well with him, clearly whatever it had been didn't bother him now.

However, although Lucas wasn't worried, suddenly Patricia was and she didn't know why. She regretted sitting down, having to look up at him.

She thought of her sisters' warning. She did sense there was something he was hiding, but she'd figure it out later.

"Tomorrow at two," she said. "I promise I won't forget."

She expected him to grin, but instead his features stilled and he said, "If you change your mind, I'll understand. Just let me know."

"Why would I change my mind?"

He hesitated, shifted his gaze to her wall unit before he looked at her again and said, "Right...I'll see you then."

She stood. "Great. I'll walk you out—"

His hand shot out with the power of a sea god able to stop an ocean wave or cause a tsunami. "Sit," he said and she followed his command without thinking. She stared up at him stunned, wondering what had just happened.

"Sorry, I didn't mean..." He touched the side of his

glasses, chagrined and softened his tone. "I don't want..." He cleared his throat. "I mean you don't have to follow me out. I've taken up enough time."

Patricia could only nod in response and watch him go.

Seconds later her sisters rushed into her office. Monica spoke first. "What did he say?"

"What does he want?" Melody said.

Patricia leaned back in her chair, intrigued. "Not sure yet. But tomorrow I intend to find out."

20

Shit, something was wrong.

Lucas sat inside his car and rested his forehead on the steering wheel, trying his best to control his temper... and lust. Aunt Wynette was up to something and Patricia was the key.

But he couldn't think about that right now.

Why had his aunt sent him there?

First the location was all wrong. Unlike the other two properties this one made no sense. Why would his aunt have him look at a business on the third floor when she owned the entire building (the first two floors held a tax preparer and temp company)?

Second, there was nothing special about the third floor office. Chance of expansion was limited and the point was to work with a location that could be discreet, perhaps even provide an opportunity to install an extra storage space or a place to hide what the owners wouldn't want others to know about. There was no such opportunity at Gardner's Contractors. The roof wasn't easily accessible, the vents were too small for someone to hide or escape, the closets and rooms would have to be made smaller rather than bigger to accommodate any changes.

Third, Gardner's Contractors was the only legitimate business in the entire building.

The only things legitimate about the other two supposed businesses in the building were the signs on their front doors. From the brief sense he'd gotten, they felt as empty as robbed tombs. He knew, with not much investigation, he'd confirm his suspicions and find out that his aunt used them for something else. She could easily let Damian use one of the other offices.

But Lucas could let that all slide if he hadn't spotted the cameras.

The tiny one in the right corner of the main area hadn't surprised him, however the one on the light fixture and another in the left corner had.

Why were there so many cameras for such a small space?

Patricia didn't seem to know about them, which made his suspicions grow. When he casually mentioned the cameras he saw no recognition in her gaze or her two associates. So either they wanted to pretend they weren't there because they didn't want to spook a potential client or someone had installed the cameras without them knowing.

And if someone was watching, why were they?

Lucas tried to get a sense of how much Patricia knew about his aunt's other life or about the building, but any code words he'd tried to feed her met with a blank stare. He opened himself up to questions Patricia didn't ask him, referred to jealous exes that she didn't have, gave her a chance to change her mind, which she didn't seem inclined to do.

Lucas lifted his head off the steering wheel and swore.

Patricia was the most dangerous variable and he didn't know why. And he couldn't get involved with her until he could figure out what part she played.

She was completely different than the other three property owners.

If only that was the only thing that made his mind race.

It was her reaction to him. In all the times he'd opened his senses to read a building he had never touched someone and had them respond. Most times only he was aware, which was why he liked to have few people around him, and if he had an unpleasant shock, the other person remained unfazed.

But not her.

Lucas absently rubbed his arm, remembering the heat that had passed between them. He remembered the quick intake of breathe; the scent of lilacs and wood polish, he'd watched her lick her lower lip and he imagined the taste of her tongue, then he'd met her eyes— she'd looked shocked, frightened, scared.

And, to his horror, it aroused him. With the animalistic desire of a predator he'd wanted to pounce.

His gaze fell to the way her figure filled her rose colored T-shirt, a heady mix against her chestnut skin. The sight made him think of sweet strawberries drizzled with chocolate, he salivated at the thought.

She tried to make light of the moment and it only aroused him more. And disgusted him. It was the part of his nature he tried to hide.

He quietly tried to warn her, but she stared back, not understanding the danger. Innocently, teasing and taunting him. She thought it was a game. If only it was that simple.

He quickly excused himself before he did something rash—like stealing her innocence and introducing her to sin —and tried to forget her. He took deep breaths, but the feeling didn't go away.

All his mind kept repeating was: *You know her name now. Don't let her go.*

He'd thought of the woman in the elevator and now he knew where she was. Who she was.

And he wanted her.

He tried to focus on the building but there wasn't much need to since the office wouldn't suit Damian at all.

He should have left then. He should have passed by Patricia's office without a glance. He shouldn't have looked inside and seen her sitting there. He shouldn't have been affected by how sad and vulnerable she looked. He shouldn't have wanted to wrap his arms around her and hold her close.

You are no good for her. Stay away. Stay away. You have nothing to give.

But he ignored that warning and knocked on the door of her office (his self made hell) daring fate to stop him.

He told himself if Patricia looked at him again with even an ounce of fear he'd walk away. He wouldn't hurt her. He didn't want to hurt her.

He braced himself, ready to apologize for frightening her, but she didn't look frightened.

She looked ready, as if to say, *I'm not scared of you.*

And his hunter's blood fired up. He motioned her to sit but she didn't.

She watched him, wary, one hand gripped in a fist as if she were ready to fight him off.

He didn't blame her. He could barely keep hold of his

lust and knew he wouldn't last long if he wasn't careful. She wasn't willing, not yet, so he had to be cool, patient.

Although he felt as hot as a furnace.

He remembered standing in her office and running his hand over the wooden shelf of her built-in wall unit, trying to ease his tension.

Touching it had been a mistake because her essence was all over it. Not only did he know she'd built it, he could feel her passion, her obsession, this feeling felt familiar (but he couldn't place where) and it felt good (too good). His palm burned against the smooth surface, and he craved to touch her. To slowly strip her down and run his hands all over her warm, bare flesh.

He managed to get his thoughts under control.

She wasn't afraid.

That aroused him even more.

But until he understood more he had to tread carefully.

He was close to the end of his tether when she offered to follow him out. He hadn't meant to frighten her, but he couldn't have her close to him. Not when he wanted her as much as he did.

Lucas sighed and pulled out his phone. He had to call Alex.

When the call connected to his PA, Alex Tran, Lucas heard loud music in the background, as if someone was murdering an electric guitar and screaming their pleasure, which wasn't a surprise. Alex liked extreme sounds. "I need you to find everything you can on Patricia Gardner in an hour."

The volume of the music dipped. "Sorry, didn't hear that. Did you say in an hour?"

"Yes."

The music stopped and silence descended before Alex said, "Anything to do with the monster?"

I hope not. "I don't think so."

"Anything else I need to know?"

"Wynette's involved."

Alex swore. "And she's connected to Patricia Gardner?"

"Yes, but I'm not sure how. On paper she's her landlord, but something's not right."

"And I'm guessing you don't want your aunt to know you suspect something?"

"I knew you were smart."

"And you want me to find out info on Patricia without her knowing." Alex released a long sigh. "That's going to be hard."

"If it was an easy job it wouldn't be fun."

Alex groaned.

"I believe in you," Lucas said with a grin. "Make Daddy proud."

21

———

There were some things that could only be experienced in real life. When Patricia drove up to the magnificent farmhouse, a baby blue colored jewel sitting in front of a looming forest on acres of green pasture, freshly mowed, the sight of the magnificent structure made her gasp and drool.

Seeing it on paper and online was nothing compared to seeing it in real life. And Lucas wanted her to work on this.

This job was a career maker. A job like this would change her life forever, but the moment she followed Lucas and he stepped inside the grand foyer her heart crashed to her feet and shattered.

"You can't live here."

Lucas quickly spun around with the smooth ominous grace of a street fighter. The motion surprised her; he had a cold brutality that his fine designer clothes couldn't hide. "Why?"

Patricia swallowed. She'd whispered the words she hadn't meant for him to hear them. She'd nearly scared him away once and she'd promised herself she wouldn't do so again. She certainly didn't want to make him angry. She sensed his energy and it was as tense as a coiled snake. His bite would be venomous.

She'd seen him vulnerable once, but he wasn't vulnerable now. "What?" Patricia said, hoping to feign innocence.

Lucas shoved his hands in his pockets, the action should have made him appear smaller, but it made him seem more lethal somehow, less predictable. "You can't live here," he repeated in a casual tone that belied the heat in his gaze. "That's what you said. I want to know why."

She made a dismissive gesture with her hand, her heart thundering in her chest so hard it hurt. She could not lose this opportunity. She briefly glanced down at her pink colored boots, trying to gain strength. It didn't matter what she thought. That's not what he'd hired her for. "No reason."

He loosened his collar.

Patricia noticed the motion and felt her unease growing. "Why don't you wait outside and let me look around."

"Why would I do that?"

"Because the house knows you."

He narrowed his eyes. She realized she'd said too much. She needed to keep him as a client. "I mean the way you move around as if you've been here before."

He shook his head. "No, that's not what you meant."

She bit her lower lip, cleared her throat. "I promise that I will do everything you requested on time on budget and... Are you sure you don't want to meet outside?" she finally said when he loosened the top button of his shirt.

"Do I bother you?"

"I'm not watching you strip down again."

He grinned. "I was wondering how long you were going to pretend you don't remember me."

"I thought you'd want it that way."

He blinked slowly as if to say, *You thought wrong.*

She glanced away and cleared her throat. "Let's—"

"I didn't get a chance to thank you."

"I'd rather you didn't."

He folded his arms. "You don't like this house."

"I didn't say that."

"You don't need to. It's all over your face."

"What I think doesn't matter. It's your needs that—"

"And you don't think I should live here."

Dammit! "I'm sorry I said anything."

"Tell me what you mean."

Patricia let her shoulders sag. Just lie. He won't believe you anyway and what does it matter that he'll be miserable here? He's rich he'll get over it.

"Whatever you say you won't lose me as a client."

"Famous last words."

"I mean it."

Of course he didn't mean it but it was too late to turn back now. The rapport she'd tried to build was gone. She'd lost his trust, she might as well lose it all the way and stop wasting both their times.

"You're right. You heard me say you shouldn't live here and the reason is..." She took a deep breath. "I sense the house's energy calling to you. I can't quite explain it but I can sense objects and energy and whether something is meant to be with something else. Especially when it comes to buildings. It's like a sound when someone is in a space that's meant for them it's a sound of harmony, but when it's not, it creates a terrible discord. When you stepped into this house it was like the high pitched screeching of a train scraping on tracks, metal on metal, grinding. This house. It's not good for you and I don't think there's anything you can do to make it work."

She waited for him to tell her she made no sense, to say they were through. Instead he turned away and said in a casual tone, "What else do you see?"

"It's not that I see anything. I just...sort of sense things."

He tugged on his collar, impatient. "What do you sense then?"

She wanted to say, That we both should leave here right now because the house is slowly draining the life blood out of you? But instead said, "You wanted the bathrooms done first, correct?"

He nodded.

"Then I think we should go upstairs."

22

Upstairs was worse.

Patricia couldn't take in the luxurious décor—the sleek wood and polished stone, the white and black accents that gave the interior a modern feel—because every step Lucas took hurt, like a high pitched screeching sound. *Get him out of the house,* a warning voice said, but she ignored it because she needed this job. He wanted to redo all 3.5 bathrooms and the kitchen. Possibly two of the six bedrooms. He even hinted at a guest residence.

This was a goldmine. If she kept her mouth shut.

He can't live here!

"You weren't quite clear about everything," Patricia said, desperate to combat the warning voice in her head. "Will you be living here by yourself?"

"No."

Oh, so he had someone. Of course, which was also why it wasn't right that she'd been fantasizing about him since last night. At least if he was with someone maybe that person would balance things out for him. Perhaps it wasn't so bad after all and she was overthinking things. "A wedding present, perhaps?"

Lucas sent her a questioning look and she felt her face burn. It was a joke referring to the extravagant gifts rich people liked to give each other but it had fallen flat. "Never mind."

"Do you think it should be?"

"It's not my place to say."

"My brother wouldn't accept it anyway," he mumbled.

Brother? Was this house part of a family estate? None of her business.

Get him out of the house now! The money's not worth it. "I can find my way to the bathrooms and—"

"We're almost there."

"I know and I—"

Her words caught in her throat when they passed by a closet. Lucas passed by first and the discord was so terrible Patricia briefly covered her ears.

She felt the sensation of being shoved forward and falling into the small space, although she knew she couldn't fit. It wasn't happening to her, but someone else. She heard the door close behind her, she heard a key lock. She felt heat and tasted fear.

It was a memory, but not hers.

Get him out of the house!

She shoved him forward, past the closed door, as if the closet was about to spring open and swallow him. It was only when Lucas stared at her stunned that Patricia realized what she'd done.

"Did you just push me?" he said.

She looked down at her hands. "I'm sorry."

"Why did you do that?"

"I don't know." She couldn't say, I think whatever's inside that cupboard was trying to get you. That made no sense, neither did that strange memory. That had never happened to her before. "Just eager to see what's inside I guess," she said with a nervous laugh, quickly opening the cupboard before slamming it shut. "I think—"

"You're scared."

For you, yes. "No. It's nothing."

He adjusted his glasses. "What did you sense?"

Not see, but sense. He believed her. But she felt uncomfortable sharing what she'd sensed. It felt too intimate. Everything about this house felt too close.

Years ago, on a job with her uncle, Patricia had used her ability to help a newly married couple. Patricia worried because the woman didn't harmonize with her new husband's house. The couple sensed it and that's why the couple had hired her uncle to help them renovate the kitchen. But no matter what they tried—new cabinets, countertops, flooring—something felt off.

Until one day, Patricia decided to walk around the kitchen alone with the woman to figure out where the disharmony was coming from, because she blended well with the rest of the house. It took some tuning, but Patricia finally discovered that the texture and color chosen for their kitchen reminded the woman too much of a bar she used to frequent when she was drinking too much.

Patricia told her uncle what she thought and together they were able to persuade the couple to come up with a design that suited them both.

But there was no such happy fix here. Something dark and sinister lurked in this elegant farmhouse and it hated Lucas.

"Tell me," Lucas said softly. "What do you sense?"

"I think you should sell this house and move on." she braced herself for his anger or annoyance.

He laughed. "You wouldn't be the first to think so."

She stared, confused. "Then why won't you?"

He shrugged. "Stubborn I guess."

But she sensed it was deeper than that. He held onto this house for a darker reason. She watched him walk ahead, the sounds of his footsteps like the terrible high pitched strings in a horror movie.

She didn't want to care.

He had his reasons for staying.

The first bathroom was only a few yards away. If she made it there, perhaps everything would be okay.

She took a step forward then paused at a sound. Not a noise. Nothing like the discordant noises that had been following her. This was a specific sound: The careful sound of footsteps. "Wait."

Lucas spun around again with that cool lethal grace that made the hair on the back of her neck bristle. It was then she realized he also moved with not only speed but silence.

She dropped her voice to a whisper. "I think someone's here."

He flashed a lethal grin. "That's interesting."

She didn't find it interesting at all.

He gestured to the stairs. "Think you can make it out without them spotting you?"

"Yes, but—"

"Then go."

"Go?"

He nodded. "Yes. Go home. We'll discuss the renovations another time."

23

———————

Lucas expected Patricia to argue, even offer a token protest, but she disappeared faster than a flash of lightning.

He didn't want to admit that hurt.

Of course she'd be eager to leave him (how could he blame her?) she thought the house was creepy and probably thought he was too.

He rarely brought anyone here, not even his brothers, but the women he did, usually gushed and told him how beautiful the house was and marveled at all of its finery. He could see in their eyes a hungry ambition to marry him and become lady of the manor.

That was exactly what he'd wanted at the time.

When he used to believe he might have a chance at an ordinary life, a family perhaps, he'd used the house as a lure to win women over. Sex was easy, settling was hard. The house was there to help bridge that chasm for him.

It worked for a time. Lucas knew he was handsome and charming and that charm lasted long enough for the women to try to convince themselves he was safe. He could bypass their natural instincts not to trust him.

Because he couldn't trust them.

And it was a flaw he hadn't managed to conquer.

Twice he'd proposed, fully aware the women he asked had fallen in love with the house, his wealth, the prestige, rather than the man.

He was fine with that.

Fine with the lies they told themselves about him. Fine that they tried to pretend not to fear him.

Why would anyone love you? You're filthy. An animal. A dog.

All that mattered was that they said, Yes.

And to his delight, two did.

But the charm Lucas depended on only lasted so long.

Because no woman could truly love you. Not once they know who you are.

Soon the casted spell began to fade and the money and the house wasn't enough to keep them. They discovered he wasn't the man they wanted.

The first engagement ended after a month in a sea of tears. Floods of regret.

The second, with Lania, lasted nearly three months and ended with screams and shouts of accusations.

You lied to me. You're not who I thought you were!

If only Ericka hadn't...

But he wouldn't think about them.

And now Patricia was gone. Any hope he'd had in that department was sealed shut.

She wanted nothing to do with him.

He couldn't blame her.

Fortunately, her swift exit made things a lot less complicated.

He felt almost giddy. Eager for a fight.

Only moments before he'd felt as if he'd been suffocating, he hated the ghastly house, but he'd brought Patricia there as a test.

You can't live here.

He remembered her words with a feeling of dread. He had no plans to live there, but how did she know that?

From what Alex had been able to find out about her, she shouldn't know anything. Alex hadn't managed to find much about Patricia at all. Everything seemed above board. Her parents and siblings were dead ends too. Although the fact her sisters were twins intrigued him.

But Aunt Wynette hadn't chosen Patricia's business by accident and now Lucas knew why.

She had a gift. It wasn't like his, but it was useful.

Patricia had managed to see past the house's gorgeous façade. It had disturbed her and she'd told him so. Warned him.

It was one of the properties he'd gotten to spite the monster. That's why he kept it, although he hated every inch of it.

And now there was someone else inside it.

Lucas walked downstairs at a leisurely pace.

He'd been waiting for one of the monster's men to strike. And he was in the mood to hurt someone.

He casually wandered around on the main floor, making himself an easy target. He rambled around the kitchen, sat in the living room. He gave whoever was in the house plenty of time to come up behind him, to catch him unawares.

But they remained stubbornly hidden.

After ten minutes he got tired of waiting.

He listened and heard movements upstairs.

Seemed he'd have to go to them.

Great.

He walked back upstairs, a weapon poised and ready, and heading down the same path where Patricia had first alerted him of hearing something.

He paused when he heard footsteps.

Finally, his prey had fallen in the trap.

24

Patricia watched Lucas spin around as if in slow motion before she heard something whiz past her ear. It lodged into the wall behind her with a hard whack.

Lucas' eyes widened in fear then roiled with the anger of a thousand gods. "What are you doing here?!" Before she could respond he said, "I thought I told you to go home." She opened her mouth and again he interrupted her. "Never... Ever... Ever. Sneak up on me. Do you understand?"

She nodded, speech impossible.

That deep, commanding voice was back, but there was something more that amazed her: His fury.

So this is what he looks like when he's angry. She'd thought he'd be the type to shout, but his anger was strangely cold, villainous, lethal.

She saw a fight and fire in his gaze that her father never had. She realized there was a difference between being weak and having a weakness. He may have weaknesses, he may be vulnerable sometimes but he was far from weak.

There was nothing weak about this man.

It was sexy as hell.

"You've got to get out of here." She tried to pull the object from the wall. It looked like a pen. But how could someone throw a pen with such force that it would be stuck in the wood boards?

"You shouldn't be here. I told you to leave."

She continued to struggle to remove the lodged pen from the wall. "But you have dangerous people after you."

"I know that." Lucas sighed and removed the item from the wall as if it was as easy as pulling a twig out of a loose hole.

Patricia held out her hand. "Let me see that."

"No." He tucked it inside his jacket pocket.

"Do you regularly carry lethal pens around with you?"

"Patricia, I—"

She covered his mouth and listened, then she grabbed his hand and raced down the hall. She stopped at the closet.

She felt him stiffen when she opened the door. "No, don't—," he began to say, but she didn't give him time to finish. She shoved him inside then followed behind and gently closed the door.

Lucas frantically tried to reach behind her for the handle; she could hear the fear in his voice. "You're trying to kill me."

"Shh..."

"Let me out. I can't—"

"I said shhh," she repeated, blocking his effort to escape. "There are really bad people out there."

"I know that," he snapped. "I can deal with them."

"They have guns. That's why I couldn't leave. There was a guy with a gun near my truck."

Lucas groaned. "I'd rather face a gun than this."

"Be quiet."

He reached for the handle again. She knocked his hand away.

He swore. "Patricia, please. You don't understand. I can't—"

She covered his mouth and said in a low voice, "Yes, you can. They're close, but they don't know where we are. Just trust me."

She could feel him shaking, but he fell silent. After a few seconds he mumbled, "Shit, I think I'm going to pass out."

"No, you're not." She couldn't slap him because that would make a sound. If she moved her arms to pinch him it could rattle the hanging items in the closet. So she thought of a compromise.

She licked under his chin. She felt him stiffen, but he seemed more alert than before.

"A little longer," she whispered when she felt him waning. She licked him again. He jerked to attention, if she wasn't terrified she would have found it amusing. But at the moment she had to keep him attentive because she couldn't afford him making a sound and if he fainted she couldn't catch him.

She heard footsteps pass.

"I'll check here," a voice said outside the door.

"I've already done that, they're not there."

"They have to be here somewhere."

"They might have escaped out the basement."

They heard the footsteps fade, but waited. The house told her it wasn't safe yet.

She felt something heavy fall against her, she swallowed

a cry as Lucas's body landed on her. She sank beneath the weight of him.

"What was that?" the voice outside the door said.

"I think it was the closet," the other replied.

She felt guilty. She'd pushed him past his limit. She probably shouldn't have pulled him into the closet with her. He probably would have done better escaping, but she'd ruined his plan and now they'd both be killed.

She gripped her hand into a fist. She wouldn't let that happen without a fight. She would cover him with clothes and then open the door and run, they wouldn't think to look for him there.

With effort Patricia lifted Lucas to a sitting position and whispered, "Forgive me." She turned to open the door, but then heard a deep voice say, "No, forgive me," before she was thrust against the back wall of the closet.

It spun around and she found herself in another room.

She turned. The wall closed. She pressed her hand against it, but the wall wouldn't budge. "Lucas?"

Her voice seemed to echo. What was this room?

Why hadn't he followed her? If they found him in the closet, they'd kill him. But they'd probably opened the door by now. To go back for him would make his sacrifice futile.

Patricia found herself in darkness, cool concrete beneath her palms, biting into her knees, the smell of old sweat and musky sheets. She fumbled around, first on the ground then she stood and reached above her head. A soft string brushed against her hand.

She pulled on it and a dim light revealed a cubed shaped grey room with no windows. It was infinitely worse than the closet had been because at least the closet had a door. Here she couldn't find one. She only saw a cot. This wasn't a room.

It was a prison.

And nobody but Lucas knew she was there.

If he was killed she was trapped there. Was that why he'd asked for his forgiveness? He'd doomed her to this terrible fate?

No, there had to be a way out.

25

———————

ut after what seemed like hours she realized there wasn't another way out and she couldn't open the wall that had swung open like a secret door. It seemed to only work one way. A door that let you in but didn't let you out.

The room was built to absorb screams. To silence cries. No one would hear her.

She could break the metal leg of the cot and chisel away at the wall knowing there was something behind it, but she didn't know how thick the wall was.

She paced. She wouldn't panic. She had to think.

And the practical pig knew what to do. The practical pig always knew what to do.

Patricia inwardly laughed, remembering the words of that made up story. She didn't know why it had come to her, but the words and the story behind it gave her courage.

She remembered a boy teasing her when she'd said she wanted to build houses when she grew up. "Girls make homes, they don't build them," he'd said with a laugh.

Later that day, she'd overheard her aunt rifling through Melody and Monica's large children's book collection searching for stories to entertain the kids at the hospital. She worked as a nurse and knew that keeping the kid's spirits up helped them heal.

At that moment, eight year old Patricia decided to come up with a story about a pig who builds houses and the wolves who needed her. She called it: The Practical Pig and the Three Little Wolves.

She added pictures to her story and then asked her mom to give it to her aunt.

To Patricia's surprise her aunt said the story had been a hit with the kids at the hospital and asked for more. The task gave Patricia a sense of pride. So Patricia wrote and drew other stories for them. She wasn't a good student, didn't have friends, but her aunt made her feel useful.

But as Patricia stared at the grey walls, she didn't feel useful now. She hadn't helped Lucas at all. She'd made matters worse for both of them.

But feeling sorry for herself wouldn't work either. And the heroine of the first story she'd written wouldn't have given up. She was practical and always helpful. She would come up with something.

Patricia checked the corners and the length of the floor. She pounded on the wall with her fist. It didn't make a sound and the wall didn't budge. She kicked it. Still nothing. Shoved it. Nothing. As a last ditch effort she ran into and hit the wall with her shoulder and finally it shifted an inch. She felt triumphant then paused when she realized the wall continued to move. Her efforts hadn't made it move, it was something else.

She saw Lucas's hand and it motioned her forward. "It's safe now."

Patricia reached out to grab his hand, but he pulled it away before she could. She didn't know if the action was intentional or by accident, and she briefly wondered if he was angry with her, but she didn't let herself worry about it. She scrambled out of the grey cell into the safety of the closet, pleased to feel the sensation of clothes hitting her face and the wooden floor pressed against her palms. A shaft of light entered the closet when Lucas opened the closet door. She stood and walked out then paused at the sight of a man sprawled on the ground in the hallway with his feet bound and his hands tied behind his back. "How did you—?"

"No time to talk," he said his voice low, focused.

She expected him to head down the stairs so they could both get out of the horrible house, but Lucas headed to one of the bedrooms then disappeared inside.

Patricia found him peeking outside the window, careful to quickly dodge out of view. "You said there was someone by your truck?"

This Lucas was different. Although he'd fought the man in the hallway, he didn't have a mark on him. His clothes looked unruffled, his face untouched.

"Patricia!"

She blinked, his harsh tone snapping her out of a daze. "Yes?"

She saw his impatience, sensed his frustration with her. "I asked you a question."

"Yes, right, right. Sorry."

He softened the tone. "I need to know what's out there to keep you safe. One got away."

He wasn't angry, he was worried. She was beginning to understand him. "I know."

He glanced out the window again. "Tell me where you last saw him. If he's still there, I'll take care of him, then come and get you."

"Okay, so I kinda lied."

He sharply turned to her. "You lied?"

"There's no guy with a gun. At least not anymore. When I went to my truck he was there, so I snuck up behind him and took him out and then returned to see if you were okay."

Lucas blinked. "Excuse me?"

"Which part did you miss?"

"The whole thing."

Patricia sighed. "There was a guy with a gun—"

"Where's the gun now?"

"In my truck."

"And he didn't see you put it there?"

"No, I told you. He's knocked out. It's no use. You can't see him from here," she said when Lucas returned his gaze to the window.

"Because he left?"

"No, because I knocked him out."

"He might have woken up by now."

"Even if he did, it'll be hard for him to leave. I keep rope in my truck." Before Lucas could ask her what she meant, Patricia motioned him forward. "I think I'd better show you."

26

He mustn't touch her.

Lucas had almost made that mistake when he'd opened the secret door and freed her. He'd almost grabbed her hand and pulled her close and held her. But he'd pulled away just in time.

However, the danger still loomed. He had to keep his distance.

Because she'd come back for him.

She'd left the house to get help, knocked a guy out and tied him up and then she'd come back for him.

And he mustn't touch her.

The chirp of a cardinal echoed through the trees as Lucas stared down at the man who lay on the grass near one of the truck's large tires with both his hands and feet bound, his jeans covered in grass stains.

He lay as still as a fallen log. Lucas bent down and checked his pulse. He noticed the cigarette burns on his neck.

"I didn't kill him," Patricia said.

"Better to make sure. After you hit me, I saw stars for days."

"I really wish you wouldn't bring that up."

Lucas stood. "But I don't think you hit him hard enough," he said then kicked the man in the back of the shins.

The man let out a yell and jerked with pain. Lucas grabbed him by the collar of his T-shirt and lifted him to a sitting position. "Your acting is still garbage."

The man cast Patricia a superior look. "I fooled her, didn't I?"

"Where is she?" Lucas demanded recognizing one of the monster's men.

"Don't know. You never find her, she finds you and she—"

Lucas cut him off not wanting him to reveal too much in front of Patricia and said, "Yeah, enough of that." He looked up at Patricia. "I'll take it from here. You can go."

She didn't move. "Can I speak to you for a minute?"

Lucas looked at the man, considering what his options were. He really didn't have time to chat. "Can it wait?"

"No."

Lucas sighed. The man grinned. "I've got nowhere to go. Though I wouldn't mind you loosening these knots a bit."

Lucas shoved him against the truck then stood and led Patricia a few yards away. "What?"

She rested her hands on her hips, which he found distracting in a way he didn't want it to be. He shifted his gaze to her hands and noticed the knuckles were bruised. Dried blood had crusted on the side of her palm. Guilt seized him.

She'd probably tried to pound her way out of the cell

he'd pushed her into to keep her safe. She probably wanted him to explain why he'd done that to her. He didn't want to imagine her terror, her fear. He didn't want to remember his own.

He watched her slowly touch her bottom lip with the tip of her tongue. He swallowed, he didn't want to notice her tongue. "I'm sorry," she said in an unsteady voice, "I don't mean to bring this up but—"

"You're right," Lucas said, steeling himself against her anger. He adjusted his frames so he wouldn't reach out and try to comfort her. He had no comfort to give. He mustn't touch her no matter how much he wanted to tend to her hands, to bandage them. To check if she was injured anywhere else. "I'm sorry I put you through this. I'll pay for any kind of distress—"

"No, that's not what I mean."

"I've got really delicate skin," the man called out to them.

Lucas ignored him. "What do you mean?"

"Are people trying to kill you?"

He pointed to himself. "Me?"

"Yes, you. Who else?"

He grinned, amused by her concern. "No," he said but when she looked doubtful he added, "they want to scare me."

"And are you scared?"

"Do I look scared?"

"No."

"Can you two hurry this up?" the man said.

Patricia folded her arms. "That's all? You're being warned?"

Lucas nodded, unsure about the reason for her questions. She didn't seem angry, but he could tell she was scared. "It's complicated. But don't worry, you're safe. No one will hurt you."

She bit her lip.

He sighed. "You don't believe me."

She let her hands fall to her sides.

"What?"

"You're sure you're okay?"

"Why are you asking him?" the man called out with a moan. "I'm the one hurting here."

Patricia reached for his arm, Lucas instinctively pulled away, he couldn't risk her touching him. Not yet. It was too soon. "Sorry," he mumbled when she stared at him stunned. He looked at her bloodied hands and her gaze followed his. She gazed down at her hands in horror then quickly hid them behind her back ashamed. "Oh, sorry."

He took a step forward, hating that she felt ashamed, then stopped himself. "No, don't be."

"I just wanted to make sure you were okay."

"I'm fine," Lucas said.

Patricia released a sigh of relief. "Great. I wasn't sure after..." She waved the thought away. "That's good. I'm sorry about the closet. I wasn't much use to you."

He paused. "You're worried about me because of the closet?"

"Yes. I know you don't like closed spaces."

Lucas looked at her for a moment then jerked his finger at the man behind him. "So this doesn't bother you?"

"Hey, hey, *this* has a name," the man said offended.

Patricia shrugged. "You said you're fine, so the rest is none of my business. However, you'd better get rid of the guys with guns before my crew shows up."

He grinned, surprised she still kept her humor. "There will be no guns."

"Good."

"And you're right about this house."

She tried to hide her disappointment but Lucas saw it and his grin widened. "I have plenty of other projects in mind. I'll let you know."

"Okay."

"I feel my life blood draining away," the man said.

"You should go," Lucas said.

To his relief, she didn't argue.

After Patricia drove off, Lucas turned his attention to his unwanted guest.

He watched the truck leave. "Who is that?"

"What do you want?"

"When did you hire a bodyguard?"

"What do you want?"

"What I always want. Peace and love, bruh."

"You know what happens when I lose patience."

"I'm just checking on you."

"With a gun?"

"I wasn't holding it or nothing. I had it hidden for my protection. She overreacted."

"She doesn't overreact."

"Seriously, who is she?"

No need for him to know. "Have you spoken to Mum?" Lucas asked.

The man sighed. "She's got something planned for you. She didn't tell me what it is, but there are signs."

Out of the corner of his eye he saw movement, by the time he'd turned, the figure had disappeared in the trees.

Just like the cameras in Patricia's office, he knew someone was watching.

27

The Darjeeling tea was weak. But no weaker than the sniveling rodent standing in front of her desk. She hated weak things. And men were the weakest of all.

Her father had thought he was strong. He smashed dishes and shouted until he lost his voice. He'd left enough bruises on her mother and brother to show his dominance. Raising up liars to hide his reign. But he didn't hit her. No, he called her his 'special little girl.' He showed her how special she was to him by sneaking into her bed at night and covering her screams. Until one day she stopped screaming. It was the day she realized her father's true form: he was a beast. A beast that needed to be killed.

She didn't give him a chance to scream. The long kitchen knife appeared from under her pillow and smoothly went into his jugular with the speed of a serpent's strike. She giggled at the horror on his face, the fear in his eyes. The beast was no longer strong as his blood dripped onto her white nightie with the yellow flower blossoms. A nightie he'd bought for her and one she hated.

She removed the knife from his neck then sliced it through his abdomen like wire through clay, smooth and quick. On reflection that probably had been overkill and had swayed the jury's verdict against her. The knife to the throat had done the job, but she'd been young and impulsive. She was more mature and careful now.

It had been a pleasure to watch him die.

She didn't pretend to be remorseful. That had also been a mistake she later learned (again, in her defense she was only nine and didn't know better). She learned that men were weak and didn't like strong little girls who could kill their fathers without fear. Who didn't cry. Her mother cried a lot through the trial. She later learned she was crying more for the beast than for her daughter, but she forgave her mother because women were brainwashed into believing their worth was nothing without a man. And soon her mother found another man who sent her pathetic little soul to heaven only eight years later.

Her brother had turned religious. She'd gotten tired of his visits to the prison and little pamphlets telling her how to save her soul. But by then she knew he was a weak man, so she smiled and listened. And listened and smiled, which was the only way most men wanted their women to behave.

It disappointed her a little, but she didn't blame him. He had the blood of the beasts, all beasts, and he was doing his best to deny it by cloaking himself in the love of a God that hadn't been there to save her.

Her brother never thanked her. She had changed his life. She knew he'd been fostered into a good family. The bruises were gone from his face and he dressed well, he ate well. His hollow cheeks filled out and she realized he wasn't a bad looking man.

But he was still weak.

Weak enough to catch a disease on one of his missions to some Asian island and die there. She pretended to cry when she was told about his death, but it clearly wasn't convincing enough because she was denied parole that year. She learned to hone her skill. It took another couple years, but she managed.

After she got out of prison the first time, she knew how she needed to act. Her second, third and fourth visits to the pen—money laundering, attempted kidnapping and mortgage fraud—fortunately hadn't been long sentences. Her attorneys always knew how to depict her as vulnerable and unassuming. She looked a decade younger than her real age, stood barely five foot three and had innocent doll-like features. When she spoke, she kept her tone light and sweet.

Men liked sweet things. She knew how to be sweet.

Shanelle Sherwood set her tea cup down on the desk and smiled at the useless vermin who was wiping his nose with the back of his hand. She motioned to her assistant to hand him a tissue.

The rodent blew his nose and thanked her.

"So you lost him?" she said.

"I talked to him. The other one came out of nowhere. I didn't know what hit me."

Shanelle didn't care. "What did he say?"

"That he's ready for you."

Of course he would say that.

She motioned to the door. "You can leave now."

He hesitated.

"What?"

"Should I look into the woman?"

The rodent was trying to think now? How adorable. "No, that's not necessary."

He hesitated again.

Shanelle sighed with impatience. "What?"

"It's just...she reminds me of someone."

"I don't care. She's not important to me." Yet. She'd find out how to use her if that was necessary later, but it wasn't something she needed to share with anyone. "You can go."

He left.

Without closing the office door—good boy.

Shanelle rose to her feet and crossed over to it. Closing doors was one thing she loved to do. In prison she couldn't close doors, as a child she couldn't close doors. But now she could close doors as much as she wanted. To keep people out or lock people in.

"You should be careful," her assistant, Marlene said.

A warning from anyone else would have annoyed her, but Marlene always gave her pause.

She wore a beautifully tailored, emerald colored suit. Her short cropped afro was peppered with grey. She looked down at her tablet, biting her full lower lip. They were lovers —on and off. Mostly off because she liked sex more than people and Marlene was fine with that—-not that Shanelle had given her much choice.

She knew Marlene was seeing someone else right now (a dentist with a bright smile and an ass that could stop traffic) but Shanelle didn't have the interest or curiosity to be jealous. Lovers were always easily replaceable. But assistants were different and Marlene made a brilliant one. Her loyalty to Shanelle remained strong through Shanelle's stint behind bars. Marlene had come into her life at an opportune time. Shanelle had been a month out on parole for a kidnapping conviction, when she'd found herself thinking murder (because she shouldn't have been caught, let alone convicted) while standing in front of a row of loose leaf teas in the Caribbean market.

Marlene had grabbed the jar of Darjeeling tea and held it out to Shanelle and said, "The only way to best a bad mood is with this paired with a slice of dark chocolate cake."

Shanelle stared at the woman amazed, having a strange feeling of déjà vu. As if they'd met in another lifetime.

It was as if Marlene knew what Shanelle needed.

Shanelle slept with her that night (all thoughts of revenge gone with the help of said tea and chocolate cake) and hired her the following day.

Marlene had helped soothe her rage. Helped her to see clearly again. Years later, that hadn't changed.

Shanelle returned to her seat and sipped the tea, now cool and weak, which was just an insult to her tongue, and said, "Why?"

"Lucas has been spotted with her more than once."

Lucas, she bristled at the name. It wasn't the one she'd given. The one that suited better. The one she always wanted to remember. Lucas. Such a crass, horrible name from the one she had given him. One that had been so sweet and melodic just like the baby that had come from her. The one who always smiled. From the first moment that gummy, toothless grin had stolen her heart.

It would have been so different if...

Shanelle brushed the thought away. She'd lived a life of 'if onlys' when she'd been a child. But she wouldn't do that now. No one would ever convince her that what she'd done was wrong. Was it wrong to want the best for your child? To fix any defects that could destroy their lives?

It was only because she loved too much, that's what she was being punished for. Her love was too strong for the world to understand.

"Lucas," she said, using the name that left a bitter taste in her mouth. "Always has a woman." The reports had been similar on that. Clearly he liked sex as much as she did. She couldn't fault him for that.

"But I still think you should keep an eye on him."

"Not hard to do." Shanelle shrugged. "The other one made it easy," she said her skin burning at the thought of him. Of his betrayal.

"I wouldn't underestimate either of them."

"Very well. You know what to do."

She wasn't too worried. But the rodent and Marlene taking interest meant it was something not to ignore.

She knew what needed to be done. The one called Lucas needed to be reminded of a few things. And she needed what rightfully belonged to her. She was tired of having things snatched away from her. She'd served her time, and now time was on her side. She'd used it to her best abilities.

The one called Lucas had plenty of weaknesses and she planned to exploit them all.

28

————

Lucas expected the nightmares to come the night he returned home from the farmhouse and they didn't disappoint.

They came with a fury, battering his mind with thoughts of being drowned, trapped, crushed.

But the nightmares proved different this time. Usually he was alone, different remnants of his childhood terrors, but this time around, the nightmares featured Patricia.

She was in danger and he couldn't get to her. Each time he failed to save her and he woke up screaming, breathing heavily, covered in sweat.

Night after night.

But in the day he could think of nothing else, except her.

He still couldn't believe she'd come back for him. That she hadn't been angry at him for putting her in that awful room. She'd understood he'd been trying to keep her safe.

But she hadn't needed his help. She'd taken down one of the monster's men by herself. She could fight. But not as a boxer. The man's face hadn't been bruised, so she hadn't punched him, she'd disabled him another way. That took training. How come that hadn't shown up in Alex's report about her?

It took him a week to get over the farmhouse visit and memories buried there.

Another week to start thinking clearly again.

His rational mind told him to stay away from Patricia. There was too much to unravel about her and he still didn't understand her connection to his aunt, but the ache, the longing was too strong. He needed to see her again no matter what the risk. He couldn't stay away.

Unfortunately, he hadn't come up with a good excuse yet. He hadn't thought of the right job to hire her for.

By the third week, Lucas managed to get a good night's sleep again, and wandered downstairs, way past noon, ready to start the day.

He strolled into the kitchen then stopped when he saw Alex, Julia and Carter standing around the island, chatting. They all fell silent and turned to him shocked, as if he'd come in on a secret rendezvous.

He looked at them confused. "What?"

"What are you doing here?" Alex said.

Lucas frowned at the absurd question. "In the kitchen or in my own house?"

"You're not supposed to be here," Carter said.

"How could you do this?" Julia said.

"Do what?" Lucas said. "Why wouldn't I be here?"

"Your father," Alex reminded him. "You're hosting his bon voyage party."

Lucas looked at them with growing dread. "Please tell me it's not today."

"It was two hours ago."

Lucas swore, pulled out his phone and saw the series of messages. "No, it can't be today."

"I even reminded you yesterday at the store," Carter said.

Lucas frowned. He didn't remember going shopping or talking to him about the party.

"And I even sent you an alert," Alex said.

"I was distracted." Lucas held up a hand. "Don't ask."

"Tell them you're sick," Julia said. "You don't look well anyway."

Lucas shot her a look. "I'm fine."

"This is the second time you've—"

"I know," he said through gritted teeth. "I'll deal with it." He pointed at Alex. "How do things stand?"

"The event planner and caterers arrived on time, so the guests should be taken care of."

"Great. Tell Damian I'm on my way."

He dashed out of the kitchen but not before he overheard Carter whisper, "Looks like the nightmares have gotten bad again."

It was perfect.

The moment Lucas opened the front door to his father's house, and saw the stylish decorations and the scent of curried rice and fried plantain floating through the air, he knew a crisis had been averted. Everyone ate and chatted comfortably in the living and dining rooms, his father waved hello before resuming a conversation with an attractive older woman.

Lucas hadn't ruined his father's day, someone had rescued it.

He discovered who when he entered the kitchen. He saw Rosaline talking to the event planner before turning to one of the catering staff. He waited for the conversation to end before he rushed up behind her and kissed her on the cheek. "I adore you."

She groaned. "And I'm silently dying inside."

He knew she wasn't joking. While he enjoyed being around people, Lucas knew how much Rosaline hated crowds. With her gift, being around so many people could prove overwhelming. He wrapped his arms around her as a makeshift shield and hugged her with affection. "I'll make it up to you."

He released her. "I'm really sorry."

She turned to look at him and her gaze searched his face. She frowned. Lucas playfully held up his hands and blocked his face. "Don't read me right now. It's not the time or place."

"You met her again, didn't you?"

29

His hands fell and Lucas stared at Rosaline stunned. Before he could ask her how she knew, Damian barged into the kitchen followed by Ian. Rosaline offered Lucas a look of sympathy before she hurried away.

"You're late. Again," Damian said.

Lucas opened his mouth to apologize, but no words emerged. Rosaline's revelation about him seeing Patricia again had rendered him speechless and also took the bite out of his brother's words. Damian was annoyed and Lucas didn't care.

Patricia. How had Rosaline known about Patricia? That must be a sign.

"Are you even listening?"

Lucas nodded, cleared his throat. "Right, sorry. I've been busy getting my um...balcony redone."

Damian frowned. "None of your properties have a balcony."

"I mean the deck at my main house."

"Didn't you just get that renovated?"

"It was long ago."

"It was last year."

"Excuse me," one of the catering staff said, trying to reach around Damian. He moved so she could grab a tray.

Lucas looked at Ian. "How's your bathroom?"

Ian swept his hand through the air as if to say, "It's fine."

Lucas turned to Damian. "Would Rosaline like a new studio?" before Damian could reply, Lucas said, "Of course there's the Oceanview property, but that's out of state." He rubbed his chin.

"What are you on about?" Damian said.

"Pardon me," a caterer said this time to Ian who moved out of the way of the fridge.

"I need a place to renovate," Lucas said.

Damian sighed. "Why?"

Another caterer tried to weave her way around them to get to the glasses.

Lucas moved to make room for her. "I found a new contractor."

"You're cheating on Craig?" Damian said referring to the family's long term contractor.

Lucas grinned. "I never promised to be exclusive."

"What's the project?"

"Don't know yet."

"Then why hire a contractor?"

Rosaline appeared, exasperated and grabbed Damian's arm. "Will you guys get out of the kitchen, you're in the way."

Lucas snapped his fingers as a thought came to him. "That's it! Dad's kitchen." He looked around the room. "It could use an upgrade."

"He'd never agree to it," Damian said, letting his wife drag him out to the back patio where only a few of the guests had roamed.

"True," Lucas said following them.

"He's going on holiday," Rosaline said.

Lucas clasped his hands together. "Right. Perfect."

Ian pulled out one of the six patio chairs positioned around the regular metal table and sat.

"No, it's not perfect," Damian said. "Even though Dad's got money he doesn't like spending it on repairs. We all know this."

Rosaline released her husband's arm. "But it's still not a bad idea."

"Dad doesn't need a new kitchen."

Ian crooked his finger, motioning her towards him. She bent down and he whispered something in her ear that made her smile.

Damian folded his arms. "What did he say?"

Rosaline gently patted Ian's shoulder. "He's reminding me to keep Eldin away so he won't overhear anything."

"There's nothing to hear, because nothing's going to happen."

Lucas ignored him. "How long is Dad's holiday?"

Ian held up three fingers.

"Even better."

Damian waved his hands. "Wait a minute. What are you planning?"

"Dad needs a—"

"I can smell your crap from a mile away. Don't lie. Tell me what you're up to."

Rosaline tugged at Damian's collar, forcing him to bend so she could whisper in his ear, "Listen before you judge."

He opened his mouth to argue and she pressed her finger against his lips. "Promise." He nodded and she tenderly cupped the side of his face, softening his harsh expression. Lucas stared, still amazed by the soothing affect Rosaline had on Damian.

Her gaze met his and he quickly looked away, embarrassed. He didn't want her to see his longing, his wish to meet someone like her. Because they both knew the truth, he wasn't good for any woman. Not in the long run.

Lucas studied an ant crawling up the leg of the patio chair and heard Rosaline say, "Remember to play nice boys," before going back inside the house.

After two beats, Damian said, "Rosaline knows something."

Lucas met his brother's suspicious gaze, sighed then said, "I met her again."

"Who?"

"The woman in the elevator."

When Damian sent Ian a look in question, Ian tapped his cheek, then puffed it out to make it look swollen.

Damian stared at Lucas wide eyed. "Are you talking about the woman who turned half of your face into grape jelly?"

Lucas shook his head. "It wasn't that bad."

"She hit you like a boxer."

"Because I wanted her to," Lucas snapped.

"Not like that."

"She didn't mean to hurt me."

"How do you know that?" Damian said. "Why are you defending her? You hardly know her."

"Neither do you."

"I can say the same."

"I know her enough." Lucas took a deep breath. "She's a contractor and does good work."

Damian shook his head. "This is a bad idea."

"I already hired her."

"I thought you didn't have a project."

"I do now."

"Dad's kitchen?" Damian guessed.

"Yes."

Damian looked at Ian for assistance. "Tell him why this is a bad idea."

Ian shrugged as if to say, Maybe it's not.

"Listen, I—"

"Do what you want." He opened the door.

"You promised Rosaline you'd listen."

"Don't bring her into this."

"I will if you lied."

Damian slowly turned, their eyes met in battle.

"No," Damian said in a quiet voice. "I leave the silver tongued lies to you."

30

———

*L*ucas took a step back as if he'd been struck. Damian didn't know everything about Lucas's past but he did know Lucas had once lived as a liar and a thief. Two things Lucas never wanted to be known for again.

"That's not what I meant," Damian said, reading his brother's expression. He walked over to his brother, draped an arm around Lucas's shoulder then hit Lucas hard in the chest in a way that hurt, but also felt good. Damian understood Lucas needed that pain to combat the psychological wounds that had yet to heal. "You know that."

Lucas lowered his gaze. "I shouldn't have mentioned Rosaline."

"She's family now, she's not off limits. I know how much you love her and if you think I'm wrong about something, you can tell me."

Lucas met his brother's gaze. "You're wrong."

Damian playfully hit Lucas on the back of his head before he stepped away. "I'm not wrong." He rested his

159

hands on his hips. "What do you know about this woman?" He held up a hand. "Besides what she does for a living and how attractive she is."

"How do you know she's attractive?"

"Because you're interested."

Ian cleared his throat.

Damian rolled his eyes. "True, he'd be interested even if she wasn't attractive, but I'll guess she is."

"This isn't about looks," Lucas said. "She's also smart and you should have seen the way she handled herself when—"

"When what?" Damian demanded when Lucas abruptly stopped.

Lucas hesitated. He didn't want to mention what had happened at the farmhouse property. Her ability to fight was information he wanted to keep to himself for now. "When the elevator stopped."

"She punched you."

"And she kept me calm."

"Sure, a real Florence Nightingale," Damian said his voice dripping with sarcasm.

"I only want to hire her."

Damian held up a hand. "I told you not to lie to me."

"Okay, I am also interested, but it probably won't go anywhere."

"Lie number two."

Lucas sighed. "Okay, I'm not sure. She's different."

"How different? She'll physically hurt you instead of mentally? You're attracted to a different type of pain? Someone who will stomp on your chest instead of your heart? Maybe—"

"Enough," Ian said in a quiet but firm tone.

"Is it?" Damian challenged. He stared at Lucas. "Is it really?"

Lucas spread his arms wide and smiled, determined to lighten the gloomy atmosphere. "You know what you need? Some food. It smells delicious. Have you eaten yet?"

Damian made a dismissive wave of his hand and said, "I give up," then stalked back inside. Lucas turned to Ian and clasped his hands together like an attentive waiter. "Want me to get you something?"

Ian rose to his feet and slowly walked past him.

"You don't know what you're missing," Lucas said to his brother's retreating back.

He sat in his brother's vacated seat and briefly shut his eyes. After a few seconds, he felt something cold and wet touch his hand. He glanced down and saw Methuselah. The sight of the old dog lifted his spirits and Lucas patted the dog's head with affection, then, like a creeping vine, dread spread over him. If Methuselah was here that meant...

31

"Hello, Lucas."

He inwardly groaned then reluctantly lifted his gaze to stare up at his Aunt Wynette. "I didn't expect you to be here."

She sent a pointed glance at a chair. Instead of dutifully rising to his feet and pulling it out for her, Lucas remained seated and pushed it back with his foot. Wynette smiled amused by his petty rebellion and slowly sat. "Thanks for the invitation."

"I don't remember sending you one." He caught the eye of one of the catering staff holding drinks and gestured towards his aunt.

"I'm sure you forgot."

"Yes, must have slipped my mind." He watched the waiter hand his aunt a cool glass of lemonade.

"You're looking well."

Lucas rested his chin in his hand and pretended to fall asleep.

She kicked him in the shins.

He feigned a look of hurt and rubbed his leg. "What do you want?"

"What did you think about Patricia?"

Lucas felt his blood go cold. She was probing for a weakness and Patricia had become his.

When his aunt had asked about the other property owners she hadn't referred to them by name. This time she was being oddly specific. She didn't say, What did you think about the owner of Gardner's Contractors? She'd used Patricia's name for a reason.

Lucas searched his mind for the best way to reply.

He could feign ignorance, but that would make Wynette extra cautious; he could appear nonchalance, but that would also make her wary because Lucas was rarely nonchalant when it came to women. Or he could tell her what he thought.

But he wasn't ready yet to ask his aunt what she was up to. He couldn't reveal his suspicions about Gardner's Contractors and Patricia. Fortunately, Alex's search hadn't left any crumbs so Wynette didn't know he'd been digging, but he knew he was on borrowed time. Wynette didn't stay in the dark for long, something would trigger her interest.

He decided to use his reputation to his advantage. "I don't kiss and tell."

Wynette stared at him open mouthed. "You slept with her?"

"Was I not supposed to?"

Wynette stared at him like he'd soiled something precious and the thought pierced through his heart.

He prepared himself for her to say words that had been hurled at him in the past. *You disgust me. Animal. Dog.* But although his aunt remained silent, Lucas could imagine her thinking those words and others. Patricia mattered to Wynette more than he did. Lucas hadn't played the game she'd wanted him to play. He'd spotted a hint of disappointment in his aunt's face, but he wasn't sure if his aunt was disappointed in him or Patricia for supposedly falling for him.

Lucas patted Methuselah's head to hide his hurt. Wynette reaction had been unexpected and although it pained him it also intrigued him.

Patricia was a complication. He wasn't sure how.

While his brothers thought Patricia was bad for him, his aunt clearly thought he was bad for Patricia.

This was proof he should stay away.

But he still didn't want to.

"Will you see her again?" his aunt said.

He leaned back in his chair, glanced up, shielding his gaze from the bright sun. "I have a job in mind I'm thinking of using her for. Looks like she needs the work." He wouldn't tell his aunt about his dad's kitchen. They were too close and Lucas didn't trust his aunt to keep it a secret.

"There's no reason to do that."

He stood. "I'll keep that in mind."

She lifted up her cheek.

Lucas gripped his hands into fists. "No."

She tapped it. This time her nail sparkled with glitter.

He growled.

She smiled.

He bent and placed a kiss on her cheek. She grabbed the front of his shirt into her fist and pulled him closer. She spoke, her lyrical voice soft and lethal. "Careful there."

He winked. "Are you worried about me?"

A flash of fear entered her eyes before she released her

grip. She stood, lifted up Methuselah, said, "Don't forget to visit," and went inside.

Lucas smoothed down the wrinkles in his shirt, unnerved by the look on her face. He'd never scared her before. She'd said she cared about him. He didn't believe her now. There was something about him that had frightened her. There was always that point where a woman...

But he wouldn't think about that. He had his dad's bon voyage party to enjoy. Lucas returned inside determined to enjoy himself to the fullest.

Lucas spent the rest of the afternoon flirting with the wait staff, flattering the event planner, indulging in food and drink, while also laughing, joking and charming all the guests.

He was in his element, surrounded by people, and he'd never felt more alone.

32

—————

*A*pricot touched the blue sky by the time the party came to an end. Lucas hugged his father and wished him a great trip before he slipped him a box of condoms.

He darted out of reach before his father could hit him. He casually walked down the porch steps, relieved the party had been a success.

"Lucas, wait."

He turned to see Rosaline. He was weary and exhausted but the smile he gave her was real. "Thanks again for everything."

To his surprise, she grabbed his hand and held it between her own. She peered into his face, her voice urgent. "What's her name?"

Not her too. He didn't want to fight anymore. Wynette hadn't wanted him to be with Patricia. Perhaps his brothers were right. Patricia should remain off limits. He'd been wrong about Lania and they'd seen the aftermath.

You're no good for her. Stay away. She's better off without knowing you.

He had nothing to offer Patricia and so much he still didn't understand.

Beast. Animal. Filth.

And for the first time he'd seen fear in his aunt's gaze.

Rosaline didn't need to remind him of the reality they both knew—he wasn't good for any woman. He didn't want to know the dark aura she likely saw around him.

The darkness that Lania had seen.

The feeling of exhaustion descended, threatening to flatten him. He noticed the deepening shadows on the ground, their slow, sinister creeping lengths, the slight chill of the approaching evening.

He'd forget about Patricia. His life was fine as it was. There were plenty of ladies willing to warm his bed and help him forget this hollow, aching lonely feeling for a few hours.

Rosaline squeezed his hand. "Lucas. What's her name?"

He didn't want to say it. She didn't need to know. "Don't worry. I won't—"

"What's her name?" she tugged on his hand. "Tell me."

He hung his head. "Patricia."

"And you think she can fix Dad's kitchen?"

"Yes, but—"

"Then this is your chance."

His head shot up. He blinked, stared. "My chance?"

"Yes."

He paused. "Are you talking about the kitchen?"

Rosaline shook her head.

His heart began to pound. Was this a trick? Was she teasing him? Did she know what she was saying?

She still held onto his hand and he felt the warmth of her hands. "I look forward to meeting her one day."

She made it sound possible, like a foregone conclusion, as if she expected him to succeed.

"But I'm no good—"

"You're fine."

"You don't think—"

"I think she'll be lucky to have you."

Lucas searched Rosaline's face unsure, no longer feeling alone, but also afraid to hope. "You're not worried that I'll—"

She bracketed his face with her hands and held his gaze. "I'm not worried at all."

She trusted him. Believed in him. there was no fear or unease in her open, penetrating gaze. Her words were the salve he needed to hear. Exhaustion fell away, allowing joy to flood his veins.

Lucas pulled her into his arms and hugged her. Rosaline gasped then laughed. She hugged him back. "This is your chance, Lucas. Seize it."

"I really do adore you," he said with feeling, placing a quick kiss on her cheek.

His gaze dipped to their entwined silhouettes on the lawn, the shadows no longer looked as dark as they had once seemed. He lifted his gaze and saw Damian watching them from the porch. His brother stood with his arms folded, his face a granite mask.

Lucas did what he always did best. He met his brother's disapproving expression and smiled.

33

He hadn't called.

It had been nearly three weeks since Patricia had last spoken to Lucas outside the farmhouse.

The first week when she hadn't heard from him, she feared he'd lied about the men only wanting to scare him. That they'd returned and he hadn't gotten away. She wondered if they'd hurt him, imprisoned him or killed him.

She thought of coming up with a reason to call her landlord, Mrs. Clemmens, and find a roundabout way of asking about her nephew.

But she didn't have to. The following day, she'd caught sight of Lucas leaving a convenience store. She'd been on the opposite side of the street, stopped at a traffic light while listening to music in her truck, when she saw him. Unfortunately, the light changed and he disappeared down a side street before she could call out to him. At least she knew he was alive and well.

The second week, she started to mistake other men for

him. Twice she'd seen well dressed black men and thought it was him, but had quickly realized she'd been mistaken.

But the third time had been almost uncanny. Patricia had walked into her building after a long day (she'd had to deal with a kitchen cabinet that had been measured wrong on a job that had already gone over schedule and budget due to a client's indecisiveness) and headed towards the elevator when she saw Lucas wearing a tailored dark olive suit pushing one of the buttons.

She raced up behind him and said, "I never thought you'd ride this again."

He spun around with a smile that made Patricia step back dismayed. The man wasn't Lucas, just someone who looked remarkably similar. "Oh, sorry, I thought you were someone else."

The man looked surprised, in the same particular way Lucas would have if he had been Lucas, but since he wasn't Lucas, it wasn't exactly the same. "Someone else?" he said in a velvet tone that even sounded like Lucas's but was also a shade different.

"Yes, sorry about that," Patricia said with a nervous laugh as the elevator doors opened. She stepped inside then turned to him. "What floor are you going to?"

He took a step back, staring at her with a touch of unease. "Uh, I think I'm in the wrong building," he said then turned and left.

Patricia rode the elevator alone, embarrassment burning her cheeks. She hoped he hadn't been a potential client. She was seeing Lucas even in places where he wasn't and scaring poor strangers away.

By the third week of not hearing from him, she'd come to

the conclusion she didn't want to face: She'd scared him off for good.

Lucas hadn't even wanted to touch her to help her out of the sealed room, and had jumped out of reach when she'd tried to move him away from the man she'd tied up, so that he couldn't overhear what they were saying.

He kept his distance for a reason. She repelled him.

But he was too polite to admit it, but her reading of him and the house and then her actions with the intruder had scared him. Perhaps he'd offered to give her another job just to be polite when he had no intention of doing so.

It bothered her that she felt more depressed about not ever seeing Lucas again, than the prospect of losing him as a client. If only she'd kept her mouth shut, if only she hadn't shoved him in that closet, if only she hadn't returned to try to save him.

It was over now. She'd eventually forget about him as she should. He'd taken up too much space in her mind already.

By the end of the third week, she'd pushed thoughts of Lucas aside with the help of a day buckling under the weight of a series of mini disasters. A job went over schedule resulting in a client's meltdown; she got stuck in traffic and then learned one of her favorite suppliers was retiring.

By the time she reached her office near the end of the day, she was in no mood to meet her sister's grinning faces.

"Guess who's here," Melody said in a sing-songy voice as Patricia passed by the receptionist desk, which was crowded with textbooks.

"We left him in your office," Monica added.

"You can thank us later."

Lucas was here? Patricia hurried towards her office eager

to see him again, desperate to find out what had kept him busy for so long. What project did he have for her this time?

But when Patricia walked into her office, all those thoughts fell away. The man sitting in her office wasn't Lucas. However, the handsome man with a trim goatee was just what she needed: A dose of reality and comfort.

He stood, the top of his head nearly reaching the ceiling, and held out a coffee and blueberry muffin.

"I will love you forever," Patricia said, taking the muffin and giving him a hug.

Her best friend Jeremy hugged her back. He gave the best hugs. "Hard day?"

"Terrifying." She took a large bite of the muffin then a sip of the coffee, before she set them both down on her desk. "I was afraid I wouldn't make it."

He leaned against the desk. "But you did."

"Barely."

He held his arms out to her again. "You know my hugs are powerful weapons, right?"

Patricia laughed and fell into his warm embrace. "Yes, they can defeat the worst bad day."

Jeremy was her only friend. He'd been bullied starting in elementary school, although the taunts took a different tone than the ones thrown at her. He was topping six foot in the fifth grade and looked much older than his age. He'd been mistaken for a substitute teacher and had been too embarrassed to say he wasn't so he taught the class the entire day. He was such a success that most of the students wanted him as their babysitter so he made a lot of extra money that way.

That's how they'd met. Her sisters had been in his 'class' and had begged their parents to hire him. Patricia had returned from one of her dreaded piano lessons to see him playing with her sisters and had immediately bonded with the sweet, friendly giant of a kid who smelled like raspberry gummy bears.

However, more than twenty years later, Jeremy was no longer the tall, skinny kid who could easily be bullied. He'd grown and filled out. Although he was not aware of how people looked at him. He was still self-effacing and sweet.

And smart. He'd sold two businesses by the time he was thirty, so he didn't have to work, but he liked to keep busy so he helped her, on occasion, letting her know about jobs to bid on, paying for advertising, managing her online business profile, and hiring her for odd jobs around his house since she wouldn't accept a loan from him. But he also liked to surprise her with food and offer himself as a sounding board. Or he would follow her on jobs as a supportive sounding board for her ideas.

He was always what she needed. Patricia sank into the comfort of his bearlike hug.

She felt him stiffen then he shoved her with such force she stumbled back into someone, whose strong hands wrapped around her arms to keep her from falling. They held her just a shade longer than necessary before releasing her.

Patricia stared up at Jeremy stunned. "What the—"

But Jeremy wasn't looking at her. He was staring at something—or rather someone—behind her. He looked scared.

"We're just friends," Jeremy said quickly. His tone surprised her, he sounded like the kid he'd used to be, the one who'd offer up his lunch money before the bully could even ask for it.

Patricia slowly turned then took a quick sharp breath.

Lucas stood there, staring at Jeremy with an unreadable expression.

34

Her eyes drank him in, she caught the scent of mint, her skin remembered the warmth of his hands when he'd briefly touched her. She swallowed, her mouth suddenly dry, her heart aching with joy. He'd come back. She hadn't frightened him away.

She rushed over to Jeremy then turned back to Lucas eager to introduce the two men. "Lucas, this is—"

"I've known her since elementary school," Jeremy added. "We've only ever been friends."

Patricia nudged him with her elbow and said in a low voice, "Jeremy, he doesn't need to know that."

But Jeremy wasn't looking at her. His gaze didn't leave Lucas' face.

Lucas in turn nodded, but didn't reply.

"I should go," Jeremy said inching, sideways towards the door like a crab.

Patricia grabbed his arm. "You just got here."

Jeremy cast Lucas a nervous look. "I'm not sure—"

"If you're busy," Lucas said in a smooth tone, "I can come back later. I should have made an appointment."

"No," Patricia said, grabbing his sleeve before quickly letting go.

Why was he acting so formal? And the look he sent Jeremy was inscrutable. What was wrong with these two? "No," she said again. She glanced at Jeremy but he wouldn't meet her gaze. She'd find out what was going on later. "There's no need, you're fine," Patricia told Lucas. "Glad to see you're still in one piece," when Lucas didn't smile she sighed. "Forget it." She turned to Jeremy and said in a low voice, "This won't take too long, wait for me." Jeremy nodded then ducked out and closed the door. Patricia turned her attention to Lucas and motioned to a seat. "How can I help you?"

He hesitated. For a moment her heart grew cold. Had he changed his mind about working with her? But he wouldn't have come all this way to say that, would he?

She tried to lighten the mood with humor. "I'm glad to see you're okay."

He remained standing and looked at her perplexed. "Why wouldn't I be?"

If he'd forgotten that she'd left him with a man sprawled in his hallway and another tied up, she wouldn't remind him. "Never mind."

His gaze shifted to the window. "Are you okay?"

"Why wouldn't I be?" she retorted in the same careless tone.

His gaze returned to her face, a soft smile on his lips, and he looked at her in a way she couldn't quite interpret but made her face burn all the same. "Good."

Patricia hurried behind her desk and sat feeling self-conscious. Cool and professional. That was what she needed to be. She would not notice that he looked like he'd lost a little weight. She wouldn't look at his hands and remember them sliding along her wall unit with the care of a lover. Patricia straightened in her chair and cleared her throat. "You didn't have to come here on my account. Next time, tell me the job site and I'll meet you there. It will save time."

She motioned to a chair again, but he didn't sit. He folded his arms. "You think I'm wasting your time?"

"No, no I just thought it'd be more convenient. You must be busy...I wasn't sure I'd hear from you again."

He walked up to her desk and stared down at her muffin. "Sorry I kept you waiting."

She moved the muffin and coffee to the side. "I'd given up on you." She lifted the muffin. She wasn't hungry but needed to do something beside look at him. "Mind if I eat this while you talk?"

"Go ahead." Lucas tapped the desk with his forefinger. "This job may be a little tricky."

She sipped her now tepid coffee. "I'm up for the challenge."

"My father is going on a three week holiday and I want to surprise him with a new kitchen. Think you can get it done in time?"

"Depends on the state and size of the kitchen, what changes you want and a host of others issues, but I think I can manage it."

"I'll make it worth your while."

Music to her ears. "When does he leave?"

"This Saturday." He placed a folded piece of paper in front of her. "Here's the address."

Patricia opened the note and scanned the address. She

had a working knowledge of the area and imagined the job would be manageable, but she still didn't have much time to waste. She noticed he'd also added his phone number. That surprised her. She lifted her head to tell him so, but he'd already disappeared.

35

Once Lucas had left, Jeremy rushed into Patricia's office, folded his large frame into a nearby chair, holding onto the handles as if on a rollercoaster, and glared at her. "Why didn't you tell me you were seeing somebody?"

Patricia's brows shot up. "Because I'm not."

"You can admit it."

"There's nothing to admit it. I'm not seeing anyone."

"Are you sure?"

"Of course I'm sure. What's wrong with you?"

"I'm not sure he'd agree," Jeremy mumbled.

"He who?"

Jeremy jumped up and raced over to window. "Yeah, there he is."

Patricia stood beside him and scanned the lot to see what her friend was pointing at until she noticed a well dressed man walking to a Mercedes: Lucas.

Patricia laughed. "He's just a client." She'd have to remember to text him a time when they should meet.

"Are you sure? You don't know him from before today?"

"Well, yes, I've met him before, but I don't really *know* him. I mean I tied him up once…but only because he asked me to." She held up her hand. "That came out wrong."

Jeremy blinked, nonplussed. "I'm not here to judge. But that one night stand might have meant more to him than you thought."

Patricia turned away from the window and sat behind her desk. "No, no. It wasn't like that." She explained the elevator incident.

Jeremy paced. "I find it hard to believe he's afraid of anything."

"But he was. I wasn't going to tell you because I'm not sure he'd want anyone to know. But that's it. He's grateful I helped him."

Jeremy shook his head. "No, that's not it. The way he looked at me was rival territory." He put his hand against his throat. "Like he would go for my jugular. He's willing to fight for you."

"He's scared of me."

Jeremy stopped pacing and pointed at her. "He may be scared of elevators but he's not scared of you."

Patricia laughed without humor. "You don't know him like I do."

"I don't think you know him at all. He wants you and it's not for business."

Patricia rubbed her forehead, feeling a little sorry for her friend. His love for her was making him delusional. "I don't know what you're talking about. A man like him would never be interested in a woman like me. Why are you smiling?"

"Because you're so very wrong."

"I am not."

He sat down and clasped his hands together. "When

whatever job he's hired you for is over I think you should ask him out."

"Why would I do that? If Lucas was really interested, he'd ask me, wouldn't he?"

Jeremy looked at her surprised. "His name is Lucas?"

"Yes, Lucas Wolff."

His brows shot up. "Lucas Wolff?"

"Yes," Patricia said slowly. "Do you know him?" She paused as a horrible thought came to her. "Did he bully you in the past or something?" Jeremy had a running roster of those who had hurt him in the past and Patricia kept tabs.

"That can't be him," Jeremy mumbled. "Does he have a brother?"

"How would I know that?"

"You're right. Forget it. He can't be the same one."

"Same one, what?" Patricia sat back, defeated and dismayed. "I won't work with him if he hurt you in the past and—"

Jeremy waved his hands. "No, no. He wasn't like that. He was great. I know people change, but he doesn't seem anything like the kid I knew. He was one of the nicest kids I'd ever met."

Nice? That wasn't the first thing that came to mind when Patricia thought of Lucas. "I'm sure it's not him."

"Even if it's not, whoever that man is, he's interested."

"Lucas is not shy. If he were interested in me, I'd know. I told you, I scare him."

"Then he likes being sacred and you're too dense to notice."

"I'm not dense."

"You didn't even see the way he looked at you."

"Because he was behind me and he's probably worried that I wouldn't keep his secret."

"He couldn't care less about that, he didn't like seeing me hugging you."

"You're making that up."

"I'm not." Jeremy wagged his finger at her. "You're scared to ask him."

"He's a client and I need the work. Stop smiling like that."

"You're scared," he said drawing out the last word.

Patricia bit into her muffin. "I'm not scared," she grumbled. "I'm not interested."

"How long is the job?"

"Three weeks."

"You can ask him out after that."

"I'm not asking him anything except for a referral."

"Why not ask for both?"

"I don't want to embarrass myself."

He took out a Montblanc pen from inside his jacket and set it on the desk. "I bet he's interested."

She pushed the pen away.

He placed the keys to his BMW on the table.

She pushed the keys away.

"There's an amazing sauna in the Bahamas. You'll get a week of luxury."

She yawned.

He frowned then cast a glance at her older model desktop then her expectant face. "Okay," he said reading her face, "if you win I'll buy you a new business laptop with a large display, touch screen with long battery life and personal upkeep for six months on the software that will help make your business run more efficiently."

"A year."

He sighed then held out his hand.

She shook his hand. "You're on."

He held onto her hand. "But if I win you have to renovate my bathroom for free." He noticed her hesitation and grinned. "Not so confident now, are you?"

She snatched her hand away. "I am."

"When the three weeks are over I'll find him and ask him for you."

"No, you might bribe him so that you can win."

Jeremy looked hurt. "I'd never do that."

She felt guilty. She knew that was a low blow. She trusted him as a friend. He'd never do that to her because he'd had it done to him when his well-meaning father paid to have someone go out with him. "I'm sorry. I didn't mean—"

"Sorry enough to let me ask him?"

She narrowed her eyes seeing the crafty businessman he was. He wasn't as hurt as he'd pretended to be. "If that will make you feel better."

"It will."

"You'd better be prepared to lose."

Jeremy stood. "I'm a grown man now. I don't lose easily anymore."

36

———

Jeremy's confidence sizzled like an ice cube under a blazing sun when he saw the dark figure leaning against his car.

Lucas made a dangerous opponent.

His heart picked up, he reminded himself he wasn't eleven anymore and he didn't have to run from kids throwing rocks at him and calling him names.

But Lucas made him forget that. Although Lucas wore corrective lens, Jeremy couldn't imagine anyone in school calling Lucas names and living to see another day. He never imagined a slender, well dressed guy could look so intimidating.

Then Lucas smiled.

It wasn't malicious, but still dangerous.

"I was hoping I'd see you again," Lucas said.

"Same."

Jeremy's response surprised Lucas. His eyes narrowed. "Why?"

"Because I wanted to talk about Patricia."

He folded his arms, a calculated move that made him only seem bigger than he was. "Go on."

Jeremy swallowed. Lucas was not a man he'd want as an enemy. "This is probably not the time, but since you're here..."

"Yes?"

"She's been hurt in the past."

"Are you warning me off?"

Jeremy felt his heart lift. Yes, Lucas had seen him as a rival. He knew he'd been right about Lucas' interest, this confirmed it.

"No, I'm opening the door."

He nodded. "Go on."

"If you're interested, after this job is done, I can arrange a date with her."

Lucas shook his head. "I don't need you to arrange anything for me."

"But you do."

"Why?"

"Because...it has to come through me. Otherwise she won't believe you."

"Why wouldn't she believe me?"

"She's...she's very cautious."

"Because she's been hurt," Lucas said.

It wasn't a question Jeremy had to answer, but he did anyway. "Yeah."

Lucas let his arms fall. "I don't like the thought of you being an emissary."

"If you want her as much as I think you do, it's the only way."

He rubbed his chin. "What do you get out of this?"

"You have a brother named Ian, right?"

He stilled. "I do."

Jeremy grinned. "I thought it might be you, but I wasn't sure."

Lucas pointed to himself. "You know me?"

"Yeah. It's okay if you don't remember."

"Jog my memory."

"I met Ian years ago in the children's ward at the hospital."

Lucas snapped his fingers and pointed at him as if he suddenly remembered, "You were a doctor."

"No, I wasn't a doctor."

"You were a nurse."

"No, I wasn't a nurse. Will you let me finish?"

Lucas nodded. "Go on."

"My sister was there for treatment and she was supposed to be moved to another hospital but she didn't make it. We were all set to move and everything, but...anyway I didn't take it well. I ran out of the hospital room and found a corner in the hallway, sat on the ground and started crying. I don't know how long I was there but when I finally looked up, there was this kid sitting next to me.

"One leg cocked up but the other was stretched out with this metal thing on it. I honestly thought he was some cyborg kid at first, his face emotionless, his movements still. But when he looked at me, it was strange, I suddenly felt better. Not happy or anything, just better. He didn't say anything. Didn't do anything, but it felt like he'd done all that I needed.

"Then you came. You scolded him but he didn't seem bothered. You led him away."

Lucas shrugged. "Touching story."

"But you don't remember it?"

"Sorry, no."

Jeremy let his shoulders drop. "Didn't think you would."

"But I'm sure Ian does," Lucas said. "He talked about you."

Jeremy blinked, surprised. "He talks? I thought he was mute."

"Yes, he gives that impression," Lucas said with a knowing grin. "He doesn't talk often, but he does talk." He rested his hands on his hips. "And while that story is sweet, what does it have to do with me?"

"The tissues. Seconds later, a nurse found me and she carried a box of tissues. She told me that a bossy kid with glasses told her that I needed them. I'll never forget that."

Lucas looked sheepish. "Yes, that sounds like me but, sorry, don't remember a thing."

"I'm not surprised."

"But how did you know our names?"

"Nurse Gayle couldn't stop talking about you two."

"Nurse Gayle?"

"Yeah, Patricia's aunt was really popular at the time."

"Patricia's aunt?"

"Yeah, you might not have remembered her, but she remembered you."

"That's interesting."

"I still know her. I could tell her—"

"Don't." Lucas softened his tone. "I'd rather not bring up my past right now. It might muddy things."

Jeremy couldn't see how, he only had fond memories of them, but wouldn't argue.

"Did you tell Patricia about me?"

"No, I wasn't even sure it was you."

"Good." He paused, met Jeremy's gaze, he hadn't moved

close, but Jeremy felt as if his collar was tightening around his Adam's apple. He held Jeremy's gaze and kept his voice low, "but she doesn't need to know about us meeting before today. So let's keep this conversation between us."

Jeremy nodded.

Lucas lowered his gaze and Jeremy released a long breath. "You're a good man, I know you want to protect her."

He nodded again.

Lucas' eyes pierced him like a laser. "But you can't protect her from me."

37

Patricia looked up in surprise when Jeremy came breathlessly through the door only minutes after he'd left. "I win."

Patricia shot to her feet. "How? When's the date?"

"Um...there's not going to be one, but—"

She felt the sting of hurt, annoyed that she'd half hoped Jeremy had been right. It was her fault for believing him even for a millisecond. She should have trusted her instincts. At least she'd get a job and some money as a consolation.

She sat back down embarrassed. "Then you didn't win. How did he turn you down?"

"He didn't exactly turn me down. He just..." He let his words trail off knowing he couldn't reveal the rest, he hated the look on Patricia's face and wished he could tell her the truth. "He doesn't like dating."

"The guy was made for it. He was trying to let you down lightly. It's okay. I was a fool to think—"

"I'm trying to warn you that after three weeks—"

"Nothing will happen, why you are bringing it up?"

Jeremy sighed. "You're as bad as he is, will you listen?"

It wasn't like him to get frustrated with her. "Okay."

"Whatever happens, I want you to give this guy a chance."

She stared at him confused. "Okay."

"I mean it. I just spoke to him outside. He's a little scary but nice, caring. He used to be so funny."

Patricia frowned. "*Used* to be?"

Jeremy quickly corrected himself. "I mean...is. He *is* funny. A great guy I admire."

She nodded again not sure how to interpret what he was saying. "What happened in less than fifteen minutes to change your mind?"

"Nothing, just trust me. This is your chance, don't blow it."

"Right."

"You don't believe me."

"I believe that you want to believe he's interested in me because you have a guy crush on him or something."

"That's not—never mind. Just...give him a chance, okay?"

She nodded because lying to such a sweet, earnest face would be wrong.

GETTING information from Ian always took strategy. It usually involved a soothing location and food. Lucas watched his brother finish his large artisanal soft pretzel as they walked leisurely around the lake in the botanical garden. "Want to take a break?" Lucas said, pointing to a gazebo where they could sit.

Ian nodded and headed there.

Lucas waited for his brother to sit then cleared his throat before he approached the topic he wanted to discuss. "About twenty years ago, when you were in the hospital, did you sit in the hallway with someone who was crying?"

Ian blinked.

"Alright, I know there were a lot of people crying, but this was a particular person. Do you remember me getting tissues for somebody when you were in the hospital? I don't remember that. But he remembers you."

Ian cocked his head in interest.

"I'm sure he's nothing like he was back then, he said he wasn't a doctor or a nurse, but he must have worked there. He's not bad looking, twists, brown skinned." He held up his hands. "I know it's a terrible description. I just thought you should know you made an impression."

Ian looked smug.

"I know, you always do. Even though you don't say a word."

Ian lifted a brow.

Lucas read the meaning. "Right, cause you don't have to. Smug bastard," he said with affection. "Oh, wait I forgot he's huge."

Ian's eyes widened. "Jeremy?"

"Yeah, so you do know him."

"He didn't work at the hospital. He was just a kid, but he looked like an adult. I learned that from Nurse Gayle."

"He mentioned her too." That she's related to Patricia but his brother didn't need to know that.

"How did you meet him again?" Ian asked.

"He's a friend of Patricia. The owner of Gardner's Contractors. One of Aunt Wynette's tenants."

"That's interesting. Are they close?"

The image of Jeremy hugging Patricia flashed through Lucas's mind along with a feeling of jealousy. Jeremy was a good looking guy, but unlike the giant he'd fought at the dentist's office, he didn't know it.

Ian read the expression on his brother's face and said, "Leave it alone."

"They're not together. I made sure. I even spoke to him."

Ian looked doubtful.

"I'm not lying. I wouldn't cross the line if—"

"Yeah, you would. This one's different than the rest."

Lucas rubbed his chin. "You're right. Fortunately, I don't have to. The path is free and clear."

Ian leaned back. "What aren't you telling me about this woman?"

"I don't know..." Lucas let his words fall away under his brother's piercing gaze. "What do you want to know?"

"This isn't about the elevator. You found out something else about her."

"She took out one of the monster's men."

Ian sat up. "When? Where? Why didn't you tell us?"

"I handled it. It was at the farmhouse. Completely unexpected." Lucas explained what happened. "And then I find him there tied up."

"I have to meet her."

"Not yet."

Ian stilled.

"The times' not right," Lucas said.

Ian frowned.

"You will meet her, I promise."

38

Patricia didn't expect an audience.

When she arrived at the location Lucas had given her—a modest colonial house with a porch—she saw two other cars besides the one Lucas was leaning against. He wore sunglasses and looked like a man who thought breaking knuckles was an art form.

Patricia tugged on the collar of her raspberry colored T-shirt before she walked up to him. "I thought your father would be away."

"He is," Lucas said through clenched teeth, his eyes dark. He was not a happy man. "They're not supposed to be here."

They? "Should I come back at another time?"

"No," he said stomping up the porch steps. "Give me a minute." He disappeared inside.

Minutes later she heard raised voices. She could only make out a few of the words such as 'Sneaky.' 'Trouble.' 'Falling again.'

Since the loud voices didn't ebb, Patricia jumped back in surprise when the front door opened. A tall, handsome man with skin like almond butter and mesmerizing brown eyes motioned her inside. She glanced to where the shouting was coming from then back at him. He shook his head as if to say, *Don't worry about it,* and once again motioned her forward. "I'm here to look at the kitchen," she said. He nodded as if to say, *I know.* His energy was so calming she no longer felt bothered by the shouting.

Patricia cleared her throat and stepped inside. Before she could tell the man what she planned to do, he turned and walked down the hall. She had no choice but to follow him. He had an interesting gait that wasn't quite a limp, but wasn't a swagger either. She followed him down the short hall past the living room where the shouting was the loudest.

He passed the room with barely a flinch or glance. He must be deaf, she reasoned, that's why the shouting didn't seem to bother him.

"Lucky man," she mumbled, "Those two are like angry rams."

She glanced inside the living room and saw Lucas shouting at another man. What surprised her was that there was no heat or cruelty behind the words. They were arguing but it wasn't the vicious fighting like her parents used to do. The two men were angry but they still cared about each other.

Patricia turned away and quickly followed behind the man to the kitchen.

The man held out his hands as if to say, "Here is it. What do you think?"

She bit her lip. Three weeks would be cutting it close, but she'd manage depending on what they wanted done.

"Do you have any suggestions?"

He shook his head.

She set her things on the counter and searched her mind for her limited American Sign Language and haltingly signed. "My name is Patricia."

He nodded then quickly signed back.

She waved her hands. *Sorry too fast for me.*

He nodded then slowly signed again and she read his words aloud, "My name is Ian."

Patricia smiled in recognition, pleased she'd understood this much. *Pleased to meet you, Ian.*

He signed some more and again she read his words aloud. "I...am...not...deaf." She puzzled over the words for a second before she quickly looked up at him, startled by what they revealed. "You're not deaf?"

He shook his head.

"Oh, sorry I thought. Forget it." She froze. "Wait...so you heard what I said in the hall?"

He shrugged, his brown eyes bright with amusement and understanding, but she still wished the floor would swallow her. Flustered, she reached for her bag to get her business cards and knocked it on the ground. Cards and papers scattered to the ground. She scrambled to pick them up and noticed that he didn't bend to help her. No surprise, he was probably used to others picking up after him.

"Sorry about that—" Her words died on her lip as she saw that he held his hand out to her. She stared. Nobody had ever offered to help her before. It was a foreign feeling. As if in a trance, she placed her hand in his and let him lift her to her feet as if she weighed nothing. She wasn't one for receiving simple, considerate gestures but this one moved her.

"What are you doing?" a sharp voice said.

Patricia turned to see Lucas coming into the room and

began to reply before she realized he wasn't talking to her. The other man grinned.

Lucas pointed at him. "I hate you," he said, his words containing fire but no heat.

The other man's grin widened.

A third man entered, big, broodingly handsome and built like a bulldozer with skin like beige hardwood flooring. "You think sneaking her in would make things, better," he said, also talking to the grinning man before he cast a look at her with such suspicion she felt her skin grow cold. *He doesn't like me.* That wasn't new to her, but she couldn't imagine what could inspire his immediate distrust. Did he not like female contractors? She never thought she'd have to convince more than one person to do this job.

But she was also surprised by how much harmony was in the home. She'd expected one of the men to give off a sour note but each one harmonized with the space, especially Lucas. This was his space. She wouldn't have thought such a simple place would work, but it hummed around him.

She could already image the kind of kitchen that would suit them all. They probably saw her as a threat and she had to allay their fears.

"Let me tell you how things will work," she said then briefly told the three men the steps involved. She took out her tablet and stylus and began sketching an idea. They all watched her in silence. She felt powerful as all three stood in front of her waiting for her to finish.

Finally she showed them. "This is only rough but—"

She paused when Ian held out his hand, palm face up. She handed him her stylus. He made a slight change to her design for the counter top then looked at her in question. "Yes, yes, that's good," she said, "I can do that." She smiled at him. The smile froze on her face when she noticed the other two weren't smiling at all. The Bulldozer stroked his beard before he sent Patricia a look then spun away. Lucas glared at Ian, who rested a heavy hand on his shoulder before affectionately patting Lucas on the head.

Lucas swatted his brother's hand away and Ian released a low, warm chuckle. He waved at Patricia before he left.

39

Patricia didn't dare move. What had just happened? Did she still get the job? "As I said this was a real quick sketch and I'll have to provide you with some estimates and—"

"You don't have to sell me," Lucas said, "and price isn't a problem, as long as everything's done in three weeks."

"It will." She licked her lip. "So...the job is mine?"

"Yes. Why wouldn't it be?"

"Because they don't like me. Well, I mean one seems to like me but the other—"

"Don't worry about Damian," Lucas said, taking off his jacket and placing it over a chair. "I'll make sure he doesn't get in your way."

"He really doesn't like me."

"Damian doesn't like most people."

"This felt personal. Is it because I'm a woman?"

Lucas sighed. "Yes."

Her brows shot up. Her fighting blood rising. This was the kind of challenge she was used to. "He doesn't think I can be in charge of this job because of that? Don't worry, I've—"

Lucas shook his head. "He knows you're capable."

"Then he thinks I'll overspend, right? I can tell by the way you dress you're more casual with money than he is. He's probably upset because of the expenses. If you'll let me show you the estimates I can assure him that I won't be ripping you off."

"He's not worried about that either." Lucas closed the distance between them. He glanced down at the tablet. "It's nothing like that." He met her gaze. "It's your effect on me."

"My effect?" Patricia repeated the words, wondering why her breath felt trapped in her throat. Then she realized it was tension. She didn't want to lose this job. It wasn't because of Lucas standing so close to her, his penetrating gaze seeming to peer inside her, the scent of rosemary soap reminding her of his bare chest, and the mark under his right nipple. She sighed. "Oh, he thinks I'm manipulating you about what needs to be done. Well, if you'd let me—" She stopped because Lucas was shaking his head and looking at her with what looked like pity.

"You don't think I can win him over?"

"I don't care if you do."

"It'll be easier if—"

He glanced down at the tablet. "You don't need to worry about him."

"But—"

"Trust me. The only person you need to worry about is me," he said in a velvet whisper.

He looked at her. It was brief. Almost a flash. But it held her still nonetheless. It was heated. Not with anger. Anger she was used to. It was something else: Lust. No man had ever looked at her as if they wanted to strip her naked and take her against the wall.

Or maybe she was imagining it because that was what she wanted him to do. Soon the look was gone, he shifted his gaze back to the tablet, but her skin still tingled.

It had to be nothing. Why was she even thinking about him in that way? This was Jeremy's fault. If it hadn't been for the bet she'd not even consider that Lucas would be interested. There was no way. What was wrong with her?

"You look flushed," Lucas said in a low voice, one that reminded her of dark caves and deep oceans, "are you okay?"

A voice that reminded her of the last time she'd briefly touched him that first time in her office and the spark that she'd felt. Patricia pressed a hand to her cheek, not that she needed to check. Her skin still burned. "No, it's just I didn't sleep well."

"Do you need to sit down?" he said, but he spoke to her with the voice of a lover, seductive and alluring, as if he were offering her something intimately more.

He was close enough to touch. Why was he so close? He smelled good too. If she leaned in a little closer, she could feel the heat of his body. Or was it hers? She closed her eyes. "You're too close."

"What?"

Patricia took a step back. "Nothing."

Lucas bit his lip. "I'm not sure I can wait three weeks."

She stared at him stunned. "You need the job completed sooner? If that's the case, I can reduce some of the plans..."

"It's not that. I—" His phone rang. He softly swore, glanced at the number then said, "Excuse me," before he left.

Patricia collapsed onto the kitchen chair. Damn Jeremy for putting foolish ideas in her head.

She glanced at one of the chairs and saw Lucas' jacket. She wondered if the lethal pen was still inside.

She quickly looked around to make sure she was still alone before she stood and lifted it up.

"What are you doing?" Lucas said.

40

Her first instinct was to say nothing, but the fact that she was holding up his jacket would take some explaining. She brushed off a sleeve. "I accidentally knocked it on the floor and was cleaning it."

He blinked unconvinced.

"I just want to see that weapon."

"Weapon?"

"The one you threw at the wall. The one that nearly killed me."

His face hardened. "If I'd meant to kill you, I would have. It was to scare you." He held out his hand.

Instead of handing the jacket back to him, she replaced it back over the chair. The voice of the lover was gone replaced with the one that had scolded her at the farmhouse. She had no thoughts of bare flesh and warm beds when she looked at him now. She'd gotten her imagination under control. He was a client. "I'm sorry," Patricia said. "I didn't mean to insult."

"Insult me? You took years off of my life, that's what you did."

"What is it?"

He picked up the jacket. "Nothing."

"Just one wrong move and it could have gotten me right here." She jabbed her neck.

He sent her a cutting glance. "You don't need to know what it is."

Lucas looked mean and annoyed, but for some reason that expression excited her. She remained unafraid. She pressed her hands together, pleading.

He scowled.

She fluttered her lashes. Something she never did.

Lucas sighed and pulled out the object. He rested in her upturned palm.

It felt light and didn't look scary. "It looks like a pen. Can I try?"

He shrugged.

She went outside and aimed at a tree. She threw it and it bounced off the trunk and fell to the ground.

She picked it up and frowned. "Are you sure this is the same one?"

He nodded.

She tried again, with the same effect. "It's not the same," she accused him.

Lucas calmly lifted the object and threw it at the tree. It stuck.

She stared.

"What did you do?"

He walked over and pulled the object from the tree. "Nothing." He opened his jacket to tuck it away, but Patricia snatched it before he could.

He stared at her. "Did you just—"

She studied the object. "That's amazing."

He took a step towards her and reached for the pen, playfully she shoved him away.

Lucas stared down at his chest then up at her amazed. "Did you just *push* me?"

"Yes,"

He slowly walked around her with the steady pace of a predator. "You wouldn't want to do that again."

"Actually I would," she said following him with her eyes. She waved the object. "What is this?"

"I'm not telling you," he continued, slowly circling her.

She gripped the pen in her fist. "I'm not giving it back then."

"Okay," he said then lunged at her, but when she moved to block him, he moved with such speed only the tips of her fingers managed to brush against his shirt, before he spun out of reach. He appeared behind her, wrapping his arm around her waist.

She seized his arm, spun away and flipped him over her back.

He somersaulted over her and landed on the ground with a thud, his legs and arms outstretched like a fallen scarecrow.

Patricia knelt beside him, hoping she hadn't hurt him too badly. "Are you alright?"

"I am now." He waved the weapon in his right hand.

Patricia glanced at her empty hand where the weapon had been then stared up at him shocked. "How did you?"

He flashed a sly grin, reduced the size of the object to the size of a keychain and slid it inside his pocket before he sat up. "You should be more careful."

She didn't move. Neither did he. If she moved a little closer...

"You've got a call," Damian announced from the patio.

A flash of annoyance crossed Lucas' face. "It can wait."

"It's Dad."

He sharply turned to his brother and she saw alarm, frustration then sadness touch his features before he sighed in resignation.

Patricia stood. "I should go," she said and reached out her hand to help him up, but he ignored it. And her, his gaze remained on his brother.

She hesitated. She hated that she'd have to walk past Damian, who loomed like Mount Kilimanjaro, to get into the kitchen and gather her things, but she had no choice. She hurried over to the patio door. Damian had the grace to step back and let her pass. She bit her lip and thought of trying to say something to win him over, but the look he sent her told her it was best to stay silent.

She went in the kitchen, quickly picked up her things and left.

41

"Don't ever do that again," Lucas said, meeting with his brothers in the living room where Damian had retreated after his false alarm. Lucas had wanted to walk Patricia to her truck, but she'd dashed from the backyard and out of the house before he could. He didn't blame her.

"I saved you from yourself," Damian said. "I saw how she threw you."

"I let her."

"I know."

"I can handle myself. Don't get in my way." Lucas sent Ian a look. "I bet you're pleased with yourself for finagling a chance to meet her. You nearly scared her off."

Ian rested his head in his hand unfazed and blinked as if to say, *If I'd wanted to scare her I would have.*

"Want to know what I think?" Damian said.

Lucas glared at him. "I already know what you think. And she does too. You couldn't even pretend to be a little civil."

Damian sniffed. "I didn't tell her to leave, *that* was me being civil."

"I'm going to approve her plans and we'll get started on the kitchen before Dad returns." Lucas pointed at Damian. "Don't interfere."

"I don't care what she does with the house. It's you."

I can't believe you're giving me such a hard time with all I'm doing for you."

Damian sniffed. "Doing for me?"

"Yes, your request to Aunt Wynette? I'm helping her with it."

Damian frowned. "What request?"

"Is it supposed to be a secret or something?"

"I don't know what you're talking about."

"I know it's been awhile. About six months ago."

"I don't think—"

"You need another location, right?"

The look on his brother's face told him more than he ever wanted to know. His aunt had tricked him. There was no urgent need. She'd had him running around for some other reason.

Lucas surged to his feet. "That crafty old—"

"She must have her reasons."

"She always has a reason. I'm going to get her for this."

"She hasn't really caused you any trouble though, has she?"

"Not yet," Lucas spat out. "But she will."

He stormed out of the house and pounded down the porch steps so focused on getting to the bottom of what his aunt was up to he almost didn't see Patricia waiting by her truck.

He halted when he saw her.

She lifted up a hand and waved.

Lucas cautiously walked over to her. "What's wrong?"

"I don't want to get in-between you and your family." She pointed at him. "Don't smile. I'm serious. I know family is important." She nodded towards the house. "And this place means a lot to you. You belong here."

"And I know you need this job."

"I won't deny that." She leaned forward.

Lucas jumped back before Patricia could touch him. He laughed impressed. "You almost got me. Nice."

"You like that move?"

"Yes."

"How about this one?" Patricia said then shoved her hand down his trouser pocket. She closed her hand expecting to grab his pen, but gripped his thigh instead. The pen wasn't there. Her hand frantically searched his pocket and found nothing.

She froze. It took the space of a heartbeat to realize her mistake.

Her *real* mistake.

Not only had she chosen the wrong pocket, but now she didn't know how to remove her hand without embarrassing them both.

She knew Lucas wore well-fitted trousers, but never imagined the pockets to be deep, tight and hot. She felt as if she'd sunk her hand into a furnace. Except it wasn't the pocket that was hot, it was the man.

"That was a mistake," Lucas said in a voice that dropped to ocean depths.

Patricia felt her paralysis extend to her breathing. She swallowed, trapped, unable to move; any action seeming to hint at sexual harassment. Even the barest movement caused her fingers to brush against the muscle of his thigh, her cheeks flushing at the delicious way the fabric clung to his body.

She hung her head, squeezed her eyes closed. Her pounding heart made it difficult to speak. "I'm sorry."

"Did you really think I'd put a pen in my pocket?"

Patricia opened her eyes, but didn't lift her head. "I saw you—"

"You mean you *think* you saw me." Lucas opened his jacket and briefly showed her the head of the pen.

"But I was sure..." She stopped. She couldn't deny that he'd tricked her with the art of misdirection. "Never mind," she said, inching a bit closer to make sure she didn't tear the fabric of his pocket when she tried to pull her hand out. "I'm *really* sorry." She began to pull her hand free, but the effort felt achingly slow, her ascent becoming a smooth, sensual slide upward awakening all of her traitorous senses. She became aware of every aspect of him: his scent (a mixture of honey and spice), the sound of his breathing (shallow), his body (hard). A low strangled growl escaped him, when she finally broke free.

"I didn't know you were so curious," Lucas said, when Patricia quickly stepped away.

She didn't dare look up at him. She kept her gaze settle on his shoulder, then his neck. She held her burning hand behind her back, flexing her tingling fingers. "Yes. Too curious. I'll make it up to you."

She knew how much he hated her touching him. That didn't stop her from wishing she could touch him more. He'd felt so hot, probably burning with anger. But his tone didn't reflect that when he casually said, "It's a knife. It's activated with biometrics so it only works with my thumbprint, that's why it didn't work for you. Satisfied?"

She let her hand fall to her side and forced herself to meet his gaze, prepared to face his anger.

But the eyes that met hers, held no anger, instead she saw the heat of arousal. One so tangible that when Luca's dark gaze dipped to her mouth, they left her lips tingling before they returned back to her eyes. "You shouldn't have done that," he said.

She nodded, bit her lip. "I wanted to see it. I couldn't help myself."

His eyes fluttered closed as if she'd said something sexy and dirty. He softly swore. "Neither can I," he said before his lips covered her own.

42

———————

"**S**he's kissing him!"

Ian yawned.

Damian pounded the arm of the couch with his fist. "And he's falling for it."

Ian rubbed his eyes.

"Right after we warned him!"

Ian scratched his chin and mumbled, "You don't have to shout."

"But she's kissing him—"

"Bet you he's kissing her—"

"—where everyone can see them."

"You're probably the only one who's looking."

"Dad wanted us to look out for him. Protect him. Remember he's been kidnapped twice."

Ian sighed and looked away, the resulting silence allowing them both to sink into a shared memory.

It had been a harrowing event for the entire family. First Lucas had been taken when he was nine years old (at a festival) then again at thirteen (at a bus depot). With his quick wit and dark humor, Lucas managed to turn being bound and gagged and tossed into a trunk into an exciting adventure story only he could find amusing. One kidnapping lasting five months, the other nearly a year.

Nearly twenty years had passed since then, but Damian didn't want to give the monster a chance to outwit them.

Damian turned and headed for the front door. He stopped when something soft hit the back of his neck. He looked down at the thrown couch pillow then glared at his brother.

Ian pointed to the sofa as if saying *Sit down*.

Damian picked up the pillow, squeezing it between his hands. "You cannot be as calm as you look."

Ian folded his arms.

Damian sat in front of him. "She's a freight train."

Ian narrowed his gaze in censure.

"I'm not making fun of her size," Damian explained. "I mean she's a steamroller. She'll hurt him."

Ian paused then said, "She took down one of the monster's men."

Damian leaned his head back against the couch and gazed up at the ceiling. "Why are you talking in riddles?"

"I'm not."

"She took down one of the monster's men. What does that mean?" He sat up and stared as the realization hit him. "Really?"

Ian nodded.

"Then she can be more dangerous than we think." Damian put the pillow cushion back in place.

Ian nodded again.

Damian studied his brother for a moment. "That's why you wanted to meet her."

Ian smiled, pleased.

"So you could see the kind of woman she is and keep an eye on her?" Damian concluded.

Ian clapped his hands in applause.

Damian let his shoulders fall. "It still complicates things." He pointed towards the window. "She's supposed to be working for him."

Ian shook his head and pointed to himself.

"She's working for you?" Damian guessed then inwardly groaned when Ian lifted a brow. "You're right. If we know Lucas, she soon will be."

43

She'd never felt so happy to lose.

She didn't push him away. She thought she would. Her rational mind told her the moment Lucas closed the distance between them and wrapped his arms around her she should resist. But she didn't.

She didn't think about having to renovate Jeremy's bathroom for free. All the labor and costs she'd have to swallow.

She didn't think at all.

Instead, she opened her mouth a little wider, welcomed the weight of his tongue, indulging in the hot wild sensation of lust as his intoxicating scent lured her to lose control, the pounding of his heart an echo of her own.

She spread her hands against the expanse of his back, wishing she could slide her fingers underneath his shirt and feel his bare flesh. She knew what he looked like half-naked, but now she wanted to know how his skin felt, when he wasn't tied up or passed out. But like this: completely alert and eager.

She knew the shape and muscle of his thigh by touch,

now she wanted to strip off his trousers and see them. She pressed her body close, still shocked at the heat that radiated from him—burning hot. She wondered if he'd leave her fingers singed as they scaled over his body, she imagined the weight of him on top of hers, thrusting himself inside her the way he was doing with his tongue. She couldn't get enough.

She wanted to devour the crumbs life had to offer her. The scraps of affection she managed to gain. She knew this incredible moment wouldn't last so she would wring it dry to the last drop.

But Lucas didn't let her. He pulled away and said in a breathless rush, "Slow down."

But she didn't want to. She wanted more. So much more than these mere seconds of pleasure, she didn't have the luxury of taking her time. For her, time was always the enemy.

She lifted her hand to cup his face.

He flinched.

She snatched her hand back, feeling as startled as he looked. "I'm sorry."

"No, I'm sorry," he said quickly. "I didn't mean to do that." He swore. "I've never done that before."

"It's okay, the last time—" She was going to mention the time she'd punched him, but he didn't give her the chance. His lips smothered her words and soon she forgot them.

She kissed him back, then touched his face and he winced.

He swore. "It's me."

"No, it's not you. It's because I've hurt you."

Lucas shook his head and said with an amused grin. "No, it's not that. I've had worse." Before she could ask him what he meant, he pressed a finger over her lips. "I'll get over it, but not today."

She pushed his hand away. "Maybe you don't like me touching you."

He started to laugh then blinked. "Oh, you're serious."

Patricia gazed down at her hands in dismay and she felt the passionate moment fade away. She swallowed back her bitterness. "Must be my hands."

"Don't talk about your hands or I'll be thinking about them all day. Are you trying to torture me?"

She began to teasingly say yes, but saw something move out of the corner of her eye and saw his brother Damian at the window before he darted out of sight.

He reminded her of how wrong this all was. What was at risk. She needed this project more than she needed a relationship.

"We need to stop." She pressed her hand against his chest. "You're a client."

"From now on you'll work for my brother." When she looked at him alarmed, Lucas quickly clarified and said, "Ian." He moved her hand away. "So now there's nothing to worry about." He drew her close. "Can I see you tonight?"

She wanted to say yes, but knew the wonderful moment was over, it couldn't be recaptured. She couldn't offer him more. If only he hadn't pulled away, if only he hadn't flinched when she'd tried to touch him then maybe she'd have had a chance. But she couldn't go further than this. Not with a man like him. While his tone was carefree, his gaze wasn't. It was intense. It didn't make her feel calm; it didn't assure her that everything would be alright. His gaze was hungry, vulnerable. And that vulnerability frightened her while also igniting deep desires inside of her. He had a weakness she didn't want to see. Didn't want to be responsible for. She saw flashes of her father's pain and her mother's disdain.

Attraction to such a man could destroy her...and him.

Patricia let her hands fall to her sides, defeated. "No, I have two bids to look over."

"How about this weekend?"

"I've got plans," the words fell from her lips even though they weren't true.

Lucas fell quiet a long moment and Patricia held her breath waiting for the abuses to begin. For the cold superior smirk to distort his lips and a spiteful gleam to enter his gaze that said, Who do you think you are? You think you're worth waiting for? She expected him to say 'Fat pig' and add 'Bitch' for good measure.

As it had happened too many times before.

She waited for her lie to protect her and reveal Lucas' true nature, his true intentions: that he only wanted sex and he could get it elsewhere. She waited for him to tell her this fact in exquisite detail as many others had. To expose her as a liar.

But instead Lucas looked puzzled, "Okay," he said, disappointment clear in his tone, "Then let me know when you're free." He gave her a jaunty wave then turned.

She grabbed his sleeve without thinking and quickly let go when he looked at her. "I'm sorry," she said with feeling, surprised by how much she meant it.

He smiled. "Don't look so worried. I understand you have a busy schedule."

"You don't think I'm lying?"

He tilted his head. "Why would you lie?"

She lowered her gaze to his shoes. "I don't know," at least that was true.

She felt him lean in close, felt the flutter-light brush of his lips against the curve of her neck, the resulting tingling of her skin, his warm breath against her ear when he whispered, "When you're free, call me. I'm not going anywhere."

She watched his shoes disappear from view and heard his car door slam before he revved the engine and drove away.

And Patricia watched him go wondering why he'd believed her. She wasn't busy. Far from it. And she hadn't had plans in years, but he hadn't questioned her. Why would he think a woman like her would be too busy for a man like him? Wasn't he used to women being at his beck and call?

She almost wished she hadn't lied. But as she climbed inside her truck she told herself she already knew the ending.

She'd end up alone.

44

*L*ucas would have preferred a night with Patricia, but Aunt Wynette would prove a useful cold shower.

He entered her house and nearly tripped over Methuselah who came to greet him. It was an unexpected and annoyingly affectionate greeting since it didn't make it easy for Lucas to stay enraged when the old dog's grey snout brushed against his hand and licked it.

The maid (olive toned, mid-fifties with amble hips that swayed like a metronome) led him to what his aunt liked to refer to as 'the office', but was really her conservatory with a large grand piano. She sat at the enormous black instrument wearing a bright orange dress, looking as harmless as a toddler. Her fingers expertly moved across the keys creating, his emotions moved by a beautiful classical melody he'd never heard before.

"This tune was created by a female composer, you know," Wynette said, clasping her hands in her lap. "If not for her gender it would have been more widely known."

He wasn't in the mood for a women's history lesson. He knew more than most all the ills men have done in the past and present. "You lied to me."

She began to play again. "About what?"

"Damian didn't ask for your help."

"Did I ever say he did?"

"Yes, that's why you had me looking at different properties for him."

"I said your *brother* needed help. I don't remember being specific."

"I'm not playing this game."

"It's not a game."

"Everything with you is a game."

"Only because life is. You have no choice."

She scooted over on the bench then patted the empty space beside her. "Come and play something for me."

He thought of refusing her then decided to sit down and play Chopin's *Funeral March*.

She laughed. "That's not very original."

Lucas began to play "Back to the Dust" by The Angelic Gospel Singers.

Wynette clapped her hands in delight and began to sway side to side in rhythm.

He continued to play. "Tell me what you want."

"To stop you from having regrets."

Lucas laughed without humor. "You're not helping there. I regret talking to you, I regret—"

"Do you regret meeting Patricia?"

He stopped playing and looked at her. He narrowed his eyes. "What do you know about that?"

"Didn't you enjoy sleeping with her?"

He focused on the keys. He'd almost forgotten his lie.

"Your brother needs help."

Lucas stiffened, ready to act. "The last time I spoke to them, Damian and Ian were fine."

"I'm not talking about them."

He repeatedly hit the C key with his forefinger, bored. "I only have two brothers."

"*Lucas* has two brothers."

He played the scales with one hand. "Exactly. And that's who I am now."

"You can't hide from your past."

"I'm not hiding. You don't need to hide from something you've buried."

"He's going to get you in trouble."

Lucas yawned.

"I don't have all the information yet, but he might have something your mother wants. Might be evidence that could send her back to prison, or gold she's tucked away."

"Then he should give it back to her."

"I had you look at the three properties because I wanted to see if he'd follow you—and he did."

"I didn't see him."

"I know."

He thought of the figure he'd seen darting behind the trees at the farmhouse. That could have been him. But something else bothered Lucas more. He bit his lip. "What do you know about the cameras in Gardner's Contractors?"

Her brows shot up. "There are cameras there?"

"Security cameras," Lucas said, wondering if he could catch his aunt in a lie.

"I don't know anything about that. She must have reasons to put them up."

He returned his attention to the piano, and ran his

fingers along the keys. His aunt didn't know about the surveillance cameras. That meant someone else was watching, but who? And why?

"What does Patricia mean to you?"

"I think you should worry about your brother more. We think he'll approach you first."

Lucas's fingers faltered on the keyboard. He'd prepared himself for never seeing his brother again. There was no need to see him. They had nothing to say to each other. It wasn't that he wished him harm. He didn't wish him anything. The thought of him only gave him pain. He also knew his aunt had evaded his question about Patricia. She was hiding something, but he wouldn't press.

"Your mother thinks he'll approach you too, that's why she's looking for you."

"I don't care."

"You owe him. Your brother helped us find you after the second kidnapping. It's because he stayed close to your mother and knew her contacts and had his own. He took a dangerous risk."

Lucas gritted his teeth. "I already repaid that debt."

At least he tried. In his mid-twenties, Lucas had reconnected with his biological brother. He'd offered him a chance to get out of their mother's world (and the dark world his brother had created for himself), but his brother had refused. He always refused.

"It's not that simple," Wynette said.

"Never is."

"You're bait."

"That's nothing new." Lucas gently closed the piano lid over the keys. He stood. "I think we're finished."

"No, dear," Wynette said with a tired sigh. "If it involves your mother and brother, things have only begun."

45

———————

*H*arsh sunlight streamed through the bathroom windows, casting sharp shadows on the floor. Patricia studied her handiwork, satisfied. She'd been called back to Maya's Hair Salon to replace several tiles after a plumber's apprentice had ruined a few when installing a new sink.

The work was a welcome distraction. She didn't want to think about the kiss or Lucas.

She also wasn't in the mood to tell Jeremy he'd been right. She would wait until the end of three weeks and then tell him. Perhaps he'd forget all about the bet by then.

The salon wasn't busy. She heard the rush of water as one of the salon attendants washed a patron's hair and amicably chatted while applying hair foils.

Patricia found the owners in the breakroom and raised her hand to knock on the door, but stopped when she heard Deena say, "Wish I could convince Lucas to come back for another 'inspection.'"

"Oh, Lucas," Samantha said with a wistful sigh. "I can't stop thinking about him."

Patricia shook her head. Great, now she was hearing his name everywhere. Of course there were plenty of men named Lucas.

"I almost called Mrs. Clemmens to come up with an excuse to get him back here."

Mrs. Clemmens? Were they really talking about Lucas? Her Lucas?

"I know. That nephew of hers can make a woman believe in heaven on earth."

Deena released a low, throaty laugh. "Or that hell has its benefits."

"Yes, there's something sinfully delicious about Lucas Wolff."

Patricia decided to knock on the door. "I'm heading out."

"Thanks for coming by," Stephanie said.

How well do you know Lucas Wolff she wanted to ask them, but didn't have the courage to do so. She waved and then left, her mind reeling.

Lucas had been with both of them and they weren't bothered? They missed him?

Had she misread his kiss? It wasn't anything more than an invitation to sex? The vulnerability she'd seen in his gaze hadn't meant he'd wanted a relationship with her. He only wanted some fun. How could she have read the mood so wrong? Of course he wanted nothing more.

That made him safe. She couldn't hurt a man like that. He wouldn't expect or want commitment from her. There would be no demands, no way to disappoint him or let him down.

Just sex.

No fuss, no mess, no worries.

Patricia left the salon happier than she'd felt in a long time. She jumped in her truck and pulled out her phone.

I'M FREE TOMORROW.

Lucas stared at the text from Patricia for a long moment, unsure of how to respond. He watched as Alex paid for a new suit Lucas didn't need (but wanted) because Lucas liked to shop. Shopping helped him to think and after he'd left his aunt's house, Lucas went to several name brand shops and bought something for his two brothers, his father, his sister-in-law, Carter and Julia, then stopped at a toy store to purchase various gifts to give to the children's ward at the local hospital. He then decided to go to the mall and purchased several outfits to donate to a local women's shelter then thought of his troublesome 'brother' and purchased some suits to donate to a halfway house.

Once Lucas and Alex decided on the logistics of how they'd donate the items, Lucas thought he deserved a treat and went to his favorite shop. That's where the new blue pinstripe linen suit came in.

"Is something wrong?" Alex asked him.

He wasn't sure. "The suit's yours."

"What?"

"You heard me." Lucas turned his cheek and Alex playfully kissed him in appreciation. Lucas motioned him away. "Now go and find a ride home."

"Are you sure you'll be okay?"

Lucas met his assistant's worried expression with a grin. "Yes."

He waited for Alex to leave before he returned his attention to the phone and typed: *Not tonight?*

Patricia: *It's late.*

It was only 8PM. Lucas: *Not that late.*

She didn't respond right away. Perhaps he'd pushed her too much. He began to type then her words appeared on his screen.

Patricia: *Where should we meet?*

Lucas took a deep breath. A bad day was about to turn into something wonderful. *Anywhere you want.*

Patricia: *Where are you now?*

Lucas: *Where do you want to meet?*

Patricia: *Can you come to my place?*

Did she really need to ask?? Lucas: *Send me the address.* When she did, he quickly replied: *Okay, give me an hour.*

46

*L*ucas arrived at her door breathless, with sweat glistening on his skin. "Did I pass?" he wheezed as if he'd completed a marathon.

Patricia blinked, confused. "Pass?"

"You... live on... the seventh floor."

It took Patricia a moment to realize what he was talking about. She covered her mouth in horror. "Oh no! You took the elevator?"

Lucas wiped his forehead. "I wouldn't risk it tonight. I took the stairs."

"I'm sorry, I forgot." She'd asked him to come to her condo because she didn't want to be distracted by how well or not he harmonized with his own surroundings. She hadn't thought about him getting to the seventh floor to reach her condo might be a challenge for him. "Do you need something to drink?"

He didn't move. He looked at her in a way no one ever had before, as if he were a hungry carnivore and she was fresh meat. If eyes could salivate they'd look as dark as onyx and penetrate like a sharpened sword.

"I didn't come here to drink," he said in a low voice, "or to eat anything or to talk. I came here for one thing and that's to sleep with you. Understood? No, don't nod. Say it."

"I understand."

He took a deep breath. "Are you ready to let me in?"

Patricia opened the door wider and he walked past her. She closed the door behind him. "I can get you some water at least." She turned.

He seized her wrist and spun her around to him. "I told you I'm not thirsty," he said in a low growl before his lips descended on hers.

She couldn't call it a kiss: A kiss felt too tame a description. His lips carried more heat, more power than it had before. She'd never been kissed like this. She felt marked, branded, claimed in the most delicious sense. He made no secret what she meant to him. This was an action, a declaration, she couldn't deny.

She touched the button of his shirt. He swiftly covered her hand, stopping her.

"Not here."

She turned and headed for the bedroom.

She turned on the lights and almost turned them off again. She'd forgotten how her tropical themed room could look to a stranger. How would Lucas respond to the wicker furniture woven from bamboo—from the king sized bed to the drawers and side chair? And the soft grey carpeting and royal blue decorative accents couldn't dim the shocking shades of pink— the peach colored walls, the coral bedsheets, the matching strawberry lamps with white shades sitting on the side tables, and the hot pink pillows. She turned to him to tell him they should do it in the dark, but she gasped when she saw him. He didn't look bothered at all. He looked...comfortable.

He'd already taken off his shoes and stripped off his shirt. He carried it slung over his shoulder. She hadn't even heard him. "How did you?"

He pressed a finger to his lips then tossed the shirt over a chair. He walked over to her and reached for her shirt, she let him pull it over her head.

She saw a flash of surprise even a little disappointment in his gaze before it was swiftly hidden. Her heart grew cold. "What is it?"

"Nothing."

She slid out of her jeans and again saw the same expression before he glanced away and removed his trousers. He tossed them aside then gently pushed her towards the bed.

She pressed a hand against his chest. "Tell me what's wrong."

Lucas looked sheepish as he looked at her bra and panties. "I thought they'd be pink."

Patricia laughed, relieved. She glanced around the room. "What gave me away?"

Lucas wrapped his arms around her and whispered. "It wasn't the room that gave you away."

That surprised her. "You noticed I liked pink before today?"

"I've noticed a lot of things about you before today. Want me to list them?"

"No," she said delighted he'd even imagined the kind of underwear she wore.

He removed his glasses and rested them on the side table. "I can buy you a set if you don't have any."

"Of course I have a set."

"I look forward to seeing them." He didn't say 'next time,' but when he slid off her panties and covered her body with his they both knew he didn't have to.

Patricia didn't know when she drifted off to sleep, but she woke in the middle of the night. She was disappointed, rather than surprised, to find herself alone in the bed. She saw the light on in the hallway and a triangle of light from the partially opened door.

She crept to the door and peered through the slit. She saw Lucas, with a towel around his waist, standing in the hallway talking on the phone. "I'm still here," he said. "She's asleep right now." He listened for a few seconds then said, "No, she doesn't know yet and I don't want her to." Lucas turned towards the door as if he'd heard a sound. Patricia quickly moved out of sight. "It's nothing," he said. "I thought I heard something."

Patricia returned to the bed not wanting to hear more.

She'd learned from experience it was never a good idea to hear what someone had to say about her. This wasn't high school anymore. She didn't have to worry about a bet, but she also knew she wasn't someone who mattered to him. She was just one of the women he wanted to sleep with. He might even have a rating system. She didn't care. The sex had been amazing.

Whatever the reason he had to be on the phone, she didn't want to know.

The light in the hallway went dark and she heard his approaching footsteps, she dove under the covers just as she heard the door sweep open further. She expected to see light from his mobile phone pierce the darkness in the room, but he made his way over to the bed without it as if he could see in the dark. She lay still.

She heard Lucas sigh then swear. She imagined him trying to find his clothes without waking her.

She felt the bed sink from the weight of him when he sat on the side of the bed. That surprised her. Was he putting on his socks or something?

Strange he wouldn't put them on outside. It'd be easier to creep out of the room and change in the hallway, but maybe he figured she was a sound sleeper.

She held her breath.

The bed moved, this time she felt the weight of his whole body, as if he were lying back down, but that couldn't be right. She felt the heat of his chest against her bare back, his hand rest on her thigh. "Why are you so tense?"

She didn't know how to respond. How did he know she was awake?

She felt his lips on her shoulder. "What's going on?"

Who were you talking to? She didn't feel she had a right to ask. "Bad dream," she lied, although it wasn't too far from the truth. His phone call had brought up bad memories.

"Want to share?"

She was tempted, but then she'd have to reveal too much about herself. About her fears. Her desires. "No."

"You're not alone. I have them too." He kissed her shoulder again. "If you can't sleep..."

She pushed the thought of the phone call away. She turned to him, wrapped her arms around his neck. "I don't want to sleep," she said and pressed her lips against his, surrendering to the passion of a masterful lover who blocked out the world. The past and future didn't matter. Only now. Only this.

Lucas reached across her and turned on the side lamp, causing Patricia to squint against the sudden glare. But Lucas didn't squint or blink. He hovered over her and waited for her vision to become accustomed to the light. He looked different without his glasses, younger somehow, but also more intense. She felt studied, assessed, like a foreign specimen under the microscope of a scientist. "Did I cross the line?" he said.

"Line?"

"I shouldn't have spent the night. Is that what's bothering you?"

Patricia stared at him surprised. She hadn't even thought about it. Men didn't usually stay the night with her, she'd never wanted them to and they were happy to leave. Why had it felt so natural for him to stay? "No, that's not it."

"Then what is it?"

She drummed her fingers against the mattress. She didn't want to tell him that she'd overheard his phone call. That would sound too much like a jealous lover. He had his life outside of her. "I was surprised to see you gone." She lightly touched his chest, hoping to distract him, making it easier for him to swallow her lie. "That's all."

His eyes continued to study her face. She turned away unable to hold his gaze.

The sheets shifted as he bent down towards her.

"I'm back now," Lucas said, his voice warm against her cheek. "And I'm not tired." He dragged a single finger along her collarbone. "Are you?"

She turned towards him, her body responding to his touch. "No."

He lowered his lips to hers in a kiss she felt everywhere. Heat filled her stomach, gathered between her thighs, rose up her neck. She welcomed the weight of him sinking down on top of her, the warm pressure of his lips sliding down her shoulder, stopping at her chest. She released a shuddering breath when his tongue teased one nipple then the other, before he disappeared underneath the sheets. A warm hand caressed the inside of her thighs, gently spreading them apart, before she felt the hot, slick pleasure of a tongue against her center. Shocked, her body responded instinctively, arching closer to his mouth, aching, throbbing, begging for more. Lucas didn't disappoint, pleasuring her center with his masterful tongue and mouth until she saw stars.

"Lucas," Patricia said, her voice sounding deep, breathless, scandalized. He reappeared from under the sheets and chuckled with the low seductive tone of a villain.

That wicked laugh, ignited her competitive edge. He wouldn't be the only one to have fun. She had a few moves of her own.

She rolled him onto his back. "Now it's your turn."

"My turn?" He stared up at her and the look he sent her shook her heart. Warring emotions flashed through his eyes—he was wary and eager.

Patricia shifted her gaze from his face to the bright pink pillows that lay on either side of him. The sight of his masculine frame against the frilly pillows should have appeared ridiculous and yet he looked like he belonged there—in her bed, with her.

The image so unnerved her (as well as the fierce feeling of possessiveness that followed), Patricia reached over and turned off the lights, casting them in darkness. She couldn't think of Lucas like that. She couldn't make him special. In the dark he could be any man: An interchangeable lover.

Feeling more in control of her emotions, she let her fingers trail the lines of his pecs, down his abs, feeling the rise and fall of his chest.

"Patricia, you—" She pressed her hand against his mouth because the sound of his voice (too distinctive, too *Lucas*) gave her goose bumps and distracted her. "Quiet."

She slid her fingers lower and wrapped her hand around the erect length of him. "You said you don't mind me touching you." She gently tightened her grip, rhythmically moving it up and down. "I want you to prove it."

He moaned. "You're proving it right now."

Goose bumps scattered across her skin again. Why couldn't he be quiet?

"I haven't even started."

His moaned deepened. "Patricia," he said, in the voice of a soulmate that seemed to span lifetimes and always called her name. Always called her to him. "It feels so good."

She sunk her teeth into her lower lip, to stop from saying his name, wanting to touch herself at the same time she was touching him. *Lucas, Lucas, Lucas.* Her body craved him. How did he make his presence known even in the dark? She couldn't pretend she was with anyone else but him.

Patricia sighed in surrender and buried herself under the covers, determined to give him the same pleasure he'd given her. She touched the tip of him with her tongue, before covering him with her mouth. She kept her hand in motion while she repeatedly licked and sucked and sucked and licked, harder and harder, until she heard him gasp. He urgently tap her shoulder with his hand, a warning he was about to come.

She gave him space and emerged from under the covers. She fell on her back, their heavy breathing filling the silence. He swore. She laughed.

"Patricia—"

She covered his mouth; squeezed her eyes shut. Why did he have to say her name like that? As if he were casting a spell that said: You belong to me? It was supposed to be simple fun between them, nothing more. Feelings made things messy. "You're welcome."

She felt him chuckle deep in his chest, unoffended. He removed her hand from his mouth and kissed her palm then licked it. She snatched her hand away.

He laughed again then disappeared into the bathroom. By the time he returned she'd changed the sheets.

Lucas sank down next to her and gathered her close. "You could have waited for me to help you with the bed."

"You were gone a long time," she teased him although she'd changed the bed in record speed.

"I had to recover from—"

"From what?" she pressed when he stopped. "The best night of your life?" Her body hummed, settled inside his warm embrace. She didn't know sex could feel this good. She doubted she'd be able to sleep.

Lucas kissed her shoulder with surprising tenderness. "Yeah, something like that." He sighed and soon drifted off to sleep and that was the first, of what would soon be many times, he whispered a name. A woman's name.

A woman named Ericka.

47

Ericka. She wouldn't think about Ericka.

Probably some former lover he hadn't gotten over, she wouldn't let that bother her. She knew Lucas was only with her for one reason. He'd even told her so. *I came here for one thing and that's to sleep with you. Understood?*

Maybe he wanted to forget Ericka and Patricia was a handy substitute. She didn't mind. She didn't expect anything from him, didn't want anything except his delicious body. And (maybe) sometimes his company.

After nearly two weeks of his nightly visits she'd gotten used to him. She expected to get bored of him, but her desire felt insatiable. Every time the sex ended she looked forward to more. Even after the most tiring day, she looked forward to seeing him, being with him, falling asleep beside him.

One morning she found him in the kitchen, with his arms crossed on the table and his head resting on them like a child being punished. "Your fridge is empty," he groaned.

She opened the fridge door. "Not completely. There's—"

"Beer, hard cheese and shriveled cucumbers." He sat up. "We need to go shopping. I'll pay."

"I don't need you to pay."

"I have money."

She closed the fridge door. "I know you have money. I don't need it. If I wanted a man with money, I've already got one. His name is Jeremy and he'd spoil me rotten if I let him. That's not why you're here. What?" she said when Lucas stared at her dumbstruck.

"You don't care about my money?" he said.

"Why would I care about your money?"

"Because it's part of my charm?"

Patricia laughed. "Do you really believe that?" To her surprise he didn't smile. She'd never seen him look so serious before. He looked vulnerable—lost—as if she'd stolen something precious from him and shattered it. She immediately stopped laughing, tasting the bitter crumbs of regret. Did he think she was making fun of him? He'd probably worked hard for his success and thought she had disregarded his efforts. Her parents had fought about money and her father always strived and failed to make more, thinking that a large bank account made him more of a man. More worthy.

Patricia sat in front of Lucas and held her hands together. "I'm sorry. I don't need your money, but if you really want to pay?"

He glanced away. "It's not about paying. It's just..." He sighed, met her gaze. "It's just...nobody's ever said that to me before."

Patricia leaned back amused. Now she knew the game he was playing. He was fishing for compliments. That had to be the reason for his strange behavior. She supposed every guy needed an ego boost every now and then. "Lucas, you're a sexy, smart, good looking man who cares about his family and friends. You could be a street food vendor and it wouldn't matter. Don't tell me nobody's ever told you that."

"Nobody's ever told me that."

She folded her arms unnerved. Why did he still look so serious? Why did the expression in his eyes break her heart?

"Then they were thinking it," she said, and playfully leaned forward to pat his cheek. He winced. She drew way.

He swore and snatched his glasses from his face. He slammed them against the table with such force she feared they would break until she realized most of the impact had been absorbed by his fist. "What the hell is wrong with me?"

"It's okay, Lucas."

His eyes met hers, stony with anger. "It's not okay, Patricia."

Patricia took a deep breath, knowing the anger was directed at himself not her. She stood, walked up behind him and wrapped her arms around his neck. She bent down and whispered, "You might not like my hands near your face but at least you don't mind them touching you elsewhere."

He didn't reply, instead replacing his glasses on his face, but she felt the tension within him ebb.

She straightened and glanced at the fridge. "We could order—"

Lucas shook his head. "We're going shopping."

She decided not to argue. It was the weekend and she had the time.

Usually it took Patricia less than twenty minutes to grab all she needed, and she thought with Lucas's help she could cut the time in half, but when she asked him to get a bag of red potatoes he looked at her.

"Where would that be?"

"In the produce section."

"And where's the produce section?"

"Never mind, I'll get it. You get me some ketchup and salt."

"What aisle?"

She pointed. "Just look at the signs."

He squinted. "I don't see ketchup and salt."

"You're not going to see ketchup and salt. You're going to see groups of items. Ketchup would be under condiments." She pointed to the aisle. "And salt will be in baking."

"Why not in condiments?"

"I don't know, because the store didn't organize it that way."

"But that's confusing. Salt is a key condiment when it comes to flavoring food."

"Forget it. Get me some Sriracha sauce."

"Can't you get it when you get the ketchup."

"No."

"Why not? Won't that be in the condiment section?"

"No," Patricia said with a tired sigh, "the Sriracha sauce will be found in the international section."

His brows shot up. "Hot sauce is put in the international section?"

"No, not all hot sauce is put in the..." Patricia stopped and sighed. "What is wrong with you? Don't you shop?"

"Not for food."

"I guess you only like convenience stores."

"No, I don't."

"But I saw you leaving one."

Lucas shook his head. "Must have mistaken me for someone else."

It was likely, but she didn't think so. He must have forgotten.

"How do you do your grocery shopping?" she asked him.

"I don't."

She didn't want to know. She'd already wasted enough time. "Wait here. I'll be right back."

"How long will you take?"

"About twenty minutes."

"Okay, I'll meet you here."

She'd rather he stayed put but he was a grown man. "Don't get lost."

"If I do I'll send out a distress signal."

She pulled a face then left him.

Twenty minutes later, he wasn't there.

Patricia paid for her items and put them in her truck then returned to the store. He still wasn't there.

She walked around the store and found him chatting with a man in the rice and pasta aisle who looked half in love with him.

Lucas noticed Patricia and mouthed, "Give me five minutes," before he returned his attention to the enraptured man.

Patricia returned to the front of the store where they were supposed to have met. She saw Lucas with the man in the flower section helping him choose a plant.

Patricia decided not to wait any longer and returned to the truck.

Ten minutes later, Lucas arrived. "Sorry about that."

"Old friend?"

"No. Never met him before in my life."

She didn't know how he could manage to be so friendly with a complete stranger. "But you looked like best friends."

"He asked me about something, can't remember what it was, but I saw his basket and I had to interfere." Lucas lowered his voice to a conspiratorial tone. "He was about to make a beef and potato dinner for his one year anniversary." He shivered in distaste. "I know it's a staple pairing, but unless you want to end up heavy and bloated it's something to stay away from. So I suggested rice or pasta instead of potatoes.

"Then we got talking about spices and I told him how great fish and turmeric could be. It's a fast and easy meal (not to mention delicious) and roasted chicken with garlic powder or stuffed peppers and oregano and...why are you staring at me like that?"

"Because you can hardly find your way around a supermarket but you know so much about food."

He shrugged. "I like to eat."

"And talk."

He grinned. "Yes, that too."

"Why did you two end up in the flower section?"

"Yes, well he asked my advice on a plant and I couldn't leave him hanging so..." He adjusted his glasses. "They've had a stressful year and their basement flooded. Finally got the water out and they want to renovate their bathroom."

"And you of course told him that you know an excellent contractor."

Lucas stared at her devastated, like a man who'd left a puppy out in the rain. "I forgot."

"It's okay," Patricia said, surprised by his distress. She resisted the urge to pat him on the head and reassure him.

He unbuckled his seatbelt and opened the door, ready to dart out. "I think I can find him."

Patricia grabbed his arm. "I'm joking."

"But—"

"It's okay, really."

He reluctantly closed the door, his voice heavy with regret. "I could have told him about your business and I missed my chance. I'm so sorry."

"Lucas, it's fine."

He held out his hand. "Give me a couple of your business cards. I'll remember next time."

She hesitated then handed him a few. "Don't oversell me."

"I wouldn't do that."

But several days later, she couldn't field all the calls that came in. She had to start turning people away.

Her schedule became busier, which meant less time together, but Lucas didn't seem to mind. He didn't pester her about the progression on his father's kitchen although she gave him updates anyway. Ian had approved all of her initial plans and two weeks in everything was on schedule.

Life was good until a friendly, handsome giant crashed into paradise...

48

Once a month, Patricia and Jeremy had a standing arrangement: they'd meet for pizza and a movie, alternating between each other's places.

Today it was her place. Jeremy showed up with two pizza boxes and calmly waltzed in when Patricia opened the door that Friday evening.

"Did you forget?" Jeremy said, putting the pizzas on the kitchen counter while Patricia stared at him in mute horror. "I heard from Melody that work has really picked up so I forgive you." He pulled out some plates and cups.

Patricia glanced towards the hallway, hoping she'd get Jeremy out of the condo before Lucas finished his shower. "Uh, Jeremy listen—"

"But I also hope you haven't forgotten about Aunt Gladys."

"Aunt Gladys?"

"You still haven't told me how formally dressed I'm supposed to be."

"Be?"

"Why are you repeating my words?"

Patricia sent another nervous glance down the hall certain she'd heard the shower turn off. "Actually, could we have this discussion later?"

Jeremy put several slices of pizza on his plate. "Sure, but we don't have much time to decide."

"Jeremy, there's something—"

"I know you're overworked. That's why I'm here to treat you." He took her hand and led her over to the couch.

"You don't take care of yourself. If you're not careful you'll burnout. I'm here to stop that."

He sat on the couch and pulled her down beside him. He rested an arm around her shoulders and stretched out his legs. "It's next weekend." He looked at her face and frowned. "You did forget. You're lucky I came by. Your cousins would have a field day if you missed your aunt's sixtieth birthday party." He picked up a pizza slice then stopped with it halfway to his mouth.

"What is it?" Patricia asked him.

"I have this weird feeling that someone is watching us."

"I'm sure it's nothing."

He rubbed the back of his neck. "I felt all the hairs on the back of my neck stand up. It's chilling."

"I think you should—"

"But nobody else is here..." He slowly looked over his shoulder and jumped when he saw Lucas standing in the kitchen, wearing a plum colored Henley shirt and khaki trousers, with a blank expression more chilling than the grin of an ax murderer.

Jeremy moved his arm from around Patricia's shoulders and shoved her away from him with such force she nearly toppled over sideways. "Still just friends," he said to Lucas. "Only friends."

"Why do you keep saying that?" Patricia said annoyed.

He didn't look at her. "A childhood friend," Jeremy said enunciating every word. He slapped Patricia on the back then said to her under his breath, "What the hell is he doing in your condo?"

"I'll explain later."

Lucas took out a slice from the pizza box on the counter then sat in front of them. "Did I hear you two talking about a party?"

"No," Patricia said.

"Yes," Jeremy countered.

Patricia sighed. "It's my aunt's birthday. Jeremy's my date."

"But I won't be this year."

"You said you would."

Jeremy shook his head. "I changed my mind."

"You know I don't want to go alone."

"Why would you go alone when you have me?" Lucas said.

"Oh no..." Patricia said with a laugh. "That's not going to happen."

Lucas studied them then said in a quiet voice. "You'd rather take Jeremy?"

"No, she wouldn't," Jeremy quickly assured him. "Not at all."

"It's complicated," Patricia said. "Jeremy's used to my family."

Lucas nodded. "I can get used to them."

"You'll regret it."

"You don't want your family to know about me?"

Patricia opened her mouth then closed it. He wasn't far from wrong. "It's not that," she lied. "It's just that we haven't known each other long and my family can be...a lot and I don't want to ruin a perfectly good weekend for you."

"She's trying to protect you from the nightmares," Jeremy said.

Lucas frowned. "Nightmares?"

"Her cousins. We call them Nightmare Number One and Nightmare Number Two."

Patricia rolled her eyes. "You really don't have to—"

Lucas leaned forward. "Tell me more."

Jeremy leaned forward ready to oblige him. "Aunty Gladys's two daughters. They have been giving Patricia hell since we were kids and they always like to show her up at these events."

Patricia groaned. "He doesn't need to know this."

"And you go as her date?" Lucas said.

Jeremy nodded. "Yes, I keep them at bay."

"I see."

"They've gotten so used to me always being with her that there are rumors we'll get married."

Lucas's eyes darkened. "Really."

Jeremy's voice went up a notch. "But that will never. Ever. *Ever*. Happen. Not in a hundred million years."

Patricia frowned. "You don't have to sound so adamant."

"I've never even looked at her with interest."

"Okay that's enough."

"I've found peaches more sexually appealing."

Patricia poked him. "Okay, Jeremy. We get you. You don't find me attractive."

"You should take him," he said to her. "It'd give him a chance to see Aunt Gladys again."

"Again?"

Jeremy shot Lucas a frantic look, lowered his gaze in regret and rubbed his hands together suddenly nervous. "Uh...I mean...he'd never get a chance to see her again." He forced a hollow laugh. "Her parties are memorable."

Lucas leaned forward and adjusted his glasses. "I didn't mean to put you on the spot, Patricia. If you don't want me to come, say so."

"I don't want—" she began to say but the words caught in her throat. He'd given her an out. She could tell him her honest feelings, that having him as a date made their fling feel more like a relationship and she wasn't ready for that. But another part of her wanted to find out what it would be like to spend the evening with him. "I do want you to come," she admitted.

"Then I'm there."

"You'll have to wear pink," Jeremy said.

She looked at her friend. "He does *not* have to wear pink."

"It's still your favorite color, isn't it? I'm not sure anymore," he said in a sarcastic tone. "There are certain things I don't know about you anymore."

"I don't mind wearing pink," Lucas said. "Pink really suits my skin coloring. We could match."

Patricia shook her head. "I'm not wearing pink."

"Why not?" the two men said.

Her gaze darted between them. "I don't wear pink all the time."

"Yes, you do," they countered. "You wear pink nail polish," Lucas said.

"Boots," Jeremy added.

"Belts."

"Earrings."

"T-shirts."

"Underwear." Jeremy held up his hands and swallowed when Lucas sent him a look that spelled murder. "Not that I've seen you in them." He let his hands fall to his lap. "I only know that because we went shopping one time and I saw what you bought." His voice faded away and he looked as if he wanted to dig a hole and jump in it.

Patricia waved her hands. "You've made your point." Both men were right. She wore pink every day. Different shades, she never got bored of it. "Yes, it's true I usually wear pink."

"You *always* wear pink," Jeremy said.

"But you also know that I don't wear pink to family events."

At family events they took particular pleasure making fun of her color choice and the mismatch with her career. The fact that pink was a supposedly feminine color and she wasn't. She'd gotten tired of snickers and jeers, so for the past several years she chose to wear black.

"Why do you like the color pink?" Lucas asked.

"Because it makes me feel strong," Patricia said. "But people think it's a soft feminine color so—"

"Who cares what people think? Wear it the way you want to. Give it new meaning."

"He's right." Jeremy sent Lucas a pointed look. "Other things have changed, why not what you wear too?"

He was right. What if she arrived at the party with Lucas and wore her brightest pinkest outfit with confidence? What if she didn't care what they had to say?

She moved over and hugged her friend, glad he believed in her. "Thank you."

He hugged her back and whispered, "I expect my bathroom renovation to be amazing."

"What?" Lucas said, "I don't get a hug?"

Patricia laughed. "Okay, Jeremy. Give him a hug."

Lucas folded his arms. "That's not what I meant."

"You'll thank me in a minute."

Jeremy shook his head. "I don't think this is—"

Patricia nudged him forward. "Go on."

Lucas stood and opened his arms, unfazed. "Okay, go on."

Jeremy crossed over and quickly hugged him then began to pull away but Lucas didn't let him go. Instead he drew back and seized Jeremy's biceps and squeezed them in awe. "Man. What the hell are you made out of?"

"His hugs are amazing, right?" Patricia said.

"Yeah. He's an amazing guy," Lucas said and all tension between them faded away. Lucas affectionately patted him on the cheek. "Come on, let's eat."

Lucas returned to the kitchen to reheat his pizza, Jeremy released a sigh of relief and smiled as if he'd made a new friend while Patricia tried to decide what excited her more—having Lucas as her date or figuring out what to wear to leave her cousins speechless.

49

On the day of the event Patricia lost her courage.

It had been so long since she'd dressed up that it was only at the last moment she realized she had nothing suitable in pink to wear.

Lucas arrived at her condo ten minutes early just after she'd tried on a chiffon dress that probably had never been in style but had seemed nice at the time.

She grabbed her bathrobe and went to the front door. She was supposed to drive both of them to the event (in Lucas's Mercedes he refused to ride in her truck) and she hadn't even started on her makeup yet.

Lucas stood in the door and gave her a once-over. "I'm not here to rush you but there's fashionably late, late and Caribbean time, which one are you shooting for?"

She turned away. "I'm not going."

"Look at me."

She spun around surprised by the command in his tone.

Lucas closed the door behind him then pointed to himself. "How can you possibly waste this? Don't you want to show me off?" He held his arms out to the sides as if he were a statue to admire.

Patricia laughed. Cocky, but right. He looked gorgeous in a salmon colored suit paired with a dark blue crew neck shirt. He made pink look powerful.

He let his arms fall to his sides. "Besides, your aunt will miss you."

She bit her lip.

"What's the problem?"

She opened up her robe to reveal her dress.

Lucas blinked.

He didn't visibly gasp and shudder but his expression was close enough. Patricia closed the robe and sighed in defeat. "That's what I thought."

"Never mind." He pulled out his cell phone then began texting. "Fortunately, I came prepared. Sit down."

Before she could ask what he meant someone knocked on the front door.

He opened it and four people hurried in carrying various garment bags.

Lucas led her to the sofa and pulled her down beside him before he pointed at the people and said, "Go."

As if synchronized, each person quickly unzipped their garment bag to reveal a beautiful dress in several distinct styles.

"Choose one," Lucas said.

Patricia could only stare.

Lucas delicately cleared his throat. "Again, I don't mean to rush you but we also have hair and makeup."

She turned sharply to him.

"Yes," he said reading her surprise. "Once you're done

here, I have another team waiting outside. Don't worry, they're professionals."

"It's not that." She was overwhelmed. "I don't know which dress to wear. They all look amazing."

He stood and walked up to a dress with straps. "I'm partial to this one."

Patricia jumped to her feet. "Okay."

"Okay?"

She grabbed the dress. "I'll be right back."

"You sure you don't want to—"

"I'm sure," she said before she disappeared into her bedroom.

She emerged feeling like a queen.

She found Lucas and two other people waiting at the dining table where there were makeup supplies and hair combs.

It wasn't always easy getting the right foundation for her skin tone—she either ended up looking painted or sickly—but Lucas had done his homework and the makeup artist was able to work magic on her face, making her look naturally beautiful by using complementary colors to enhance her features.

They pinned her medium length twists into an elegant upward style, while leaving two twists, loosely wrapped with gold twine, to hang down, framing her face.

She hadn't been this dolled up in years. Never felt so well taken care of.

Of course Lucas had also managed to get matching shoes, a clutch purse and gold teardrop earrings.

"I don't know what to say."

He kissed her and smiled. "Then don't say anything."

But Lucas' mood suddenly dipped when they parked outside of the repurposed mansion.

It was a popular destination for events. Several years back, her uncle had helped the new owners with renovations and certain repairs and her aunt loved hosting parties there. Patricia exited the car eager to join the festivities and see her aunt again. But Lucas didn't follow her. He leaned against the car and gestured her towards the house. "You go on ahead. I'll join you in a minute."

"No, I'll wait for you."

He hesitated then reached for his phone, "T-there's a call I have to take."

She hadn't heard it ring, but perhaps he had it on vibrate. However, he also looked a little uneasy. "I won't shove you into any closets, I promise. Even if I want to kiss you."

He forced a smile. He didn't usually have to. Her tone sharpened, concerned. "Are you okay?"

"I'm fine," he said, keeping his false smile in place. "Go on. Show off that dress." He lifted his phone to his ear and said, "Yeah, I'm here," stopping her reply. He turned his back to her.

But she didn't move. There was no point entering the party without him. She might as well sit in the car and wait until his phone call was over and then—

"Patricia, go inside."

She could already imagine the superior expressions on her cousins' face if she showed up alone wearing pink. 'Oh look who's trying to be cute,' Nightmare Number One would say and Nightmare Number Two would add, 'How adorable.' She didn't want that. "But I don't want to go in by myself," she told him. "That's the whole reason I brought you."

"Patricia—"

She bristled with annoyance and a tinge of panic. "I knew this was a mistake. I should have brought Jeremy instead."

The flash of hurt that crossed his features shocked her. She hadn't thought coming to the party with her had meant so much to him. She lightly touched his arm and gently said, "No, I didn't mean that." She kissed him on the cheek. "I'm glad you're here."

His sigh sounded sad. "I'm sorry that..." He took a deep breath. "I won't let you down. I-I..." He held up his phone. "Let me finish this call and I'll be with you. It's... a family issue I...have to deal with."

A thought struck her. "Is it your father? He was supposed to have come back and I haven't heard from Ian. What did he think of the kitchen? Was he angry at the changes?"

This time when Lucas smiled it was real. "No, Dad loved it. It was a complete win."

"I'm glad."

Lucas pressed the phone against his chest and jerked his chin towards the house. "Go. You don't need anyone. You look beautiful."

The look of admiration in his gaze gave her courage, but his lips looked a little pale. "Are you sure you're okay?"

He nodded. "Find your aunt. I look forward to meeting her." He returned the phone to his ear and again turned his back to her before he said, "What was that again?"

She had to trust him. She had to trust herself, she felt beautiful and she knew she looked amazing. She could face them.

Patricia took a deep breath before she stepped through

the door and into the elegance of a dark marble floor entrance, and made her way into the Grand Hall.

50

—————

*H*e'd made a mistake.

Lucas waited to watch Patricia safely go inside before he released a long sigh. He'd been expecting an ordinary house party.

Not an 18ᵗʰ century mansion that featured Georgian architecture and lush gardens. Inside he'd have to be prepared for intricate woodworking and possibly period furnishings that would try to gain his attention. He'd have to keep his gift under control. He'd invited himself and Patricia was depending on him.

He'd have to be very careful which rooms he went into, what he touched, where he let his gaze linger.

I should have brought Jeremy instead.

Patricia had no idea how much her words pained him because they were true. She should have brought Jeremy. Jeremy wouldn't be facing a minor crisis right now. Jeremy wouldn't have forced her to go inside alone. Jeremy would have stayed by her side all evening. Jeremy wouldn't have given her cause to worry.

Jeremy might not have Lucas' confidence but he had what Lucas craved—Patricia's trust. Her devotion.

It wasn't something he could buy. It wasn't something Lucas had managed to win yet.

I should have brought Jeremy instead.

Useless dog.

Lucas tucked his phone away with trembling fingers. He didn't want to lose her. He had to be strong.

I thought you were different.

Lania's words seared through his mind. But he didn't want to think about Lania or Ericka or anyone else. This night belonged to Patricia.

He hadn't had a chance to tell her the truth about his father's reaction to the kitchen. He didn't just love it, he adored it. When Ian had surprised him, his father had jumped up and down like a ten year old and shouted his delight. Patricia's design choice had made the kitchen both modern and familiar. Eldin took in every detail and begged them to let him meet her.

Few people could make his father that happy. Patricia was special.

Lucas feared he didn't deserve her, but he didn't care.

He'd become a man who did. He'd rise to the occasion.

Lucas took another deep breath.

He wanted to be the man Patricia turned to. The one she trusted, the one she thought of when she needed help.

He stared at the mansion and flexed his fingers. He hadn't made a mistake. He was glad he came. He wanted to show her off. He wanted to be beside her. He wouldn't let her regret choosing him.

51

It took Patricia about five minutes to realize that no one recognized her.

As she made her way around the gorgeous Grand Hall people she'd known since childhood and others she'd met at different previous events smiled at her. Some complimented her on her dress; others asked how she knew her aunt. She gave them vague responses, enjoying being a person of mystery at least for a little while. She'd never had such positive attention before.

So many people took a moment to chat with her that it took nearly twenty minutes for Patricia to realize she hadn't had a chance to speak to her aunt or seen Lucas. But she enjoyed being in disguise, pleased she hadn't been discovered by anyone or seen her cousins yet. She didn't have to worry about seeing her mother since she no longer had anything to do with her husband's family.

Then her sisters broke the spell.

They both rushed up to her and alternatively said, "Oh." "My."

"God."

Monica clapped her hands. "You look amazing!"

Melody looked around. "Where's Jeremy?"

"I'm not here with Jeremy," Patricia said.

Her sisters looked shocked. Monica spoke first. "You mean the rumors are true?"

"Rumors?"

"That you brought an escort."

"No."

They looked relieved. "So you came by yourself?" Melody asked.

"No, uh...I came with Lucas."

"Lucas?" her sisters asked in unison.

"Wolff," Patricia clarified.

Melody frowned. "Isn't he a client?"

"Not...technically. He's doing me a favor. But I can't find him."

Her sisters shared a look. "Now we know what the commotion's about," Monica said.

Melody nodded. "Yes, that explains a lot."

Patricia looked at her sisters confused. "What are you talking about?"

They shared another secretive glance before Monica said, "We think we know where he is."

Melody took Patricia's hand while Monica led them to the Ballroom. Once there, she weaved a path to the far corner of the room, where the animated sound of women's voices and the soft sound of male laughter caught Patricia's attention before she saw a circle of mostly women and some men surrounding something.

Patricia saw the top of a man's head. It took her a moment to realize the head belonged to Lucas. Patricia wasn't sure whether to be annoyed or pleased. Something like this would never have happened with Jeremy. First, she would have been able to spot Jeremy right away; second, Jeremy never drew a crowd.

At least Lucas hadn't gone and that was a relief. Patricia turned to leave.

Monica grabbed her sister's arm. "You're not going to say anything?"

Patricia shook her head, hoping to quietly disappear before Lucas saw her. "No. I think—"

"Patricia!" Lucas called out to her.

She inwardly cringed then reluctantly turned, while her sisters quickly disappeared into the crowd, and saw eyes filled with daggers pointed at her. Something she'd hoped to have avoided.

"Excuse me," Lucas said amicably, making his way through the crowd. He approached her completely unaware he'd put a target on her back before he said, "Where have you been? I've been looking all over for you."

She nodded towards the group of people who continued to stare at them with more than just casual interest. "You weren't looking very hard."

He winked. "Jealous?"

She gave him the once over. He looked better than he had a few minutes ago. Color had returned to his face. "How was your phone call? Is everything settled? Are you okay now?"

"Yes. Have you spoken to your aunt?"

"No, I haven't had a chance to see her yet, but let's go find her." She took his hand then gasped. It felt clammy and cold. She stared at him alarmed. "You said you were okay. What's wrong?" She pointed at him. "And don't say 'nothing.' Your hands are cold. You're not shy and not easily embarrassed, you love attention and you've got it, so what's going on?"

Lucas shook his head, pulled his hand away. "Sorry, it's the house."

She didn't know how to interpret his words. Because he wasn't the owner of the house, she wasn't able to read how the building was affecting him, but clearly it was. The rooms were large and airy, had the crowd of people surrounding him made him feel trapped?

"Do you want to leave?"

Before he could reply a familiar voice said, "And who do we have here?"

52

*P*atricia's heart lifted with delight as she recognized the voice of the woman who'd made her younger years bearable and been a comfort to her through many hard times. She turned and smiled at the older woman. "Happy Birthday, Aunty."

The heavyset, elegantly dressed woman looked at Patricia with a blank expression.

"It's me."

She blinked.

"Patricia."

Her eyes widened. "Patricia?" She let her soft brown gaze trail over Patricia's dress. "I should have known. You look amazing. Your father—" She bit her lip. "So glad you could come."

"Thank you," she said, feeling embarrassed by a sudden wave of emotion. "And this is my date Lucas Wolff."

He kept his hands behind his back and offered her aunt a brief nod of his head. "Happy Birthday."

"Are you the one to thank for this?" Gladys asked gesturing to her niece.

"Yes," Patricia said.

"No," Lucas countered. "She was eager to come and wanted to arrive in style. I only came along for the ride."

Patricia stared at him, wondering why he was lying. He'd done more than come along for the ride. He'd gotten her a new dress, shoes, earrings, makeup and had her hair styled.

When Patricia opened her mouth to disagree he narrowed his eyes, stopping her words.

"Thank you, dear," her aunt said taking Patricia's hand. "That means a lot to me. I know how hard it's been running your own business." She looked at Lucas, taking in his suit. "And you, young man, are also a sight to behold."

He grinned, tugging on his jacket with a show of exaggerated vanity. "That's my reason for living."

Her aunt began to laugh then suddenly frowned and stared at him for a moment. "I remember someone who used to say that. What did you say your name was?"

"Lucas Wolff."

Gladys narrowed her eyes. "Have we met before?"

"If we had I'm sure you wouldn't have had to ask that. I tend to be memorable."

She chuckled. "Yes, I certainly would have remembered you. It's only...you remind me of someone."

Lucas held his hand over his heart, feigning hurt. "And here I thought I was an original."

"You are, dear." She waved to someone in the distance. "I have to keep circling the room. I'll talk again later. You two enjoy the rest of the evening."

When her aunt was out of hearing, Patricia said, "Why didn't you want her to know this makeover was your idea?"

"Because it made her happier thinking it was you."

"Was your name always Lucas Wolff?"

He shoved his hand in his trouser pocket. "Why?"

Patricia shrugged, not able to put into words the tension she'd sensed in him when her aunt asked him his name. "Just curious."

Lucas began to respond, then two ladies walked passed him, one boldly sliding her finger down his arm before she said, "You can't leave until you finish the story about Bangladesh."

Lucas grinned. "I wouldn't dream of leaving you...unsatisfied."

They giggled then left.

Lucas watched them go, amazed. "I'm used to attention, but I'm surprised by how popular I am."

Patricia opened her mouth then closed it.

"What?" Lucas asked.

"I hope this won't upset you, but you're popular because people think you're an escort."

He nodded as if solving a puzzle. "That's why. I could understand the business cards, but I was stumped by this," he said, opening up his palm to reveal a phone number written in black ink.

"You let her write on your hand?"

"She was very insistent." He took off his jacket, rolled up his right sleeve and showed her his forearm where someone had written their phone number with purple lipstick. "As was she."

"How did you manage that?"

"Actually—"

Patricia shook her head. "I don't want to know."

"Okay."

"You don't mind that they think—"

"I'm flattered." His face changed. "Unless it bothers you."

"Oh, why would it bother me that people think I had to pay to have you come with me?" she said her voice dripping with sarcasm.

Lucas rubbed his chin, grim. "Put like that I'll have to—"

"It's okay. It's too late now."

"It's never too late."

"No one will believe you came here with me willingly and that...why are you looking at me like that?"

"Are you offering me a challenge?"

Patricia swallowed suddenly unsure. "No."

"Are you sure?" Lucas buttoned his shirtsleeve and put his jacket back on. "I can make sure there's no misunderstanding about our relationship."

"We don't really have one, do we?"

He lowered his voice, holding her gaze. "Depends on you."

She was thrilled and scared, unsure of what to do next, curious to know how he would show people they were together, but also afraid it would embarrass her. "Never mind. It doesn't matter."

"Actually it does." He pulled her close and kissed her.

He drew away so quickly she didn't get a chance to respond, she could only stare. By the time her thoughts and breath began to return to normal he started patting his jacket as if he'd lost something.

"What is it?"

"Where could it be?" Lucas said patting his trousers before returning to his jacket again.

"Have you lost your phone?"

"No, it's something else." He opened the right side of his jacket then the left before he sent her a mischievous look. "What could this be?"

Patricia stepped closer to see what he was referring to. Slowly he pulled out a gossamer pink scarf, seemingly from thin air, and wrapped it around her neck.

"When did you, how can you—"

Lucas grinned. "When you wear it, think of me."

She felt her face flush.

"That's my scarf!"

They both turned sharply to the voice.

53

Nightmare Number One stormed over to them, her features so pinched they looked like they'd been assembled by clothes pins. Nightmare Number Two was fast on her sister's heels, her generous lips, colored scarlet red, curved into a malicious grin.

Nightmare Number One pointed at Lucas. "You stole my scarf."

It had been years since he'd been called a thief, but he had the same visceral reaction—a desire to charm and dissuade. He didn't allow himself to feel outraged, affronted, defensive. He didn't care about trying to prove his innocence. He knew he had to manage the situation.

He wouldn't accuse, he wouldn't say she was wrong. "Did I?"

"Yes."

"When?"

"I don't know." She pointed at Patricia. "All I know is I arrived at the party with that scarf and now she's wearing it."

Lucas lifted the end of the scarf. "This scarf?"

"Yes."

"This exact scarf?"

Nightmare Number Two sniffed with disdain. "Are you dense? I guess Patty didn't pay you to think."

Lucas let the insult slide. He walked up behind Nightmare Number One and again seemed to perform magic when he lifted a scarf from behind her and draped it over her shoulder. "Yes, I'm incredibly dense because *I* can't tell the difference."

She stared, speechless. "How...how did you do that?"

"I didn't do anything."

"But you must have," Nightmare Number One said.

"Sorry for the misunderstanding," Lucas said. "Excuse me."

He left the room. Before Patricia could follow, Nightmare Number One grabbed her wrist. "Who is he? How did he do that?"

"I don't know," Patricia said, "but he didn't steal anything."

"Then how..."

Up-close Patricia could see what had likely happened. Nightmare Number One's scarf had gotten tangled with the clip of her necklace and likely fallen off her shoulders, she'd assumed her scarf had been lost.

Patricia gently untangled the scarf from the necklace, careful to make sure the scarf didn't tear. "You should be very careful next time you wear the two together." She handed her the scarf.

Nightmare Number One looked rightfully embarrassed. "Oh."

"You can apologize later," Patricia said ready to find Lucas.

But Nightmare Number Two didn't want Patricia to have the last word and couldn't stand her sister's humiliation so she said, "Nice dress, Patty."

"Thank you."

"Although the shoes and purse *and* scarf is a bit much, don't you think?"

"No, I think they look great."

"That's no surprise. Your family always had a problem when it came to moderation."

Nightmare Number Two's cruel words hit their mark.

Nightmare Number One sent her sister a look and Number Two feigned a look of chagrin. "Oh, sorry. I guess I went too far. Enjoy the rest of the party."

Patricia watched her cousins turn, glad Lucas hadn't been nearby to overhear anything. She didn't want to tell him about her father's drinking and certainly not how he died.

She glanced down and caught sight of the scarf, and then her dress and remembered what the color pink meant to her. It meant strength.

Jeremy and Lucas believed in her. She didn't have to feel ashamed or act small. It was time to believe in herself and stand tall on her own.

"I will," Patricia called out to them.

The two cousins turned and looked at her, surprised she'd spoken.

Patricia rested a hand on her hip. "I will enjoy this party and do you know why?" She didn't give them a chance to respond. "Because I'm wearing this wonderful dress in my favorite color, I came with a gorgeous man who makes me happy and I finally realize I don't care what you think about me anymore. I think that's the best reason of all." She wiggled her fingers at them. "Goodbye." She turned and walked away triumphant.

PATRICIA FOUND Lucas in the lounge, standing near a table nearly buckling under the weight of wrapped gifts.

"Sorry about that," she said. "But I did warn you."

"You did." He lightly touched the bright red ribbon on one of the gifts.

"How did you do it?"

He glanced at her, his gaze cautious. "Do you think I stole it?"

"Of course not. It's just how you made it reappear was amazing."

He shrugged. "I have a flair for the dramatic. I saw it hanging on her back, the pattern matched her dress so it wasn't easy to see at first, but it was attached to the necklace clasp by a thin thread."

"I noticed too. You left her shamefaced. You didn't have to leave. You could have waited for an apology."

He smiled. "I know when a performance is over and it's time to exit the stage."

"Do you want to go?"

He held out his arm. "No, I want to stay as long as you want to."

Patricia looped her arm through his, eager to extend the extraordinary evening, then kissed him on the lips. "I'm so glad to hear that. This has been one of the happiest nights of my life."

He looked doubtful. "Really?"

"Yes. The Nightmares came after me and I stood up for

myself." She shook her fist in the air. "Tonight's the first time I won a fight without punching someone."

Lucas laughed. "Congratulations."

Patricia placed a hand over her heart and meekly bowed her head. "Thank you." She took his hand, glad it wasn't as cold as it had been. "It's a big deal. I usually either fight with my fists or retreat. With my cousins, I always retreated but this time when she made fun of my dress—"

"She made fun of your dress?"

"And spoke about my father—"

"What did she say about your father?"

"I didn't back down." Patricia jolted to a halt then realized Lucas had stopped walking, but still held her hand. She turned to him and saw all humor had left his eyes. "What?"

"What did she say about your father?" Lucas asked in a too quiet voice.

Patricia sighed. "My father had a problem with drink."

"I see," Lucas said but he remained still and held her gaze, willing to listen. She was tempted to share more but didn't feel ready yet.

"One day I'll tell you all the boring details," she said, keeping her tone light, "but not tonight."

Lucas gave her hand a gentle squeeze. "Fair enough."

They walked in silence until they reached the corridor. "I'm glad you came with me."

Lucas winked. "I aim to please."

Patricia playfully nudged him. "Don't say things like that. No wonder people think you're an escort."

"Maybe." He stopped and turned to her. "But who cares what other people think?" he said before he kissed her and led them both back into the Grand Hall.

THE PARTY ENDED BY ONE, but neither Lucas nor Patricia wanted their time together to end. So Lucas didn't go home that evening. Instead he spent the night and the following day, basking in his success. He'd survived the night, he hadn't lost Patricia and she'd been glad to have him by her side.

Lucas was still in high spirits a week later. He whistled his way to his car on his way to an appointment with his accountant. He sat inside the car and began to start it, but paused when a familiar scent wafted towards him.

The scent of Darjeeling tea.

The scent that always followed the monster.

54

"Hello Lulu."

He hadn't been called that in years. Hadn't heard that name. He'd been Lulu for the first six years of his life. He didn't turn. He knew better than to turn and face her, instead he looked at her through the rearview mirror.

She frowned, disappointed. "Aren't you going to say hello?"

He ran his hand over the steering wheel.

Soon he felt small, greedy fingers sweeping along the nape of his neck. "Oh, why did you have to cut your beautiful hair?"

He jerked away from her touch. There was no need to ask her how she'd found him, or how she'd gotten into his car, the only question that mattered was, "What do you want?"

"Why must you be so impatient," she said like a petulant child.

He remembered that she rarely smiled. But if he did a good job (stole from a wealthy tourist, swiped valuables from a store) he'd get a rare glimpse of the beauty that had trapped people in her sticky web.

And when he disappointed her…

"Because I want you to leave. It's hard to forget you when you keep showing up."

Her gaze sharpened to steel knives. He saw the woman who wouldn't let him go. "You will never forget me. You are mine. You should be grateful, you wouldn't have this fine life without me."

"Really?"

"You have dual citizenship because of me."

That was true. Like her immigrant parents, she'd had him in the States before returning to Jamaica giving him full US citizenship. It had been a calculated move that allowed her to shuttled her children between both countries— keeping them out of school and away from others.

She kept her possessions and that's all anyone was to her. Something to own or use.

She never let him forget it.

But he wasn't Lulu now. He wouldn't let her think she could still control him.

"I'm a man now. Not a boy."

"More's the pity. Have you spoken to your brother?" She tapped his shoulder. "And don't lie. Remember I was the one who taught you how to lie."

"No."

"Really? He's been spotted around you."

"I haven't seen him. I'm telling the truth."

She swore. "That's a nasty habit, but I believe you."

"Then why are you here? I can't give you what you want. I don't know what he has on you or what he's taken from you and I don't care."

"You will care if he gets at Patricia."

Lucas stiffened.

Shanelle laughed. "You think she wouldn't be pulled into this?"

"She's an innocent."

"She's not as innocent as you think and your brother will use that to his advantage, but I can help you."

Lucas started to laugh.

Shanelle waited for him to sober before she said, "I'm here to warn you because a mother should look after her children."

"You almost sound like you believe that."

"I do."

"You're scared."

"Lulu, if I lose, so will you. You'd better get to your brother soon or what happened with Lania will repeat itself all over again."

Patricia had just finished putting together a schedule and expense estimate for Jeremy's bathroom renovation when her Aunt Gladys called her in distress. "I don't want to trouble you," she said. "But how well do you know Lucas?"

Patricia swiveled in her office chair and faced the window. "Why?"

"Because he called me up and asked me a lot of strange questions about your Uncle Orlando. He talked about wanting to offer him a lucrative job. He also mentioned a farmhouse."

A farmhouse? The same one he hadn't hired her for? "I don't know why he would do that."

"I didn't feel comfortable, so I didn't tell him much, not that there's much to tell, but I don't know why he called me up instead of your cousin."

Her aunt was right, Lucas calling her aunt made no sense. Orlando's son had taken over the business. Aunt Gladys had nothing to do with it. "I don't know why he would bother you. I'm sorry. It's okay if you said no."

"He seemed so different than when we spoke in person."

"I'm glad you called me. I'll see what he wants." Patricia began to disconnect but her aunt made a noise that gave her pause. "What is it?"

"I didn't want to bring this up and it might be nothing."

"Go on."

"Three of my gifts are missing. We checked everywhere, but can't find them. When we looked at the video footage Lucas was the only other person who'd been alone in the lounge where the gifts were. I wouldn't make a big deal of it because I hate accusing anyone, especially a guest you brought, but the theft didn't happen during the party, the cameras caught him much later."

"Later?"

"Yes, he came back after hours. I saw the footage myself. He was definitely there. The owners allowed me to store the gifts in the lounge until the following morning. That's when we realized what had happened. I'm truly sorry to tell you this."

"I'll find out what happened."

Patricia hung up and began to text Lucas then stopped and set the phone down.

She had to think.

It made no sense. Why would Lucas call her aunt? And how did he know anything about her uncle? She'd never mentioned him before. And when had he had time to return to the mansion? He'd been with her.

How had he even gotten her aunt's phone number?

Patricia picked up her phone as she remembered the look on Jeremy's face when he'd mentioned Lucas and Aunt Gladys. Patricia was certain he'd said 'meet her again.' She called him up.

"So what's the timeline for my bathroom?" Jeremy said.

"What do you know about Lucas?"

He stumbled over his words. "Uh...what do you mean? No more than you do."

"Are you hiding something from me?"

"Why would you—"

"Answer me."

"Like what?"

"You said you've met Lucas before, but you also seem to know something else about him."

Jeremy released a long sigh. "It didn't seem like a big deal, but he didn't want you to know that he'd met Aunt Gladys in the past."

"When? How."

"Nearly twenty years ago. At the hospital. He visited his brother in the children's ward."

"Why would he want to hide something like that?"

"I don't know. I told you it didn't seem like a big deal to me."

That's why he'd seemed familiar to her aunt. Why had he pretended not to know her?

The pieces started to come together—the other woman's name—Ericka-whispered nearly every night, Lucas hiding his connection to her aunt, his hesitation entering the mansion. Had it been a guilty conscious because of what he was going to do? How he was going to deceive her?

Why steal? Why lie?

It had all been planned. He'd used her to get close to her aunt.

Why had he mentioned the farmhouse to her aunt? Had he pretended to use her so that he could get closer to her uncle?

Was he like all the rest? Had she been a means to an end?

Still reeling, she jumped when her cell phone rang. She silently groaned when she saw Eldin's name.

55

Patricia arrived at the house ready to hear what other project the older man had in mind, but when she arrived, she saw a note that said: BE BACK IN TEN MINUTES, MAKE YOURSELF AT HOME.

Patricia's gently turned the door handle, unnerved that the older man was so trusting.

Patricia walked down the hall to see her handiwork. She studied the countertop then glanced out the window and saw Lucas leaning against a tree. She hadn't seen his car in the drive, perhaps his father had taken it, it also explained why he'd left the front door unlocked.

She stormed over to him ready for answers.

If only he hadn't smiled at her. If he hadn't smiled she might have been able to hold onto her anger until later.

But he had and it broke through her like a flood.

"Are you pleased with yourself?"

His smile fell.

"I was right. I should have taken Jeremy to the party instead of you."

He stared at her stunned. "Patricia—"

"I know what you did at the mansion. I should have known it wasn't real. You've never cared about me. I know about her. Ericka. She's who you wish you were with. Did you do it for her?"

The shock on his face gave her grim pleasure. Lucas glanced away with a look of panic before looking at her again. She'd hit home and he hadn't expected that. Did he really think his true love was a secret? All doubts about the importance of Ericka disappeared. Her pain gave her words extra fire. "I see it now. I'm a fool. I'm just a tool. You used me. You're a thei—"

Lucas held up a hand. "No, don't say it," he said, his eyes filled with fear like a puppy about to be kicked and curling itself up as small as possible to stop the blow. His eyes pleaded with her as he said barely above a whisper, "Not you. Anybody but you."

That stopped her. The words—the accusations-got trapped in her throat because of the look in his gaze. She found she couldn't call him a thief and a liar because it would hurt him too much, although she felt the words to be true.

He made her care. And that angered her more because she hated the power Lucas gave her. He made himself vulnerable and weak, when he should be guarding himself. He made it so clear how much she meant to him (and yet still he'd betrayed her). She shouldn't be able to read every expression that crossed his face. She shouldn't be able to know how to hollow him out, to wound him. He'd handed her the weapon and begged her not to use it. How had he lived this way for so long? Without a shield, a barrier, to the rest of the world?

She bit her lip, trapping her words and she saw relief and hope lighten his gaze. She wanted to shake him for being so transparent, letting his feelings lay bare for her to stomp on.

She wanted to shout at him but stopped when she noticed something move out of the corner of her eye.

That's when she realized they weren't alone. His two brothers stood there.

Damian's expression was clear, Ian's unreadable. Why couldn't Lucas be more like him? Then none of this would have happened. She turned to leave. She wouldn't say what would hurt him. She'd quietly think those thoughts and never see him again.

"I don't know what's going on, but I didn't use you," Lucas said. "I'd never do that. I went to that party because I wanted to be with you. That's the truth."

"What about Ericka?"

Another quick glance at his brothers. What didn't he want them to know? "I'll explain later. But it's not what you think."

"Of course not," Patricia said bitterly.

He rushed over to her, but didn't touch her. "I mean it. It's complicated. I will tell you everything later. I can't do it here." She tried to search his eyes, but he wasn't looking at her. "I promise."

You can't believe him no matter how sincere he sounds. How could he not have known? "Why did you contact my aunt?"

"I didn't."

"But you know who she is?"

He sighed. "Yes, but—"

"Why were you at the mansion after hours? You were

caught on camera. And then some things gets stolen. What am I to think?"

"Patricia, I was with you all night."

She thought of how he seemed to make her cousin's scarf appear as if by magic. He was clearly good at deception. "You could have snuck out while I was sleeping."

"Yes, but I didn't. The theft had nothing to do with me. I promise you. Please believe me."

She felt defeated. She wouldn't embarrass him in front of his brothers. Perhaps Ericka was someone he loved, but his family didn't approve of. He tried to get over her but couldn't. Patricia just happened to be the unlucky one in this family drama. Not a heroine or villain, just a side character. He probably tried to get over her but his heart wouldn't let him.

If that was what he wanted, fine. She didn't know why she'd give him that courtesy but it seemed the right thing to do.

"Okay," Patricia said the words before she thought them through, the joy on his face made her realize her mistake. He was asking her to trust him and she said she would. She didn't trust anyone. And now it was too late to take back her words. What had she done? He looked at Damian with a look of triumph.

"You think that's enough to convince her?" she heard Damian say.

"Why are you talking about her as if she's not here?" Lucas shot back.

"She won't be in a minute."

"She has a lot to take in."

"You're fooling yourself that this isn't over."

Patricia didn't stay to hear Lucas' reply. She went into

the kitchen and collapsed on the ground. Her body shaking, tears gathering in her eyes. She was supposed to break up with him. She'd had it all planned out in her mind. It was supposed to be like all the others. She'd shout at him, he'd shrug, she'd return home heartbroken.

But that hadn't happened. Instead, she'd done nothing. She'd stared at him and let him speak and then done nothing. That wasn't like her. She was a woman of action. Why hadn't she done something?

She wiped her tears then peeked out the window and saw the two brothers still arguing. She shifted her gaze to Ian who was sitting in one of the patio chairs.

He stared right at her.

She ducked out of sight then cautiously peeked again.

He motioned her to him.

She shook her head.

He grinned then pointed at himself then at her as if to say, *Want me to come to you?*

She shook her head again.

His smile widened and then—to her horror—he started to get up.

She didn't want to talk to him. She headed for the door then paused. Perhaps it wasn't about Lucas but rather the kitchen. Or perhaps he knew what other project Eldin wanted her to do.

She heard the door open then close.

"Sorry about the scene out there," Patricia said. "Very unprofessional."

Ian tugged on his ear. "You have about a minute."

"A minute?"

He nodded. "Before Lucas comes after you. If you want to leave, do it now. I won't stop you."

Is he a mind reader? She did want to run, why hadn't she? Anger had fueled her, despair and disbelief had kept her there, but there was no reason to stay anymore.

She turned and headed down the hall. "Tell Eldin I'll talk to him later."

She'd made it to the front door when she heard footsteps running behind her.

"No, don't leave like this," Lucas said.

He didn't touch her, he didn't have to. The plea in his voice spun her around to face him, although her mind told her to walk away. To not listen anymore.

He took a step towards her. She pressed herself against the door. She closed her eyes, she didn't want to cry. "It's okay. You don't have to explain anything."

She felt him then as he gathered her in his arms, wrapping her in the scent of rosemary soap, breaking her heart with the soft pressure of his lips against hers before he whispered in a sexy, velvet tone, "I do. I owe you everything." He tightened his embrace. "Come to my place tonight."

Her eyes flew open. Patricia stared at him stunned. She'd never been to his place before. She'd see too much and she didn't want to. What if there were pictures of Ericka there? "But I—"

The corner of his mouth kicked up in a quick grin. "Don't look so worried, I'll send you the address." He kissed her again then said, "Come whenever you're ready. I'll be waiting."

56

$\mathcal{P}$atricia left with a low grade dread of seeing Lucas again because she believed him.

She believed he hadn't stolen anything or contacted her aunt. He had spent the night with her and the next day. She believed he would be able to explain everything and it would make sense and part of her didn't want it to.

She could guess what the talk would be. She'd be pushed from 'lover' to the reliable 'friend zone'. It had happened before. She never stayed in that role long, preferring to keep Jeremy as her only friend—male or otherwise.

She'd never really been seen or treated as a lover but more like a handy distraction until something better came along, or kept like a comforting blanket one took out when the mood hit and safely tucked away when it was no longer needed. She wondered how her relationship with Lucas would be after this. She still wanted to know him. He'd be the first friend since Jeremy, although she'd never had any romantic feelings for Jeremy while Lucas had carved out a special category for himself.

She'd never be the same.

She would have to distance herself for several weeks to acclimate herself into this new role. But she was also relieved that Lucas hadn't wanted to breakup with her. That made her feel special, even though she couldn't deny it didn't hurt. She wanted to be a different kind of special. She wanted to be the love interest, the one that someone dreamt about, cared about in romantic ways, but she also knew that she'd been given a gift in having someone like Lucas care about her as a friend.

He'd thank her for keeping his secret about Ericka (whatever it was) and that would be the bond between them.

Patricia didn't arrive at his place late in the evening. The sun was just beginning to set when she parked her truck in the drive of a gorgeous split level. She'd thought of going to his place in the evening, it would be easier to hide the inevitable tears on a dark ride home. But the dread of seeing him again kept building by the hour so she thought it best to get it over with. She couldn't protect herself from pain, pain followed her.

She glanced at herself in the rearview mirror seeing a stranger in the reflection. She'd pulled her hair back in a ponytail and chosen a light pink blouse and rose colored jeans. This wasn't Patricia, the lover. This was Patricia, Lucas' friend. Lucas' friend was strong and could face anything. Lucas' friend—not lover—was the steady force. Not feeling, but not unfeeling either.

Patricia knocked on the door. She heard no movement, heard no reply. She knocked again. Perhaps he wasn't home.

She walked around the back and saw him standing in the backyard looking up at the clouds. But she'd never seen him like this. His glasses sat on the patio table and he wore jeans and a plain black T-shirt. It was the first time she'd seen him dressed so plain, so casual it almost didn't seem like him.

His energy was subdued. She was used to the charisma, the quick smile, the open energy. But he looked weighted.

He turned to her but there was no recognition in his gaze. He frowned as if trying to puzzle out who she was. As if he'd already forgotten her.

That stung. She'd imagined being pushed aside but not so swiftly. Was this Ericka so important to him that she'd tortured him this much? Was this really a story she wanted to hear?

Patricia took a step back. If he'd forgotten that he'd asked her to come that would make it doubly worse.

"Wait," Lucas said and she watched him reach for his glasses and shove them on his face. "Patricia," he said pleased, dawning spread on his face. "I thought it was you but I wasn't sure."

He truly hadn't recognized her without his glasses? Either he was very near-sighted or had been lost in thought. That was a relief.

She walked over to him. "I knocked but—"

He swore, glanced down at his phone. "I'm sorry. Were you waiting long? What route did you take? Have you eaten anything?"

It wasn't like him to bombard her with questions. He was nervous? That also wasn't like him.

"I'm not hungry," Patricia said then her stomach grumbled, betraying her. "At least I wasn't until you mentioned it."

He grinned. "We can take care of that. Carter and Julia aren't here so it'll just be us."

"I don't know who those people are."

He snapped his fingers. "That's right. It's your first time here. They're my housekeeper and chef. I'll introduce you next time."

He made her believe there would be.

Unlike how he'd been at the supermarket, he moved easily in the kitchen as he prepared a simple meal. He was in beautiful harmony with his surroundings, she'd noticed the moment she'd entered his home (awash in a neutral color palette) there hadn't been one sour note. This was where he belonged.

He seemed both ordinary and extraordinary at the same time. There was something rougher, a harder edge to him than when he was dressed in his boisterous colors and business casual suits. Seeing him now made her wonder who she'd been with the entire time.

She could feel him watching her, although she could never catch him in the act, his gaze always flitting away when she looked at him.

She couldn't just sit there, so she decided to make herself useful. Although his housekeeper did an excellent job maintaining the house she'd noticed a few minor improvements she could make. She went to her truck, took out a few items and went to work.

She'd noticed a wall unit with tiny drawers that didn't slid easily so she used a block of paraffin wax and rubbed it on the drawer's slides and edges. She swapped out an old doorknob that had seen its days and lubricated a few hinges and door locks. She had started on the windows when she heard Lucas clear his throat. She turned. "I'll be done in a minute."

"I didn't ask you over to put you to work," he said.

"I don't mind."

"You can finish up later."

She was reluctant to stop what she was doing but her stomach reminded her she was hungry and the savory smells wafting towards her didn't help.

Patricia followed Lucas to the dining room then stopped and stared at what lay on the stone tabletop: deviled eggs, creamy pasta covered with chopped walnuts and parmesan cheese, and crackers with hummus plus a small garden salad. But what amazed her wasn't the assortment, it was the color.

57

Everything, from the deviled eggs to the hummus to the pasta, was a beautiful shade of pink.

Patricia laughed and that made Lucas smile. She approached the table with caution, as if unable to believe what she was seeing. Only moments before she thought her heart would break and now it had mended a little. She got a tiny boost of fight back. She couldn't believe he remembered what the color pink meant to her. He had thought of her, he did care. Her heart continued to ache but she'd remember this moment. It made her love him more. As a friend of course, she quickly reminded herself. She couldn't ever think of him as more than that.

He pulled her close and kissed her and she prepared herself for a kiss of gratitude. But he kissed her like a lover. Even more deeply than he had in the past. "Thank you for believing me," he whispered against her lips.

She didn't know how to reply so she silently sat down in the chair he pulled out for her.

"I hope you like this."

"I already love it," she said then regretted using the word 'love' but Lucas didn't seem to notice. "How did you do this?"

Lucas poured some red wine into two wine glasses. "The deviled eggs were dyed with beet root and the pasta with beet sauce. This is second hand knowledge since I didn't do anything but warm them up, but I'll take the credit for the idea."

Patricia swirled the pasta onto her fork then took a bite and indulged in the savory cream cheese, the al dente pasta and the crunchiness of walnuts and parmesan cheese. "Oh, this is heaven."

Lucas winked, flashing one of his mischievous grins. "Leave room for dessert."

"What's for dessert?"

"Strawberry brownies."

She took a sip of wine. No one had ever treated her like this before. "You didn't have to do all this."

"I didn't do anything."

"Except heat up the food?"

"Yes."

"And set the table. And choose the menu and order the wine—"

"Ordering is easy."

She noted the bouquet on the table. "And getting pink blossoms."

"You deserve them."

And he wanted to let her down easy because that was the kind of guy he was. She was one of the many women he'd have in his life. She hoped he'd keep her around longer than most. She ate some more wanting to focus on the food and not meet his eyes. She could tell he was intent on explaining. She wasn't sure she wanted to hear what he had to say, but that was why she was here.

"I'm sorry about—"

"Can we talk after?" Patricia interrupted. "I want to enjoy this food without thinking about anything else."

She also wanted to delay when their relationship would change as much as possible. She could eat this food and not have to hear about his first and only love. She didn't want to have to swallow down the food as she pretended what he told her didn't hurt. This was best.

Lucas didn't reply, so she released a breath. He was giving her time. That was good.

But too soon dinner was over and he was handing her one of the strawberry brownies, which tasted like strawberries with a soft fudgy texture.

Patricia moaned with pleasure. "This is my new favorite food."

"Until you've tried strawberry sugar cookies, strawberry bread—"

"Don't tempt me."

"I like tempting you."

She stood. "Let me help you clean up."

"No need."

"But the kitchen is a mess."

"It'll be fine."

Lucas wanted to talk, but she needed to stay busy. She grabbed another brownie. "Go on then."

She wasn't used to be handed fragile objects, especially fragile objects like feelings. No one usually trusted her like that before.

He jumped up from his chair. "I got something for you."

"Isn't this enough?" she said but he was already gone.

Lucas returned carrying a bear dressed in a pink hardhat and holding a hammer.

She stared up at him. "Why?"

"The little hammer opens up a safe filled with chocolate. It's a bribe. I know I messed up."

Patricia set the bear on the dining table. "Tell me about Ericka."

The same surprised panic look entered his face. "How did you know that name?"

"You whisper her name in your sleep. She means a lot to you."

Lucas hesitated. "Only my father and aunt know about Ericka."

That made the feeling and pressure feel heavier. Why would he trust her with a secret he hadn't even told his brothers? Who was this woman? What power did she hold?

"You don't have to tell me."

"Yes, I do." He bit his lip. "And I want to." He walked into the living room, Patricia reluctantly followed. Lucas sat on the couch and Patricia began to sit across from him, but Lucas shook his head and patted the space beside him. "You're too far away, come over here."

"But—"

"Please."

She sat down beside him and he rested his arm around her shoulders. Her body tingled from the contact but she didn't dare move away, although it was sweet torture.

Lucas stared out one of the large windows. "The first thing you need to understand is this," he turned to her and lifted her chin, forcing her to meet his heated gaze. "There is no one else for me, but you," he whispered as if stating a vow. He let his arm fall before he returned his gaze to the window. "The second thing you need to understand is I was once named Lulu and I had a brother named Ericka."

58

ucas never imagined he'd have to tell this story and as he shared it, it felt like the story of someone else's life. But he knew it was his. He told Patricia a terrifying tale about a woman name Shanelle.

Shanelle hated boys even more than she hated men. The fact that she'd given birth to twin boys outraged her, so she sought to fix that cosmic cruelty. She raised them as girls. While also reminding them of what they would become if they didn't listen to her.

Animal. Beast. Filth.

Sugar and spice and everything nice that's what little girls are made of.

She had them recite all the ills men had done in the world. And if they remained boys what they likely would do. She told them stories about their cruel grandfather, their silly uncle, their useless biological father, who she told them had abandoned them, but years later Lucas discovered he'd tried to take them away from her when they were about two years of age and had stashed them away at his mother's house.

Shanelle made him pay for that defiance by organizing a burglary that left their grandmother dead from an apparent heart attack. Although their father knew the truth (his mother had been healthy with no heart troubles) no one could prove otherwise, so to save the rest of his family (he had a sister and two brothers and their families to protect) their father stayed away.

Lucas could never understand why his mother married their stepfather, except that he owned two homes. One in Jamaica and one in the States. The one in the States was a simple colonial—with a basement, which his mother enjoyed using as punishment, leaving them there for days.

His stepfather was not someone the brothers could turn to. He pretended that everything in their house was fine. Or maybe he thought it was. He would give them sweets and call them his little darlings then disappear when Mum's temper got the best of her.

His stepfather ironed their dresses and pressed their hair and rarely said a word, even when he noticed cigarette burns on their skin.

A maid, one of their mother's many lovers, had also done her best to try and save them, trying to help them sneak out one night when they were about five, but their mother had caught them. The maid soon disappeared, her family never found her.

His mother's power was absolute. Not only had she dressed them as girls, she had also trained them to follow in her path of crime and deception. She worked hotels, shops, bus stations, any place where there were many people in constant motion who she could manipulate and lure. It was easier, she said, to raise girls. People liked girls, trusted girls. Lulu proved her right. With his smile and sweet temperament, he became an adept thief and liar. As did his brother.

But their paths diverged one spring day.

At six, Lulu decided to run, his brother decided to stay.

One ended up in juvenile detention. The other got rescued by a Jamaican businessman who Shanelle couldn't intimidate. One got adopted and changed his name.

One got kidnapped by his mother multiple times trying to break free, the other stayed in his mother's grasp whether she was in prison or out.

"And that's it," Lucas said with a sigh.

Patricia stared at him unnerved by how distant he sounded.

She didn't know how to rationalize it all. Ericka wasn't a woman. Ericka was his brother. He'd been raised as a girl. Lucas wanted her to know this about him. Things had been real between them. *There is no one else for me, but you.*

"Why haven't you told your brothers?" Patricia asked choosing the safest topic she could find as her mind tried to rationalize the rest. "I don't think they'd think less of you because of your past."

"Because talking about it is like reliving it somehow. It makes it part of me, a part of me I want to forget."

"It's not part of you anymore. But it does haunt you. You care about him. You think about him. Is he in trouble?"

"He's always in trouble. And he brings it with him. He's hanging around me for a reason and I don't know why."

"What can I do?" She felt him stiffen. She nudged him. "And don't say 'nothing.' You're not allowed to go 'lone wolf' on me. We're a team."

"Are we?"

"Yes. That's why you bribed me, right?"

Lucas shook his head. "No, I wanted to bribe you into bed."

Patricia stood and held her hand out to him, relief making her heart buoyant. He wasn't breaking up with her. "You never have to bribe me for that."

Lucas took her hand and stood. "We still have a lot to talk about."

Patricia kissed him then whispered. "We can talk later."

59

Sex was always amazing with him. But this time felt different—more intense. At first Patricia blamed the new surroundings for feeling a bit disoriented. She'd never been to Lucas's home before let alone his bedroom.

And yet the spacious room felt completely familiar because, like its owner, it offered warmth and comfort. She sank into the luxurious plum colored sheets, feeling safe and protected and eagerly welcomed his body.

But this time felt different.

The sex felt thrilling, wonderful, and terrifying. Mostly terrifying. The feel of his bare flesh against hers burned, he overwhelmed her as if he were larger somehow, invading all of her senses—he exuded a dark musky scent. Shifting against the soft sheets pressed against her back, she heard his breathing over the pounding of her heart. His hand caressed the skin on her thigh, but his palm burned with the heat of electricity. He'd never touched her like that before: slow, careful, calculated. He burned, his eyes darker than they'd ever been, and her arousal felt more acute-

verging on a pain that was more psychological than physical.

In a panic she shoved him away. Lucas flopped on his back, throwing his arm over his eyes.

Patricia stared at him alarmed. "What are you doing?"

"Trying to make love to you."

"Why?"

"Why do you think?"

She didn't want to think. It didn't make sense.

He let his arm fall to his side. "How long are you going to keep pretending you don't know how I feel about you?"

There is no one else for me, but you.

"I'm not pretending." She'd hurt him she didn't mean to. "It's a lot to take in."

"Because you don't believe me."

Because I'm scared to. "I do. It's okay," she said.

"No, it's not." He sent her a sad, indulgent smile. "You think I don't know when you're lying to me?" His smile widened. "I knew from the first time you told me you had work to do when clearly you didn't."

She froze. He knew? He wasn't as naïve and innocent as she'd thought. It felt like a betrayal, as if he'd been playing her. As if she'd been with a stranger in her mind all this time.

"If you knew why did you let me lie? Why didn't you challenge me? Confront me? Why didn't you get angry?"

He shrugged. "Because I know we all lie for different reasons." He poked her in the cheek. "Plus I found it amusing. You're a terrible liar."

Why was he looking at her as if this was all okay? How did he manage to turn the strangest of situations and make them feel...normal? He didn't make her feel awful, which she should.

Patricia shook her head. "I don't know why you'd put up with that. With someone like me."

Lucas fell quiet a long while before he softly said, "Who hurt you?"

No, that question was too tender to give a response. There were too many 'whos' to pinpoint just one. Did she lay bare all the teasing? Her mother's coldness, her father's disappearance in drink? She didn't want to share about herself, her pain in case she shone a light on parts of her Lucas hadn't noticed before. Then he'd look at her in a different way. He might like her even less. Her flaws would loom large in his mind, become something he couldn't unsee: 'Oh yes, you are fatter than I thought you were, your hands are rough and big, you do tend to trip over your words and not have anything interesting to say.'

She didn't want him to see her as others did, she would not give him their language. And yet she felt a desire to share, no one had ever asked her before. Been interested.

She glanced at him and saw his breathing had slowed. Perhaps he'd fallen asleep waiting for her to reply. That was okay, the threat was over.

"My uncle hurt me," she said, the words piercing the quiet darkness like a flash of lightning, their power shocking her. "I worked with him for sixteen years and I thought he trusted me. Believed in me. He taught me how to fight, he guided me when I was floundering, he even understood when I told him about what I sensed with people and buildings. He never made fun of me.

"I looked up to him. I thought that when he decided to retire he'd leave the business to me. But he gave it to his son instead. I'm never enough it seems. Even though I supported my family after my father died. I took care to make sure my sisters and mother didn't suffer more than they had to. Some days I went without sleep, without food (not that anyone noticed). I helped my uncle with jobs when his apprentice got sick, studied trends, improved my craft, it wasn't enough. No matter how hard I worked.

"In spite of all that I did, he left without a goodbye and gave the business to a son who wasn't even half as good as I was. But I was determined to prove myself. So I started my own business and now it's doing better than it has in years, but at times, I wonder if I really like what I do or if I'm doing it because it was the first real job I had out of high school. It's the only thing I know. I feel trapped. At times I feel drained, tired of proving myself over and over again.

"I'm tired of being let down by the people I care about. Tired of feeling like I'm letting them down. I'm tired of not being good enough."

Her voice cracked, she wiped away tears, took a deep breath.

"I don't know how long this will last but...aside from Jeremy you're the closet person I've considered a friend. I don't have many friends. Only one, really. Most people don't like me. And I've tried. I've tried with girlfriends who only find my number when they need something repaired for free, or because their partners couldn't get around to fixing it. I'm tired of men who expect me to be grateful they notice me and who always reminded me, without saying the words, of how I was teased and called names.

"Your mother lied to you, Lucas. Girls aren't sweeter than boys. They can be just as vicious. It doesn't matter how you're born, it's who you are as a person that counts.

"One time, in middle school, they'd stolen my change purse. I missed lunch that day, desperately trying to find it.

One kid shyly let me know where the bullies had put it. They'd hidden it in the field. It had rained that day so the field had turned to mud. The bullies laughed as they watched me dig it out of the ground. Pigs like mud, right?" Patricia sighed. "I'm so glad I'm not boring you with all this. I don't know how you do it. You get along with so many people and people like you. They want to be around you. I know how they feel. You're amazing. I don't know how I got so lucky that you even looked at me...

"But...I worry about you sometimes. You're too open. Too good. I know it's selfish of me to hold onto you when there's someone better out there, but I can't let you go. Not yet."

"Don't let me go."

Patricia paused. She wondered if he was talking in his sleep again. Then she felt his grip on her fingers tighten. "Please don't let me go."

He'd been listening? He'd been listening this whole time?

"I'm not good," Lucas said. "You know I'm not good and that doesn't frighten you."

She was a little frightened but not by his words. It was his tone, it was deeper, a shade darker than she'd ever heard it before.

"I want to be good." He released a bitter laugh. "But when I hear you tell me about the people who hurt you, I want their names. And I want the names of their parents and their children. And I want to make them suffer. Slowly." He paused. "That's not a good man. A good man doesn't like violence. They seek calm, consensus. They don't think about breaking someone's wrist or smashing someone's nose or even shoving someone in front of a train because they want to seek revenge. A good man doesn't start off as someone who put enough laxatives in a kid's pudding until they were sitting on the toilet so long they had to be hospitalized because said kid tripped his brother and laughed.

"I was homeschooled for a while after that. I live in the shadow of monsters, always afraid that I am one." He sighed. "I'm lucky you haven't let go yet because one day you will. You'll have to. When you truly realize I'm not who you think I am and I won't stop you.

"I got you into a mess you don't deserve. But I will fix it. My life isn't usually like this and—" He abruptly stopped. "No, this is it. I can only shield you so much, but this is it." He sighed. "You're not the only one with a strange ability. I have a...way of sensing buildings, they talk to me. That's why I'd had a hard time at your aunt's party. I didn't expect the building to be so old."

"I wish you'd told me."

"I wasn't ready to."

She turned on her side, reached to touch his face, saw him flinch and moved away.

He swore. "I don't know what's wrong with me."

"It's not you, it's—"

"It is *me*," Lucas said, his eyes flashing fire. He pounded his chest. "Want to know how I know? Because I've never wanted someone to touch me as much as I've wanted you. I dream about you touching me but the moment you do..."

"What if I tell you what I'm going to do?"

He sighed. Stared up at the ceiling. "I don't want that."

"Still want to make love to me?"

He nodded.

"Tonight?"

He nodded again.

Patricia took a deep breath. "Alright."

Lucas shook his head. "You're not ready yet."

She bit her lip. "I don't think I ever will be."

He rolled her on her back, covered her body with his. Kissed her. "I want to be inside you," he breathed. "I want you to let me in, Patricia. Really let me in."

"I thought you didn't like dark, tight places."

She felt him laugh. "As long as you're with me, I'm fine."

He had more courage than she did. She was the fragile one, by building walls around her heart she'd become brittle, easily broken. Lucas' open heart made him more resilient. She didn't have to fight, to defend. She could let go, let him in, trust him. She curved into his body, his heartbeat throbbed against her ear, but it beat too fast, his breathing ragged, his skin too hot, she could feel him shaking. She gently pushed him away. "Lucas. What's wrong?"

He laughed, rueful. He lifted his weight off her, "I've never done this before." He rested his forehead against hers. "It matters too much. I'm sorry."

"You don't need to lie to me Lucas."

He stared at her stunned. "But I'm not—"

"You've made love to me before but I've been too blind to notice." She trailed her finger along his shoulder. "I've been greedy and selfish and enjoying every minute of it. I've been taking without giving you much in return."

"Patricia, that's not—"

"And you let me get away with it because you don't expect much."

"That's not—"

"Do you want me to make love to you? No, don't nod, say it."

Lucas closed his eyes and whispered, "Yes."

Her heart hammered in her ears, his previous anxiety becoming her own. "It's my first time so be gentle with me."

"Always."

"And I'll need lots of practice to get it right."

His mouth curved into a soft smile. She felt the tension in him ease. "Patricia, you can't go wrong with me."

His words gave her the courage she needed. She didn't need to be anyone else but herself. She'd never made love before, but she knew how to build things. She rolled him on his back. "I'm going to build you a sanctuary."

She saw his Adam's apple bobble when he swallowed. "A sanctuary?"

"Yes, a place meant only for you." She slid her hand down his chest. "But you'll have to be patient because it will take some time." She pressed her open lips to his.

She didn't know sex could be more intimate. That what she'd experienced before wasn't even close to this. Lucas's skin felt different, everything about him felt new and exciting: A wonder that never ceased to amaze her. She inhaled his scent, tasted his mouth. She discovered new things about him. He had sensitive nipples, he liked when her fingers teased him there but always responded with a guttural moan that aroused her when she used her tongue. She explored his back, behind his knees, and his inner thighs, taking care to discover what pleased him, always surprised by how much it pleased her as well.

"God, Patricia, I can't hold on anymore," he said gripping the sheets, "let me inside you. Please."

"But—"

He flipped their positions and covered her body, his eyes blazed with desire. "You've built the sanctuary, now let me in."

There was a hard edge to his tone she found a little terrifying but she knew him too well to be afraid. She surrendered and welcomed him inside her, expecting him to take her hard and fast. But he surprised her. While his entrance was fast what followed were slow, decadent thrusts, each one driving him in deeper and deeper, stoking a liquid heat within her, she tightened around him, riding the delicious wave of orgasm.

Lucas shuddered in ecstasy as Patricia wrapped her arms and legs around him, pressing her body closer, a delicious moan escaping her lips.

He never imagined a woman would hold him like this. It wasn't grasping, clingy, desperate, or demanding but affectionate, tender, loving. She had truly built him a sanctuary where he could rest. He could be completely himself with her.

Animal. Beast. Dog. Her soft sighs, her tender touch, melted those words way, Patricia accepted him as he was, she brushed away his shame.

"I love you Lulu," she said.

His breath froze in his throat.

"And Lucas. No matter what you call yourself, I love you." She gently cupped the side of his face. It was only when he met the delicious pleasure of her lips that Lucas realized he hadn't flinched.

60

———————

They lay in each other's arms, neither ready to sleep. "I think I met your brother once," Patricia said breaking the silence.

She felt Lucas tense. "When?"

"He was in my building and he was at the elevator and I thought that was strange that you'd take the elevator and I think I teased you about it. But when you turned around I realized it wasn't you."

Lucas's brows shot up. "You could tell?"

"Sure. You look very similar but he doesn't look exactly like you."

"We're identical."

She shrugged. "I don't know what it is then. I could just tell."

"He met my other girlfriends too and managed to ruin things, not that it was difficult. But things with my last fiancée had been brutal."

"You were engaged?"

He nodded. "Her name was Lania and he scared her.

She didn't believe me when I told her the man she'd met wasn't me. He got a good chuckle out of that. Damian and Ian only vaguely know Ericka's role in the breakup. They blame Lania for most of it."

"So they know you have a twin brother?"

"Yes, but not that we were raised as girls. They think he's named Eric." Lucas sighed. "I can't blame him for everything, even before he showed up things weren't working out with her. I wasn't as refined as she wanted me to be. And then I showed her a side I shouldn't have."

"Can I guess what you did?"

He nodded.

"Did it involve your weaponized pen?"

He hesitated then nodded again.

"Did you put said pen through someone's hand?"

"Were you there?"

"No, I was just imagining what I would have done with a weapon like that."

"It was not a good day, she was not supposed to see that. She'd decided to surprise me that day by stopping by my home. At the time I was having a meeting in my office. It was a heated discussion because I'd discovered an associate had been stealing and I was annoyed. I don't like when people steal, especially from me. Lania came right through the door when he started screaming."

Patricia clicked her tongue. "Temper temper."

"I had warned him," Lucas said with a note of regret, "but he didn't listen. Lania stared at me in horror. Called me a bunch of names I probably deserved before she raced out of the house. I barely got her to forgive me for what she'd seen then Ericka showed up and pushed her over the edge."

"How?"

"He pretended to be me and told her that I was going to give all my money away and live simply."

"And she didn't like that I take it?"

"Not at all. She told him that she only put up with me because of the money and that I was no use to her without it. She gave me a week to change my mind or we were through."

"So you broke up."

"No, not because of that. When my brother told me what he did I was furious. I knew she cared about the money more than me, I didn't expect much. So I went to her apartment to tell her what my brother had done and I found her on the doorstep tongue kissing a guy with an injured hand."

Lucas nodded grimly at Patricia's shocked expression. "That's right, he was the same associate who'd I'd uh...argued with. They'd been lovers for months. I realized later that Lania had feared me not because I'd been violent but because she'd been afraid that I had discovered he was her lover. The fear I'd seen in her eyes was because of guilt and she was afraid I'd hurt her too. I was too stupid at the time to see the signs of her deceit. I should have."

"Because you loved her."

"No, because I wanted to love her."

"Your brother was probably trying to figure me out as well, when he came to my building, but I blew through his deception."

"Yes, that likely kept him away. But I don't know why he was at the mansion or why he approached your aunt."

"And why he'd steal her gifts."

"He didn't," Lucas said.

"But they're missing," Patricia countered.

"Not because of him. He's an easy target because he was there, but I'm afraid someone else stole them and you'll have to figure that out. Or someone lied and pretended to give a gift. And lied about it being stolen to save face."

"But it was more than one."

"All I'm saying is that someone close to your aunt is involved with the theft, if there was one. It wasn't my brother." He paused. "I found it strange how Nightmare Number One was so quick to call me a thief. It was as if she was setting the stage for one."

"But why would she do that?"

"You'll have to ask her. I might be wrong, but it's suspicious. Does she have money trouble?"

"I don't think so."

"You should find out." He pinched the bridge of his nose. "But that only answers one question. I still don't know why he was there afterhours or why my mother wants to use me as bait or what my aunt is up to or—"

Patricia pressed her finger over his lips. "Since neither of us is in the mood to sleep tonight, let's go and enjoy some more strawberry brownies and try to figure this out."

61

———

Carrying a plate of strawberry brownies, Patricia sank into the couch cushions with a contented sigh. She wore one of his many robes—she didn't realize a man could have so many—this one, a burgundy colored cashmere, embraced her body in feather-soft luxury.

"I love your house."

Lucas sat next to her dressed in a red and black plush robe with matching slippers. "Say the word and it's yours."

"You mean you'd move?"

He sent her a look filled with both shock and hurt. "You wouldn't want me here?"

Patricia grabbed the lapel on his robe and playfully shook him. "I was joking, Lucas. Why would you think that?"

"Should I tell you about the other women in my life?" he said in a dry tone. "Or would you like to hear the story about my mother again?"

She kissed him on the cheek. "I'm sorry."

He rubbed her kiss from his face. "That was a mean thing to say."

"I built you a sanctuary, remember?"

He frowned. "I think it just fell down."

She laughed. "Okay, I'll make it up to you."

"You'd better," he said sounding hurt, but the corner of his mouth quirked in a sly victory.

Patricia gasped surprised by his deception. He hadn't been hurt at all. He'd tricked her and she'd fallen for it. "You're terrible."

A slow, wicked, yet sexy, grin touched his lips. "I know," he said without remorse.

No wonder he could see past her lies, he was a master at it. She saw the cunning child and teen he'd once been. She briefly wondered if he'd been leading her to this moment the entire time. "Bet you could cry on cue as a child."

He trailed his thumb along her jaw. "Scared?"

"A little."

"Good. You scare me too."

"I'm not scary."

"Yes, you are. You know how to hurt me."

"I won't punch you."

He pinched her chin. "That's not what I mean and you know it."

That still unnerved her about him, how easily he admitted his weakness for her. "Fine. I'll do a home repair of your choosing and offer you the Duppy discount. Will that make me less scary?"

He paused. "What did you just say?"

"I'll offer you a repair—"

"No about a discount."

"Oh, the Duppy discount. I overheard my uncle say it

once and I found it funny. But when he heard me repeat it he made me promise never to say it again. But since he's gone, I don't care. Why?"

Lucas slapped his forehead. "The cameras. Of course. Your uncle is the Duppy Man."

"What?"

"He didn't abandon you. He disappeared because that's what he does. He's a legend. You go to him and he could make something appear or disappear. He probably handed the business over to his son because he wanted to keep you safe. His business was part of his cover, but anyone associated with the Duppy Man can get into trouble." He swore. "All this time he's been watching over you. Wynette probably knew all this too."

"Wynette?"

"My aunt. Mrs. Clemmens." Lucas rubbed his jaw. "But why hadn't Alex been able to make the connection, unless...?" Lucas swore.

"What? Who's Alex?"

Lucas' tone turned grim. "Someone who's going to be very unhappy to see me."

ALEX WAS COMPLETELY unprepared to find Lucas outside his apartment door the following afternoon after he came back from a quick jog.

Lucas adjusted his glasses. "You know why I'm here."

"Can I pretend that I don't?"

"Do you think that matters?"

Alex tugged on his sweaty T-shirt. "Can I shower first?"

"No."

Alex sighed and opened the door. His apartment opened into a large living room that housed his love of mixology. He had shelves lined with his extensive barware collection made up of vintage glasses, tall glasses, shot glasses and more.

Lucas casually walked over to one of them.

"Have you been on her payroll the entire time you pretended to work for me?"

"Not the entire time."

Lucas picked one vintage glass with a blue tint. "I bought this for you when I was in France, correct?"

"Yes."

"Shame if it got broken."

Alex swallowed. "I didn't do it for the money."

"Did she threaten you?" Lucas tossed the glass from one hand to the other.

"No."

He tossed the glass in the air.

Alex gasped. "Please don't, Lucas."

"Why were you working for her behind my back?"

"She said I could help."

"And you believed her?"

"No, I believed you."

"Me?"

"Yes, remember you told me that you didn't mind—"

Lucas held up his hand and swore, realizing Ericka had fooled Alex as well. "You mean Wynette didn't tell you I have a twin brother?"

"You have a twin?"

"Never mind." Lucas replaced the glass on the shelf. "I guess I'm talking to the wrong person."

"Am I forgiven?"

"I don't know yet. Help me with a puzzle."

"Okay."

"My brother has something my mum wants. And he went to Patricia's aunt to find out where the Duppy Man is. Why do you think?"

"Well, if he hired the Duppy Man he either wants to find something or hide something."

Lucas stared at the array of glasses a long moment, some offering him a reflection of himself in strange distorted proportions and hues, before he said, "Or there's another option."

"What?"

"If one goes by the folktales, the duppy is a ghost or spirit that brings bad fortune. Perhaps my brother doesn't want to find or hide anything. Perhaps he wants to scare someone."

62

The man in the grey track suit sat down at the expandable wooden table with a plate of pita pizzas topped with roasted red peppers, sautéed mushrooms and cherry tomatoes. From this seated position, he reached to his left in the cramped kitchen, and opened the fridge, indulging in the brief chill that combated the heat from the stove, and grabbed a bottle of ginger beer.

Ericka, Eric, Diane, Deon, Trigger. He responded to many names and had used many more. But there was one name no one had given him, but one he'd designated for himself: Lulu's Shadow.

He enjoyed the role. Although he'd been born first, he felt as if he were the secondary twin. That Lulu shone the brightest. Lulu was his world. Lulu tried his best to shield Ericka from the darkness of their lives. He pleased and charmed their mother and others as best he could. He didn't succeed many times, but he never stopped trying, Ericka could never understand that. Lulu always carried within him a seed of hope, a belief that life could be better. He cared about people, Ericka couldn't care less.

The only person he truly cared about was Lulu.

He didn't blame his brother for running. Lulu had tried to convince him to run away with him on one of the rare moments their mother had given them the liberty to steal by themselves.

But Ericka made his choice. He didn't believe in a better world. He still didn't.

He didn't fault his brother for escaping, for changing his name, changing his life. He didn't lie or steal. He'd turned legit, although there were rumors that Lulu's adopted Dad's initial business dealings wasn't. Ericka admired him for that. Eldin Wolff knew how the world worked and he kept Lulu safe. But Lulu didn't know how to keep himself safe.

That's where Ericka found his role.

Lulu was a sucker for women. He wasn't naïve and he didn't fall hard, but he wanted to live the pre-processed life the marketers and advertisers tried to brainwash people into believing. That there was a happy, rosier life out there if you just worked hard enough, were good enough.

Ericka knew that was rubbish.

Lulu didn't.

So Ericka did his best to show him (Lulu made it easy since he was determined to keep his twin brother a secret) by revealing the true nature of the people around him, especially women. Lulu was very adept at choosing business associates, there were the occasional mistakes but he didn't make many, but when it came to women—Lulu always settled.

Ericka didn't believe his brother should ever settle. There was no woman worthy of him. But Lulu kept searching, ever the optimist. Ericka had hoped Lania would have been the last straw.

If only he hadn't met the Duppy Man's niece. That had been Aunt Wynette's doing. She'd outfoxed him there. She'd put a worthy foe in Ericka's path.

Patricia was nothing like the others even with her family ties. But being the Duppy Man's niece put her off-limits in a number of ways, while also bringing their lives around full circle.

Lulu tried so hard to pretend he didn't exist.

It was time he formerly introduced himself.

He wouldn't let his brother deny his existence any longer.

The man in the grey track suit finished his pita pizzas and took a quick swig of his ginger beer. The temperature in the room had cooled, putting him in a calm, relaxed state.

The man in the grey track suit pulled out his burner phone and sent a text, ready to put his final plan into action.

63

Wynette always found her morning swim calming. The indoor lap pool offered the perfect temperature and classical music filtered in through carefully concealed speakers.

This morning, however, after completing two laps, she sensed someone watching her. She removed her goggles and saw a tall dark figure looming over the side of the pool and realized this morning wouldn't be like the others.

She sighed and completed another two laps (making sure to reduce her pace to one so leisurely she was almost floating) before she slowly climbed out of the pool. She held out her arm for her towel that rested on the bench. "Hello Lucas."

Lucas walked up behind her and draped the towel around her shoulders, before he lifted one end and wrapped it around her neck. "The Duppy Man," he whispered.

Wynette chuckled amused, unafraid. The pressure of the towel pressed against her windpipe in an uncomfortable way, but not enough to really hurt. "I wondered when you'd find out about that."

He released his grip and stepped back. "Is that why you wanted me to stay away from Patricia?"

Wynette took the towel from her shoulders and dried herself off. "I never said that."

"I saw it in your eyes. Your fear."

She reached for the robe on the bench. "I don't fear you. When will you understand that? I'm worried because I saw how you felt about her. It wasn't like any other woman."

"And that's a problem because—"

"Because your brother will get jealous."

"No, he—"

Wynette tightened the belt of her robe, annoyed. "Do you really think he intervenes in your love life to protect you? Are you that naïve?"

"First you tell me he needs help, now you're telling me to be afraid of him."

"I didn't say afraid."

"You don't know what you're saying—"

"He likes to keep you alone, to keep you to himself. I knew that if he sensed how important Patricia was to you it would...complicate things."

"It hasn't."

"It will."

"No, Patricia can tell the difference between us." Lucas nodded at her surprise.

"That's interesting."

"So he'll give up."

"Unless he puts your mother on Patricia's scent."

"Why would he do that?"

"He already has."

"There's no reason—"

"You need to find your brother and talk to him. You're the only one who can end this."

Lucas called Patricia, but his messages went straight to voice mail. He called Jeremy. "Have you seen Patricia?"

"What do you mean?" Jeremy said. "She's with you."

"With me?"

"You mean she hasn't reached you yet?"

"Reached me?"

"Yes, she told me she was meeting you somewhere. I think she said a farmhouse or something."

Lucas swore.

Jeremy paused. "Is something wrong?"

He didn't want to get the friendly giant involved. The combination of Ericka and the monster would be too much for him. Better to keep him in the dark.

"How long ago was this?"

"About an hour."

Lucas swore again.

"What's going on?"

"Nothing. It's alright, we must have passed each other." He disconnected before Jeremy could discover his fear.

If something happened to Patricia he'd never forgive himself.

He was too far away to reach the farmhouse in under an hour, he wouldn't be able to get there in time.

64

____

wo men received a text.

Both men received a text with one word. The same word.

The first man was lounging on the couch with his wife when the text arrived with a ping. He told his wife to ignore it, but something made her sense that it was urgent. When she saw the one word it didn't mean anything to her, so she held the phone out for her husband to look at it.

Color drained from his face and he scrambled off the couch, ready to leap into action.

The second man received a text while halfway through physical therapy. He usually turned his phone off, but had the instinct to leave it on that day.

When the message came through, a message he'd been waiting for, he calmly ended the session and immediately changed into loose fitting trousers and a black, long sleeve shirt.

The one word reminded both men of their brother

Lucas. He was the reason they'd chosen the word in the first place.

It had been a windy winter night and Lucas had dutifully checked under the bunk bed he and Damian shared plus Ian's bed for monsters. At ten he was still shaken after the first kidnapping and jumpier than usual, but tried to pretend he was fine and maintained his cheery disposition.

However, that night, instead of saying 'goodnight' as he usually did he said, "I wish I was like water. If I'd been like water she couldn't have tied me up and kept me locked up. Water can't be trapped, it can slip through anything. It changes shape too. It can become ice, or air, or steam. It can change and escape anything."

"If anything ever happens to you again," Damian said, "say 'water'. We'll know you're in trouble and come and get you."

"Nah, I don't want you to get hurt 'cause of me."

"We won't get hurt."

"But you could."

"We won't. Not with Dad's help."

"I wouldn't want Dad to..." his words fell away because Ian had pushed his blankets aside and was making his way over to Lucas's bed on the lower bunk.

He sat on the side of the bed and took his brother's hand. He held it tight and Lucas's lower lip trembled, then he started to cry.

Then he wept.

Damian climbed down from his bed and sat on the edge of the bed. He patted his brother on the shoulder. "You're safe now. Don't cry," he said before he started to cry too, remembering the terrifying ordeal and remnants of his painful past and another sibling he'd lost.

But Ian didn't cry. Not because he didn't hurt, he felt more than most, but because when he took Damian's hand too he needed all the strength he could muster to give his brothers comfort.

Soon the sound of their misery faded leaving the slight wail of the winter wind outside the window.

"Water," he said.

The two brothers wiped their eyes and nodded. That was the word that bonded them then.

And bonded them now.

65

*P*atricia's heart still raced from the cryptic message Lucas had sent her as she drove to the farmhouse. Had he decided to sell the house and wanted repairs? Had he met with trouble and needed help?

She parked her truck and knocked on the front door. It slowly swung open. She cautiously stepped inside. "Lucas? I'm here."

Silence.

She stepped further into the foyer. "Lucas? Are you upstairs?"

She heard the door close behind her. She spun around and saw a man who looked like Lucas, but wasn't him.

"Hi Patricia. We have a lot to talk about." He gestured towards the living room.

"Where's Lucas?"

"He'll be here soon. Don't worry."

The first thing she noticed when Ericka pushed himself away from the door was how much the house was made for him. Every note harmonized as he led her to the living room. "What gave me away?"

She wouldn't tell him about the house or that there was something about his eyes, his chin, the sound of his voice that was a shade bitter. While Lucas could turn anyone into a friend this man could easily create enemies, on purpose. But there was nothing chilling about him, nothing off-putting, he was very personable and friendly. One could imagine falling for him and then realizing too late he'd injected you with poison. That's how he got close to people, like the lure of a Venus fly trap.

He sat down on the sofa and gestured to the sweet biscuits on the coffee table. "This is one of the properties Lulu tried to bribe me with."

Patricia glanced at the biscuits but didn't touch them, before she sat.

"Bribe you?"

"Hmm...I guess bribe is the wrong word. Challenge. We both bought this property to challenge the other. He challenged me to go legit and I challenged him to find a trustworthy woman. Whoever won got the house." He sent Patricia a knowing look. "I guess I lost.

"Unfortunately, Lulu didn't appreciate the improvements I've made. I thought they were great reminders of our childhood. Hiding places can be lots of fun."

So the prison room was likely his idea. "What do you do?" Patricia asked, hoping to keep him chatting until Lucas arrived.

"I'm in the insurance business. If you get yourself in trouble, I insure you don't get hurt. But it'll cost you and I rarely take on new clients. "

"Why were you looking for my uncle?" She wouldn't

forgive him for upsetting her aunt when he called her asking questions.

A flicker of surprise passed through his gaze. "I didn't expect you to ask me that. Bravo." Ericka looked around the room, impressed. "So you can spot your uncle's handiwork then?"

"My uncle worked on this property?" Patricia said surprised.

Ericka clicked his tongue in pity. "He really did keep a lot of secrets from you. Yes, this was one of his masterpieces. So many hiding places."

She thought of the closet with the false wall and the dark room. "He built that cell?"

Ericka frowned in displeasure. "It is not a cell. I thought you'd have more imagination than that. Why would this gorgeous place have a grubby thing like a cell? Next you'll confuse the chains in the basement for a dungeon." He sighed as if gathering patience. "Like the other rooms, that particular *space* serves two purposes. You could say it's like a knife or a gun. They are neutral. How you use them gives them purpose. You can store things, hide things, trap things, save things. It's multipurpose."

"I see."

"Do you?"

"Yes. You're a very intelligent person. You see what others don't."

"Don't try to flatter me. It won't work."

"I'm not trying to flatter you. I'm trying to understand why I'm here. You're an intelligent man you must realize that."

"Are you angry with me?"

"No. What's the purpose of the room now?"

Ericka clasped his hands together and grinned like a delighted child. "I'm so glad you asked. It's gift for Lucas but I wanted to share it with you first."

"Why me?"

Ericka pointedly ignored her question. "There's a woman in there right now. This afternoon she sat in her kitchen nook and drank her favorite Darjeeling tea prepared by her assistant and sometimes lover. A woman she trusts, but probably shouldn't. Because this time her tea wasn't like the other ones. This time her tea made her very sleepy. Soon she'll wake up in a room with no windows or doors. But that won't frighten her."

"Why are you telling me this?"

"Because it's an interesting story, please don't interrupt."

"Sorry."

"She's going to wake up and we'll be able to watch her if we want to. But I don't think either of us cares. It will be Lucas who'll have to make a choice."

They heard the sound of tires squealing to a halt.

Ericka groaned. "Oh, damn. The other ones have gotten here first."

"The other ones?"

"His brothers." He stood. "Will you excuse me for a minute?"

Patricia shot to her feet. "I won't let you hurt them."

"I don't plan to hurt them," he said heading towards the front door.

Patricia raced past him and went outside. She saw Damian first. "I'm safe it's okay. Go back."

"Not until—"

"I mean it, he wants me here not you."

Ericka appeared in the doorway and Damian stared at

him stunned. "Lucas? When did you get here?" He walked towards him, but Ian appeared at his side and held him back.

"He's not Lucas," Patricia said.

Ericka nodded. "She's right. But I'm not a violent man. We can eat biscuits while we wait for Lucas to arrive." He turned and went back inside the house.

"Don't," Damian said when Patricia made a motion to follow him.

"Really, it's okay." She motioned them forward. "Come. He's expecting you."

Damian and Ian shared a look.

"Trust me. He won't hurt me...or you."

"It could be a trap."

"He's set a trap for someone else. His mother's inside. In a cell. I know the cell."

Damian looked torn but Ian nodded then gestured for her to go inside.

She led the brothers to the living room where Ericka calmly sat watching a documentary about volcanoes.

He held open his arms in welcome. "Ian and Damian. So glad you could join us."

The two brothers silently sat.

"I know a lot about you. But what do you know about me?"

"Not much," Damian said.

"Shame."

"What do you want?" Damian said.

"I'm already getting what I want."

"Is it true that you have her?"

"Yes." He held up a hand, but I'm not saying anything more until Lulu arrives."

Damian frowned. "Who's Lulu?"

Ericka turned up the volume on the documentary. "Shh... this looks interesting."

They waited for nearly twenty minutes in silence until Ian turned his head towards the window as if he'd heard something. Seconds later Lucas's voice filled the foyer. "Ericka!"

"In here Lulu!"

"Here he is now," Ericka said turning off the flat screen.

Lucas stormed into the room then stopped when he saw Patricia and his brothers. "What the hell—"

"Why didn't you tell them anything about me?"

"Okay," Lucas said to his brothers, "False alarm. Sorry I bothered you."

"The beautiful dresses we used to wear."

"I'll make it up to you for wasting your time."

"How we loved getting our hair done."

"Shut up."

"The dolls."

"I mean it."

"You were such a pretty—"

"What do you want?"

"I wanted to surprise you."

He shot Damian and Ian a glance. "I can handle this. Take Patricia—"

"No," Ericka stood. "I think everyone should stay. Especially her. She should see this. Shouldn't she see her legacy?"

"Her uncle had nothing to do with what happened to us."

"I didn't say he did. You make me sound like a vengeful idiot. I'm wounded."

"Shut up and tell me what you want."

Ericka sighed dramatically then led them over to the

dining table where he had a laptop set up. On the screen they could see a woman lying on the ground.

"You didn't even put her on the cot," Lucas said.

Ericka's eyes turned cold. "She's lucky there is one."

"You don't want to do this."

"Oh, how wrong you are."

"Ericka—"

"This has to end. It's either her or us. Mainly you. She won't leave you alone. I thought if I told her that I had information to send her back to prison she'd come after me, but no, just like before, she uses you to get at me. She kidnapped you. Any time I did something wrong, she punished you. I want this to end—for both of us."

"This isn't the way."

"Monsters need caves."

"You mean cages."

"No, I mean caves. She'll be fine here. No one will look for her."

"Her team—"

"Is under my control now. I've been very patient and so has Dad."

"Dad?"

"Yes, you know when grandma died she wasn't only looking after us. There had been another child, who'd hid. A cousin of ours. When she learned about Shanelle she prepared for vengeance. When she was old enough she became a close confidant and lover of hers, which made her very useful to me."

"We can't leave her there."

"Of course we can," another voice said. They turned and saw an efficient looking older woman in a tailored turquoise suit. She had a short, peppered grey afro.

"I'll take care of her until it's no longer necessary," Marlene said.

"Give us the house and walk away Lulu," Ericka said. "You can be free. This is my gift to you."

"Why did you contact Nurse Gladys?"

Ericka shook his head. "You don't want to know all about Nurse Gladys."

"I do. Why did you call her? Why were you at the mansion?"

"I called her to find out some information. She got nervous so she had to blame you for the thefts of the gifts. But she knows who did it." He turned to Patricia. "Your cousins are in some financial trouble, you may want to look into that."

"What did Nurse Gladys do?" Lucas said.

"She worked with the Duppy Man on some—containment cases. She's very good at keeping people alive using very little resources."

"Like a torturer?" Patricia said.

Ericka kissed his teeth. "Such nasty terms. She's an artist. She knows how to encourage people to (how should I put it?) tap into their higher nature. You come from an impressive family."

Patricia felt her heart grow cold unable to believe her aunt and uncle had been involved in such dark dealings and she didn't want to know more. Had her father known? Was keeping that a secret what caused him to drink?

"We won't leave her there," Ericka said. "We'll allow her to explore other rooms that have no doors to close." He flashed a malicious grin. "We know how much she hates doors she can't close."

"I wish you hadn't told me this," Patricia said.

"We're all in this together now."

Lucas rubbed the back of his neck. "You didn't have to involve her."

"Give me a number between one and fifty," Ericka said.

"Why?"

"Just give me a number."

Lucas folded his arms. "No."

"Why not?"

"Because, knowing you, it'll be the number of years you'll hold her captive."

"You're right," Ericka said, disappointed. "How long do you think it should be?"

Lucas shook his head and let his arms fall to his sides.

"I promise I'll take good care of Mum."

"You can't stay in this house."

"He wants to," Patricia said in a low voice. "The house suits him. He'll be happy here."

Ericka frowned. "What does she mean by that?"

But Lucas wasn't listening to him, his gaze focused on Patricia. "Really?"

"Yes. He's not like you."

"Would you two like to tell the rest of us what's going on? Shouldn't family be honest with each other?" Ericka said.

Lucas pointed to the image on the screen. "Is this what you wanted?"

"Yes." Ericka looked at Ian and Damian then Patricia. "This moment will connect us for life. We're all tied together forever now. You'll never forget me."

"I've never forgotten you."

"But you tried."

"Yes. It was easier to survive that way."

"Now you can survive and remember me too. I won't bother you again."

"Let her go—"

"No Lulu," Ericka said in a grave tone. "This is the end for us. I won't bother you again. I want you to live fully in your new life. I want you to walk out that front door and remember this—we faced the monster and won."

66

In the end Lucas couldn't walk away until his brother and cousin decided on an end date for keeping the monster captive. They gave him one, a couple years in the future. He wasn't sure if they were telling him the truth or lying, but it gave him peace of mind. He agreed that when they released her, he'd finally give Ericka the full deed on the house.

That night, Lucas finally told his brothers about his childhood and he felt a weight lifted.

In celebration of his mother's capture, Eldin hosted his sons, Aunt Wynette, daughter-in-law, Rosaline and Patricia at his house, proudly making a pot of red beans and rice, jerk fish and callaloo in his new kitchen.

They sat out on the patio and enjoyed the soft brush of a warm autumn.

Ian rubbed Methuselah's stomach, while three different conversations bounced around him.

Rosaline admired Patricia's pink nails.

"She even has a pink hammer," Lucas said, overhearing the women's conversation.

Patricia nodded. "Like in the story of the Practical Pig and the Three Little Wolves."

They all fell silent, but before Patricia could apologize for bringing up such a silly story they'd probably never heard of Lucas said, "How would you know that story?"

"You know the story too?"

"Of course. Nurse Gladys read it to us. How do you know it?"

"I wrote it."

Eldin burst into laughter. Ian and Lucas soon joined him. Damian stared at her stunned.

Patricia looked at the brothers confused. "What's so funny?"

"Go on, you got your wish," Lucas said.

Damian walked over to where Patricia sat and got down on his knees.

Patricia leaned back startled. Even on his knees he looked enormous. "What are you doing?"

He mumbled something.

"What?"

"She couldn't hear you," Lucas said, cupping his ear. "Say it louder."

"Thank you for writing that story."

"It was his favorite," Lucas said. "He said if he ever met the author he'd bow at their feet."

Damian stood and folded his arms.

Patricia felt her face burn. "You didn't have to do that."

He looked annoyed, but his voice was kind. "It was a really good story."

She felt a soft touch on her arm and turned to Rosaline who said, "That means he *loved* it."

Damian returned to his seat and grumbled. "Don't rub it in."

"I'm glad it was you," Eldin said. "You made my boys very happy."

Patricia straightened in her chair, pleased. Perhaps she'd found a way to get Damian to soften towards her. That was a win.

"Nah, I didn't really like it," Lucas said.

Damian sent him a warning look. "It was perfect."

Lucas stood and held out his hand to her. "I liked most of it but I always felt it was missing something."

"Missing something?" she said taking his hand and letting him lift her to her feet.

"Yes. The practical pig was always helping others. But if I were to write an ending for the story, I'd add that the three little wolves gave the practical pig something back."

"What?"

"A family."

Ian nodded in agreement and the others soon followed. Wynette and Eldin shared a knowing look. "Sounds about right," Eldin said.

Lucas looked at Patricia. "What do you think?"

A place to belong. A family to belong to. Her world had expanded beyond her mother's sadness and caring for her sisters. She could imagine inviting them to a party at Lucas's split level and including Jeremy too. Patricia's heart sang with joy at the thought of a bright future. She wrapped her arms around Lucas' neck and kissed him. "I think that's the beginning of a whole new story."

ABOUT THE AUTHOR

Dara Girard, an award-winning, national bestselling author of more than fifty novels, from romance to suspense, loves telling stories.

Born in the US to immigrant parents, Dara enjoys pulling from her Jamaican, British, Nigerian heritage and exposure to various cultures to bring what reviewers and fans call "vivid emotional stories" to life. She is best known for her popular Henson Series, the mysterious Clifton Sisters, and the fun Black Stockings Society.

You can write her at:
contactdara@daragirard.com
or
ILORI Press Books
c/o Dara Girard
1207 Delaware Avenue, Suite 3092
Wilmington, DE 19806
If you'd like to receive a reply, please send a self-addressed stamped envelope.

Visit her website to sign up for her newsletter and get sneak peeks, monthly updates on new releases, and special offers.